SHADOW OF THE ABYSS

EDWARD J. MCFADDEN III

SEVERED PRESS
HOBART TASMANIA

SHADOW OF THE ABYSS

Too long on foaming billows cast,
The battles fury bray'd;
And still unsullied on thy mast
The starry banner wav'd;
Unconquer'd will Columbia be
While she can boast of sons like thee.

-Captain of The USS Wasp, Johnston Blakeley

PROLOGUE

Mid-Atlantic rift valley, October 11th, 1814

The sloop's bow sliced through the turbulent sea, sending spray across the surface of the blown-out Atlantic Ocean. Captain Johnston Blakeley stood on the main deck of the USS Wasp, staring at a line of dark clouds that marched across the horizon to the west. The wooden boat creaked and moaned, and canvas flapped as it drove through the waves.

"Tighten that jib, Mr. Cercut," Blakeley said.

"Aye, cap'n."

The Wasp was fresh off its battle with the Atalanta, and the crew was tired, hungry and depressed. It had been days since they'd seen the sun, and the inky ocean and the whistling wind had become constant companions. The Wasp's crew had spent the last two days knotting and splicing the rigging and mending the courses and topsails. The biggest project had been the removal of four thirty-two-pound round shots from the hull and repairing the holes.

Something glinted on the ocean's surface and Blakeley pressed his spyglass to his left eye. A large white form slipped beneath the waves. Or had he been staring at the ocean too long?

"Cap'n, did you see that, sir?" Cercut said.

"I saw nothing. Tend to your duties." The sea writhed, pushing around the 117-foot, five-hundred-ton sloop like it was a toy in a bathtub. A huge wave broke across the bow, and the Wasp dipped beneath the ocean. Whitewater frothed over the gunnel, knocking over three sailors and washing them down the deck.

Blakeley shouted, "Helm, ready about." The wind howled and shifted, but he was trying to keep the Wasp moving forward. He looked through his eye scope again and saw a slick white shape rise from the sea to port. A whale? A huge shark? No, there was no dorsal fin.

"Mr. Kric," the captain said.

Rory Kric, the Wasp's second in command, stepped closer to his captain so he didn't have to yell above the howling wind.

"Ready for battle," Blakeley said.

"Sir?"

"Do it! Now!"

"Aye, cap'n," Kric said. He scrambled below deck.

The Wasp was a flush-decked, ship-rigged vessel that carried two twelve-pound long guns and twenty thirty-two-pound carronades. The crew of young Americans stood at 173, but many of them weren't yet experienced sailors or sea fighters. The Wasp was fast, big enough to engage large war vessels, durable, and had enough storage to carry provisions for long campaigns. Its current mission was to inflict maximum damage on the British merchant marine while making it difficult for the pursuing Royal Navy to determine the Wasp's position.

Blakeley said, "Mr. Carr, are we on course?"

The sailing master shook his head. "I don't think so, sir. This wind and rough sea have moved us west."

"Get us back on course, Mr. Carr."

"Aye, sir, should—"

The Wasp shuddered as if it had run aground. Blakeley gripped a handrail, but several crew members, including Sail Master Carr, slid across the deck and nearly tumbled into the sea.

"Helm, come about!" Blakeley yelled.

The helmsman barked orders and the crew scrambled. The rudder arced as the ship's thick boom swung across the deck. The mainsail flapped and cracked, then caught air and the vessel surged to port.

"Trim the topsail, Mr. Cercut," Blakeley said. Sailing Master Carr was back at the captain's side. "What have we hit, Mr. Carr? Find out if the lookout has spotted any—"

The Wasp was struck again and this time the sound of breaking wood and screaming sailors rose above the roar of the wind. With her canvas wings unfurled in the thick northwest breeze, the Wasp stood out toward the darkening west with nothing before it.

"Captain!" yelled a lookout from above.

"Aye," Blakeley said.

"To stern, sir. To stern!"

Through the fog and haze a leviathan rose from the depths, its caudal fin snaking through the rough sea toward the stern of the Wasp.

"Dear god," Blakeley said.

The thirty-foot creature sported a crocodilian jaw, stacked with ten-inch knife-sharp teeth. The beast's flat head made up a third of its length, and it sat atop a short neck at the end of an elongated torso, which tapered back to a thick tail with a caudal fin at its tip. It snaked through the water propelled by two flipper-legs.

"Ready rear long gun," Blakeley said. Whatever this thing was, he'd send it to the bottom like every opponent he'd ever faced. "Fire when ready, gunner."

A few tense moments passed as the giant sea creature knifed through the ocean, a mound of water surging before it.

The long gun boomed, and the shriek of the cannonball ended with a splash.

"We missed it, sir," said Mr. Carr.

"Again," Blakeley said, but it was too late. The beast had disappeared below the sea.

The Wasp's main bell chimed twice. Night was coming on.

"Helm, hard alee," Blakeley yelled.

The maneuver went awry, and the ship bucked as the creature breached on the Wasp's port side. Carronades erupted and poured shot into the beast at point-blank range. The creature wailed, swam around the Wasp's stern and commenced an attack on the starboard broadside.

Great jaws snapped and grabbed at the vessel as it was tossed on the roiling sea. Men screamed and fled, and Blakeley watched in horror as his officers tried to gain control of the crew and keep them on post.

The Wasp unleashed a round of shots, but the creature had submerged. A sucking sound rose above the gale, and to Blakeley it sounded as though the beast was screaming.

The ship lurched and rose from the ocean, the deck tilting at a thirty-degree angle. Men slipped into the sea as the Wasp plunged back into the ocean with a crash. Water surged over the gunnels as Blakeley fell, his spyglass falling from his hand and breaking on the deck. In the chaos he watched his father's gift roll down the deck and bounce off a coil of rope into the sea.

The creature missiled from the ocean, jaws open, glassy gray eyes rolling, flippers driving its weight. Jaws clamped on the starboard gunnel, tearing a chunk off the side of the boat. Seawater poured through the rent and the ship listed. The mainmast crashed over the side as it snapped, and the ship's hold filled with rising water.

The captain couldn't bring himself to abandon ship. They were victorious. They'd vanquished their enemies. Why had God sent this titan to destroy them? Blakeley got to his feet, searching for the creature as it came about and prepared for another attack run.

Seeing the beast's open jaws coming at them snapped Blakeley from his paralysis. "Abandon ship! Get those lifeboats in the water. Mr. Carr, bring us—"

The beast rammed the Wasp, its jaws taking another bite of the sloop. Wood cracked and splintered, and the creature's massive torso pushed over the sinking Wasp and disappeared into the sea on the opposite side, leaving the boat in two pieces.

Nails popped as the foremast came down and the carnage on the forward deck was obscured in dirty white sails. Panicked sailors jumped into the sea, lifeboats forgotten. How that it should end this way, Blakeley thought.

"Sir! Sir, let's go!" A sailor Blakeley didn't know stood beside him, yelling, but the captain didn't respond. He was in a fog. "Sir!" The man grabbed him by the shoulders. Then the deck split, and the sailor fell away into the sea.

There would be no abandoning the Wasp for Blakeley. He was captain, and that meant he would go down with his ship. He thought of his wife, his children, and for the briefest instant, sorrow washed through him. He prayed, then stopped, asking himself again why God had treated him so. Was he not a good servant? Had he not done all his Lord commanded?

The wind gusted, then calmed, and for a heartbeat the sea fell flat. A ray of sunlight peeked through the clouds.

The creature breached, landing atop Blakeley and driving what was left of the Wasp beneath the waves. He yelled, "From the rocks and sands and enemy's hands, God save the Wasp!"

Blakeley slipped beneath the deep and dark blue ocean, lost at sea without a grave, unheralded, unconffin'd, and unknown.

1

Sailfish Haven, east coast of Florida, present day

Splinter sat with his back to a palm tree, gazing out at the Atlantic Ocean. The tide was going out, and the white froth of the retreating sea crept further from him with each set of waves. Clouds of surfers sat in the consistent breaks like algae blooms, swaying and undulating with the roll of the ocean. Seagulls screeched, and the scent of rotten fish and bad eggs baking in the sun hung in the air like smoke. Thin cirrus clouds fleeted across a clear blue sky, the white streaks left behind by planes creating a lopsided checkerboard.

Sailfish Haven public beach was crowded for a Tuesday, and the concrete walkway that ran along the sand had steady foot traffic, the palm trees along its edge providing the only shade. Teenagers yelled and wailed as they played volleyball, children laughed, and waves pounded the shore.

A woman wearing a long turquoise sundress and a blue sunhat the size of a sombrero fumbled with her phone as she tugged at her son's hand. The boy was no more than two, his blonde hair matted to his head with sweat, lollypop residue around the edges of his mouth. The boy and his mom walked on the beach, and she tapped at her phone, dropped it in her purse, and jerked the boy to a stop as she fished the phone out and resumed pecking at it.

The child stared at Splinter as he walked by, and Splinter crossed his eyes. The child giggled, watching him, and tripped, the kid's face headed for rocks and sand.

Splinter's hand shot out, grabbing the boy and stopping his fall. The boy's mother jerked her head downward, radar engaging, but Splinter's hand was already back on his knee and he stared up into the woman's wide blue eyes with the innocence of a newborn puppy.

The child smiled at Splinter, and he winked. The mother gave Splinter a withering look and dragged the child away.

Splinter watched the lady stop up the beach and catch the attention of a police officer. She pointed his way. He couldn't really blame the woman. He looked like a bum. Greasy hair pulled back in a ponytail, unruly beard, and the red line of his scar, which ran up the right side of his face and around his eye like a hook. The scar was sunburned more than the rest of his face and looked fresh. And he probably smelled.

The cop's head turned. Splinter reached for his backpack, but decided to stay. He'd earned that right at least. The right to sit on a public beach in his own country.

The cop inched his way down the walkway, and Splinter waved. The officer sauntered up, hand on sidearm, eyes on everything but Splinter's face. The cop's life was so much easier if he didn't have to see Splinter as a person. "That lady said you looked at her funny," the officer said.

Splinter said nothing.

"What's your name?" the officer asked.

A large set of waves rolled in, crashing like thunder.

The cop said, "I asked you a question."

Again Splinter didn't respond. Years of experience had taught him silence was golden. Even a benign or innocent response could be unclear, misinterpreted or misheard. Best to say nothing.

The cop took a deep breath and looked to the sky, hoping God or Buddha or something would provide him patience. The officer sighed. Splinter said nothing. Hot currents of air baked off the concrete walkway, and the cop finished his visual search.

"Mind if I look through your backpack? If there's no drugs in there, you'll have my thanks and money for a cup of joe. Deal?" the officer said. He didn't meet Splinter's eye.

Splinter shrugged.

The flatfoot unzipped the big pouch of Splinter's dirty and road-beaten pink Dora the Explorer backpack and pulled out clothes. A sweatshirt with an eagle carrying an anchor on the breast, four black plastic garbage bags, a pair of gym shorts, two plain dark blue t-shirts, and some underwear. The cop held up the book on how to make weapons in survivalist situations. "You into this stuff?"

Splinter said nothing.

"Not a good sign." The officer pulled all the pack's smaller pockets inside-out, spilling Splinter's life on the walkway.

Finding nothing of interest, the cop said, "That your cane?"

Splinter's walking stick was propped against the palm tree.

"You hurt? A Navy boy?" the cop asked. "What's your name and where do you live? Why no ID in here?"

"Name's Matthew Woods, friends call me Splinter. You can call me sir, or Captain Woods. I live in southern Florida." His expired military ID and current bank card were hidden in the backpack's lining.

"What is your address?"

"Don't have one," Splinter said.

"You're a vagrant?"

"I'm on permanent leave."

"No job?"

"Not interested."

"So you're, what, a bum of leisure?"

"OK, look, I don't work because I don't want to. When the measly pension the Navy gave me runs out maybe I'll work, but now I don't want to. That alright with you?" Splinter's cheeks burned, and his neck throbbed with pain, but he wasn't done. "I don't have an address because I don't live anywhere. I move around, and last time I checked that wasn't a crime in the country I fought for." That was the most Splinter had said in months, but he felt the anger coming on.

"Where'd you fight?"

Splinter flipped the lapel on the army jacket he wore, revealing a short stack of ribbons: Silver Star, Meritorious Service honors, two Purple Hearts, and Afghanistan and Iraq Campaign medals. Splinter's heart raced. Breathe. These flatfoots who'd never fired their weapons really pissed him off sometimes. "I'll make you a deal, Officer—" Splinter leaned in to read the cop's nameplate. "Officer Peterson. When I do have an address, I'll invite you to the house warming party."

"Funny." The cop walked away, leaving Splinter's belongings in the sand. No money for that cup of joe.

Splinter's nerves tensed and pain shot down his spine. He rolled his shoulders and tried to crack his neck and back. No luck. He stuffed his belongings back in his backpack.

Something was wrong. Very wrong.

The wind picked up, and sand bit his face like tiny daggers. A gale tore across the beach, ripping at palm fronds and scattering beach toys.

The wind stopped, like the end of a great exhalation.

Splinter's anger blossomed, his vision blurring, panic filling him with fear.

An intense sucking sound rose above the yelling of panicked people. The massive pucker got deeper and louder as the ocean receded as if the laws of physics were reversed. People ran past him, dragging children and gear. The sea floor was exposed, revealing rocks, seaweed, and flopping fish.

A white line crossed the eastern horizon and grew like a nightmare.

The battle-fog took him, and Splinter vaulted to his feet and drew his speargun from inside his jacket. He grabbed his cane and screwed its end into the pistol's modified handle, turning the 1960 vintage CO2 Sea Hunter spear pistol into a rifle. Splinter put the stock to his shoulder and trained the gun on the receding sea, fanning it back and forth as if he expected an enemy to emerge from where the ocean had been.

The white line on the horizon came on, growing as the seafloor rose.

Splinter picked up his pack and ran. The wind kicked up and the ground trembled. He bolted across the walkway, people moving out of his way, fear in their eyes. He slipped the speargun beneath his coat, holding it tight against his side as he ran. He crossed a thin patch of weeds into the parking lot. Screaming filled his mind. Children crying. People ran in every direction.

Splinter raced across the public parking lot toward A1A. Cars stood still on the road, drivers and passengers staring east. He looked over his shoulder, arms and legs pumping.

A massive wave towered on the eastern horizon, and was almost to the shore.

Splinter made for the Comfort by the Sea hotel, which sat along the calm waters of the inner bay, Indian River. It was four stories tall and made of cinderblocks. Getting to its roof was the only thing he could think to do. He dodged through the throng of people packing into cars and trucks that would become their watery coffins. The tsunami would hit at any moment, and there was no car fast enough to escape it. The exits and entrance were already blocked with traffic. He threaded his way over A1A, running full speed, cutting and juking.

The emergency siren at the fire station pierced the day, its shrill cry late in coming.

People packed the entrance to the hotel, so Splinter ran through the fountain and headed for the rear of the building. Panicked people stacked ten rows deep blocked the back entrance. Splinter changed course, picked-up a stone from the edge of a decorative pond, and hurled the rock through the plate-glass window next to the rear entrance.

Louder screeching and cries as a deafening rumble blocked-out the sound of the siren. Wind tore through the broken window as Splinter jumped through. Glass shattered and wood cracked, the world spinning like a tornado. He crossed the lobby, threw open the door to the emergency stairwell, and took the steps up two at a time, chest heaving, pain stabbing his back.

The building shook, and Splinter fell. He landed hard on the metal stair treads, and blood dripped down his leg. Water shot up the stairwell like a giant firehose, and Splinter was driven upward like a cork on a rising sea. He sucked in air as the water consumed him, and he stroked up as the pressure eased, and the sea receded, pulling him back.

Splinter grabbed the handrail and held on, lungs burning, his legs braced against the wall as the undertow pulled at him. The force of the water ripped at his clothes, and he strained to keep from being sucked out of the stairwell like sewage.

He'd wished for death so many times. Now that he'd come calling, Splinter had changed his mind.

The water drained away and he lay panting on the stairs, still clinging to the handrail. Splinter unscrewed the stock from his speargun, slipped the pistol into his jacket, and strapped his cane-stock to the backpack. He put the pack on, pulled it tight, and got to his feet. He ran up the steps two at a time because he knew that rarely was there one tsunami wave. There was usually a series of them.

He exited onto the roof and ran to the eastern edge.

The sea covered everything. The light poles. Cars. Lifeguard stands. Street signs. All of it was hidden by the turbulent sea. Splinter went to the western side and what he saw there was more disturbing. Sections of Sailfish Haven were gone, the small structures sucked into the sea as the ocean retreated. The streets were canals, and the taller buildings stood in the flood, their glass windows reflecting the chaos. The wave surge pushed inland across the mangroves and consumed the inner bay, finally coming to a stop as it flooded Fort Pierce and the Old Dixy Highway.

He leaned against the parapet wall. His camp in the groves was gone. His skiff. He had nothing except what he carried in his backpack.

The sea churned as it receded, dragging bodies and the flotsam of humanity. The wind died to a faint breeze. Splinter saw the mother's blue sombrero sunhat floating in the jetsam, and he thought of the boy. All the people who'd been on the beach. Everyone that came near him died. How much longer could he do this?

Emergency sirens wailed and helicopter rotors pounded the air. Splinter ran back down the emergency staircase. He needed to disappear and find a place to sleep for the night.

2

The twenty-eight-foot Parker sliced through the Atlantic Ocean, its bow lifting and falling with the gentle three-foot waves, throwing sea spray across the surface and leaving a field of dimpled whitewater. The day was clear and humid, and heat pushed across the water like invisible waves. Boats dotted the horizon, and tuna-towers and trolling outriggers swayed with the roll of the ocean. The Parker's twin 150HP Yamahas whined when Lenah pushed down the throttle, and the boat leapt from the water.

Lenah Brisbee was a knockout, and Splinter was convinced the only reason the two mobsters from Miami chartered the boat was so they could hit on its captain, his ex-girlfriend. The two greased knuckleheads knew nothing about fishing, and spent most of their time flirting, trying to convince Lenah they were important men down in Miami. She handled them with ease, having been harassed so many times she no longer noticed when she was repelling a sleaze-attack.

"Lenah, how is it you're not married? This state filled with morons?" Sal Palmitari said. He claimed to be a made-man, but Splinter wasn't buying it.

"Yeah, bunch of fools," Brownie Keato said. He was Sal's brother-in-law and Sal made it clear every chance he got that he wasn't happy about the fact.

Sal shook his head and turned his attention back to Lenah. "Don't mind him. He's missing a few crucial parts, like a brain. Other important parts he's got, but they don't work too good."

Splinter turned to Will, the third charter, and rolled his eyes.

"How is it your boat didn't get sunk with most of the others?" Sal asked.

Lenah sighed. Six months prior, a series of extraordinary events caused a tsunami that rolled over Sailfish Haven. The mid-Atlantic Ridge experienced a violent surge of lava, which deformed the sea floor. This triggered an underwater landslide on Grand Bahama Bank, which caused the tsunami, but one good thing had come from the events; the fishing off the east coast of Florida was the best it had been in living memory. Scientists from the University of Florida studied the phenomenon, and found there was no pattern in the currents, or any other indicators that explained why fish of every breed and size swarmed to the area. Any captain with a functional fishing boat and the proper licenses migrated to where the fish were hitting, and that meant Sailfish Haven was alive, even though it was still recovering.

"I was running bass charters out on Lake Okeechobee. Soon as I heard about the fishing over this way, I double-timed it here," she said.

"Double-timed?" Brownie said.

"Move fast. Run. You are the dumbest shit I know," Sal said.

Brownie hung his head and said nothing.

Splinter moved between Lenah and Sal, and Will chuckled.

Will was Splinter's friend, a local retired cop who'd come on the charter as Lenah's guest. Like Splinter, she wanted help around because Lenah didn't trust Sal and Brownie to pick up paper on the side of A1A, let alone be her only back-up out on the water. The goombahs had offered an exorbitant fee she couldn't turn down, but her normal deckhand was sick, so she'd hunted down Splinter and begged him help.

Splinter still loved her, but he knew he could never give her what she wanted: a stable life, a husband, kids, all things Splinter once thought he could provide, but everything had changed that night in Kabul.

Lenah drew back the throttle, snapping it into neutral, and the motors fell to a distant purr. The Parker's wake broke on the transom, and seawater sprayed across the deck. Lenah fiddled with the Hummingbird Solix 10 fish finder and pulled out her phone and held it up for inspection. "Bluetooth. I can move the boat and get hit signals out on deck," she said.

Sal stepped around Splinter and got close to Lenah to look at the screen, and the captain deftly sidestepped him, opened the cabin door, and went out on deck. The four boys followed her like dutiful puppies, and Lenah handed Sal a fishing pole and Splinter put a piece of week-old squid on its hook.

"Damn," Sal said. "That's some nasty shit."

"Nasty shit that will catch you a fish. You do remember you're out here to fish, right?" Splinter said.

Sal jerked his head back, doing his best De Niro imitation. He cocked his head to the side, as if he didn't believe what he'd just heard from some dirtbag putting rotten fish on a hook.

Lenah stepped between them and put her hand on Sal's shoulder, leaning forward, letting him get a good look at her breasts.

Pain shot up Splinter's back.

"Let me show you how to do this since someone—" Lenah turned and looked at Splinter, "can't be nice."

"Yeah, go swab the deck Mr. Pee," Brownie said.

"It's Mr. Smee," Will said.

"I like Pee," Brownie said.

Will and Splinter laughed.

"You're a grade A asswipe. You know that, Brownie?" Sal said.

The short, spindly man with dirty-blonde hair and a receding hairline looked at each of them, his face twisted and confused.

Everyone got lines out and the day wore on, and the Atlantic became a desert, heat pressing on everything, the sea breeze an inconsistent nothing that slowed their float to a crawl. They waited and fished, the roll of the ocean and the rise and fall of the bow lulling Splinter toward sleep.

"Whoa," Sal said. His reel spun off line so fast it buzzed.

"Hook it now. The way I told you," Lenah said.

Splinter stopped swabbing the deck, openly staring, and Brownie and Will checked their lines and turned to watch.

The fight lasted as long as that time Mike Tyson beat Marvis Frazier. Sal climbed into the fighting chair and put the rod in the stainless-steel holder. Then he checked the reel, pulled back on the pole, and the fifty-pound braided line snapped like piano wire. The spool tangled as the pressure was relieved from the line, and Sal handed the pole off to Splinter, who stared at the man in disgust.

"What do you make of that, Splinter?" Lenah said.

"Big mother, whatever it is. Not much can snap a fifty-pound braided line," Splinter said. "Even for an amateur."

"Whatever it is? It's a fish. Shit. Even I know that," Brownie said.

Splinter saw it first, the gray dorsal fin rising from the water, cutting through the waves and coming at the boat. It was three feet tall, and that meant the shark was at least fifteen feet long.

"Start the engines, Lenah." Splinter pulled his speargun from his jacket pocket. He didn't have his stock-cane with him.

"What is it?" Sal asked.

Splinter pointed at the dorsal fin coming at the Parker.

"Oh, shit," Sal said, and pulled a gun of his own. He held the SIG Sauer P320 Sub-Compact at his side, shifting his weight from foot to foot, eyes locked on the fin as it arced past the boat on the port side. The beast's caudal fin swept back and forth, the shark's torpedo body easing through the water like a ballerina.

The creature circled the boat, then turned and headed for the Parker. It floated just below the surface, and rows of razor-sharp teeth flashed white within pink smiling gums, the shark's dark eyes watching them. It was a fifteen-foot great white, and as it fell back into the depths Splinter went cold.

With a waggle of its caudal fin the beast angled downward, diving into the blue.

Sal said, "What the hell do—"

"Ssssshh," hissed Splinter. He leaned over the gunnel, scanning the sea. Splinter started to sweat, nerves jumping, the fog coming on like a storm, his vision going red.

Breathe. Breathe.

"Who the fu—"

"Not now, Sal," Lenah said.

Splinter shook as he stared at the bubbling water. He gripped the bait bucket handle so tight it cut his hand. A gust of wind brought the scent of blood, and Splinter stepped away from the gunnel. Something was coming to the surface.

"Splinter, you OK?" Will asked.

"Yeah." Splinter didn't take his eyes off the ocean.

The sea bubbled red, and the shark's head burst from the water, rows of teeth gleaming in the sunlight. A primal screech echoed over the ocean. The shark's head rolled forward, bobbed on the surface, then tipped over and sunk beneath red sea foam. Entrails, gristle, and torn muscles swirled behind the severed head.

Waves lapped against the hull as a huge shadow glided beneath the water to starboard, and it got bigger as it came to the surface.

Sal brought up his gun and Splinter his speargun.

The great shadow passed beneath the boat and disappeared into the deep.

3

"What the hell was that?" Sal said. He'd gone white, the dark bags under his eyes puffing out like rain clouds.

"No idea," Lenah said.

Blood and fat floated on the ocean's surface, but the shark's head was gone. Most dead fish float because of their swim bladder, but heads didn't have anything to fill with air. Splinter studied the water, searching for the bigger beast.

Lenah headed for the pilothouse.

"What are you doing?" Splinter asked.

"Calling the Coast Guard. They'll want to know about this," she said.

"No go," said Sal.

Splinter's hand shot out so fast Sal never saw it. One minute the SIG Sauer was in Sal's hand, the next it was gone. Splinter held the weapon up for inspection, then tossed it in the sea.

"What the hell?" said Brownie. The skinny shit advanced on Splinter, but whether it was the look in Splinter's eyes, his stance, or Brownie's instinct, the criminal thought better of it and stepped back.

Sal wasn't so smart.

"You're gonna get your head busted for that." Sal tossed his head right, then left, cracking his neck. He brought up his fists and danced on his toes like a boxer.

Splinter smiled broadly and said nothing.

"Sal, I wouldn't go there if I was you," Lenah said.

"You're not me," he said. Then he stepped forward and threw a quick rabbit punch aimed at Splinter's face.

The ex-SEAL jerked his head, and the punch missed. Splinter stood his ground and smiled.

Sal tried two more times, only to hit air. Sal's face reddened, his eyes glowing with hatred. Splinter had embarrassed him, and in front of Lenah.

"You done?" Splinter asked.

"We got bigger problems, no? Knock it off," Lenah said.

"We ain't paying you," Brownie said. The weasel clearly thought that settled the matter.

"You already paid," Lenah said.

"By credit card. I'll cancel the payment," Sal said, supporting his brother-in-law in his defiance.

"You do that, and I'll come find you. You don't want that," Splinter said.

Silence fell. The sea breeze pushed across the ocean, the gentle waves having been replaced by steep three footers that slapped against the hull.

"Someone's gonna replace my gun," Sal said.

"Yeah, be sure to hold your breath," Splinter said.

"Now that's—"

Lenah cut Sal off. "Can we put the testosterone on hold for a minute?"

"That why they call you Splinter? Cause you're a thorn in the ass?" Sal said.

"Very original. Most douchebags go with a derivative of 'under my skin,'" Splinter said. He'd never let the asshole know that was exactly why his nickname was Splinter. He'd been a relentless taskmaster. Add to that his last name was Woods and the nickname had stuck.

A black shape floated below, and it moved lazily around the boat, fading and becoming darker as the sun went behind the clouds. Splinter barely saw whatever it was gliding beneath the waves, but he felt it, sensed the beast looking for them, taking stock, deciding if they were worth the effort.

"We gonna fish, or what?" Brownie said.

Splinter chuckled. "You see that there, dumbass? That thing down there just decapitated a fifteen-foot great white shark. An apex predator of the sea. I think we're done fishing for the day."

"Who asked you?" Sal said. "You the captain, or is she?"

Splinter said nothing. The grease-ball had a point.

Lenah ran her fingers through her long blonde hair, her eyes darting every few seconds to the massive shadow lurking portside. "If that thing breaches under us, we're done. I think we need to get the hell out of here and call the authorities. They'll want to track this thing. Interview us about the shark."

"I'm with you on the first part. Let's get underway. Then we can talk about what we should do," Splinter said.

Sal puckered his lips, but said nothing. Brownie stood by his brother-in-law like a child.

Will said, "Lenah's right."

"Not now," Splinter said. He left the fisherman and Lenah alone and entered the pilothouse. He started the outboards, and spun the wheel, pointing the boat west toward shore. The others joined him in the cabin as Splinter eased down on the throttle and the boat moved away from the bloody seas.

Will said, "What do you think, Splinter?"

Splinter didn't respond. He stared out the windshield, looking back every few moments to see if the shadow trailed them. It didn't. He checked the SONAR, and only the rainbow-colored line that marked the sea floor rolled across the bottom of the screen. He plotted a course for Fort Pierce Inlet, set the boat on autopilot, and sat back in the captain's chair.

"I can tell you I've never seen anything like that before in all my days on the sea, and those days are many. I've sailed every sea there is. Great whites are the kings and there isn't much in the ocean that can take one out."

"What can?" asked Brownie. Sal shot him a dirty look.

"An orca," Lenah said. "That's the only thing big enough. Pods of whales, other sharks, and schools of large fish have been known to repel the attacks of a great white."

"That's what you know of," Sal said. "They pull strange shit out of the sea all the time."

"Yeah, remember that sea monster they dragged in off Hatteras? The thing looked prehistoric," Brownie said. The dirty look this time made Brownie flinch, and he sealed his lips into a thin line.

A large swell rolled the boat, and Sal lost his balance and reached for the bulkhead, but missed it and tipped over.

Splinter moved like a viper, catching the man in his arms inches before the back of his head smacked the deck. Splinter eased the thick Italian back to his feet and stepped back. Sal blinked, processing what had just occurred. His forehead knitted, and he balled his fists, anger painting his face red.

As Splinter braced for an attack, Sal's face lightened as understanding washed over him. With what was clearly a great effort, the self-proclaimed mobster said, "Thanks."

"Now we're even," Splinter said.

"Even?"

"For the gun."

Then Sal did something Splinter didn't expect. He laughed.

Sal's laughter released the tension on the boat like air escaping a balloon. "OK, hotshot. I guess we are."

Lenah tuned her radio to channel sixteen and hailed the Coast Guard. "Coast Guard, this is Evenstar. Do you copy?"

Splinter stabbed the control panel with his index finger and shut the radio down.

"What are you doing?" Lenah said.

"We need to talk about this. Calling the ocean fuzz might have unwanted consequences," Splinter said.

"What are you talking about? I'm the captain of this boat, and I say we're reporting what we've seen," she said.

Her confidence and strength were two of the reasons he'd loved her. Still loved her in many ways. He said, "This is going to be news, Lenah."

"And what did we see?" Sal added.

Splinter had to admit Sal had a point. What had they seen?

"I didn't see anything," Brownie said.

Sal shook his head and rubbed his eyes.

Lenah opened her mouth to speak, then closed it. The five of them stood there, the Parker rocking back and forth.

What would happen if Splinter's name hit the news and some intrepid journalist dug up his past? There would be police interviews, the Coast Guard would want to talk to him. They'd want an ID, an address. It all made Splinter feel sick. He'd come to Florida to get away from his past. To get away from people and all the bullshit they toted with them. Instead of expressing his feelings, he said, "Sal's right, as much as I hate to admit it."

"Have you lost what's left of your mind? You saw what was left of the shark. The shadow," she said. She was pleading, but Splinter could tell by the tone of her voice that she was already starting to see things his way.

"I'd prefer not to have my name in the news," Sal said. "And what would telling the police achieve? What? They gonna come here and look for the thing? A street light has been out on my block for two years."

"They could at least put out a warning," Lenah said.

"A warning for what? A decapitated shark head? A shadow?" Sal said.

Splinter said, "And certain police might take an interest in your licenses when they find out you cater to a certain clientele."

"What's that supposed to mean?" Sal said.

"You know exactly what I mean," Splinter said.

As Splinter and Sal tried to persuade Lenah, Will stood by silently. The old cop shifted back and forth on his feet, his sunburned face twisted. Seeing his frustration, Splinter said, "What's the matter, Will?"

Will just shook his head.

Splinter relied on Will for all kinds of things. He was his connection to the real world, the person he went to when he needed help.

Will said, "I'm torn. I agree with Lenah one hundred percent, yet you fellas have a point. I've been trying to work out what my statement would say, and it's pretty damn thin."

"What are you saying?" Lenah asked.

"I don't know what I saw," Will said. "Sorry, Lenah."

"Couple all that with we have no proof," Sal said.

"Should have taken a picture or two with your fancy phone," Splinter said. He didn't own a cellphone, and never would.

Sal harrumphed, and when Brownie snickered, Sal punched him on the shoulder.

"So we do nothing?" Lenah said.

Splinter knew this was one of those moments that would come back to haunt him no matter what he did. A no-win scenario. If they tried to report what they'd seen, a shit-storm would ensue. They'd be called liars. Lenah would be accused of pimping her charter business. Their entire story would be considered questionable because two of the witnesses were wannabe criminals, and the cop on board wasn't prepared to say what he saw.

Then there was Splinter's past coming back at him like an incoming tide: slow, persistent, and never ending. He'd have to move. Disappear again. If they stayed quiet all that could be avoided, but what if someone went to the cops and the others didn't? They needed to make a pact, like he and his sister Jasmine used to. Sadness washed over him at the thought of his sister. He hadn't seen her or the kids in years. They lived up north.

"We need to agree not to say anything. Make a pact like me and my sis used to. Anyone have a problem with that?" Splinter said.

Lenah's eyes went wide. "You have a sister?"

"And two nephews. They could walk by me and I wouldn't know them," he said. "I stay away because I don't want—"

"Fine," Lenah said. "But we're heading in and I'm keeping the money."

Splinter went out on deck and stowed the poles and hosed everything down. Lenah brought the Parker up on plane, and the sea spray sent a thin mist across the boat. The sun had started its descent to the horizon, and to the south a thin band of dark clouds marched across the sky. The boat pitched and rolled in the surf, but they were still making twenty-five knots, and would be back at the dock by three o'clock.

Splinter stared down the fishtails that shot out fifteen feet from the propellers. He didn't see the shadow. He didn't expect to. The nerves in his neck tensed, and pain danced down his back. Whatever the thing was hung out in the deep water, and that's where it would stay. Most fish didn't leave their comfort zone if they didn't have to. Then the obvious smacked him.

The tsunami.

4

The tsunami sank and destroyed many boats, and the back bay of Snake River was littered with wrecks. The Coast Guard and local authorities said it would take several years to haul and dispose of all the boats. This was fine by Splinter. He'd found a half-sunk twenty-eight-foot sailboat, its bow firmly lodged in the mud on the bay bottom. The craft's deck tilted at a twenty-degree angle, but Splinter didn't mind. He'd gotten used to it.

The rear half of the boat was dry, and this was where Splinter lived. The master cabin was intact, and he'd dried out the mattress and stowed his meager belongings in the quarter's built-in armoire. He'd found an old gas camp grill wedged in the bows of a fallen tree in the mangroves, and he'd claimed it as his stove. His newly purchased ten-foot Zodiac with its 15HP Johnson beater was tethered to a cleat on the forward deck. He'd bought the craft from a fisherman who'd used his insurance money to buy a new boat with a new tender. Splinter still had his bank card, so he had a few bucks and could've stayed at a hotel, but that just wasn't his style. Too many rules and people.

Water crept up the half-submerged deck toward Splinter as the tide came in. He sat topside drinking beer and listening to the marine channels for news. The main topics of discussion the last six months had been fish and detritus. Cars, chunks of buildings, and bodies still washed-up on shore, and it wasn't unheard of for a fishing charter to come back to port with a haul of fish and a corpse or two.

The radio chattered, and Splinter took a long pull of beer. He hadn't seen Lenah for a week, and he wondered why she hadn't asked him to help again. He guessed her deck hand, Raul, who Splinter thought had more on his mind than fishing, must be over his bout of flu.

Splinter turned up the radio when he heard a report about a whale washing up on the beach at Fort Pierce Inlet State Park. He finished his beer, tossed the can down an open hatch into the flooded hold, and turned off the radio.

He wore camouflage cargo shorts, flip-flops, and a Miami Dolphins t-shirt that had more holes than fabric. He'd found the shirt in his sunken home, balled up in a corner. Most likely it had been tossed there after a big fins lose.

He grabbed the disposable waterproof camera he'd found floating in the jetsam. He'd kept it because it had four pictures on it, and if he ever saw the mystic shadow again, he'd be prepared to document the event.

He tossed the camera in the Zodiac and jumped in. He untied the lead line from its cleat and let the boat drift away from his half-sunken home with the current. The Johnson was old. So old he had to hand wind a cord around the flywheel before he could start the engine. He wound the cord and pulled but got nothing but a choke and wheeze. He repeated this process six times before the tiny outboard sputtered to life. He toggled the throttle switch, pulled the control arm to center, and headed north for Fort Pierce Inlet.

A light chop danced across the green water, mangrove trees filling in the banks on both sides of the bay. Snake River separated the mainland from the seashore, which was a meandering vacation paradise that stretched from Miami to Cape Canaveral. A1A ran its length, and Splinter saw cars racing past the beautiful scenery. He just didn't understand people anymore, if he ever had. They were always in a rush, pushing to be someplace they didn't want to be. Even on vacation.

Tiny shiners leapt from the water as the Zodiac skipped over the sea, spray coating Splinter's face. He smiled, closing his eyes and remembering when his father would take him fishing on lake Nicatous in Maine as a kid. He had those mental pictures firmly fixed in his mind, postcards that he referred to when sadness and anger washed over him. His dad had been dead for years, stricken down by diabetes. He'd been a pro football player that never got his shot because of an early career ending injury, and he was forced to spend his life selling cars and wondering what if? This never sat well with him, but Splinter remembered him as a loving father, if a bit sad.

To starboard, a wide opening appeared in the mangroves, and houses lined the shore like dominoes. Splinter passed the opening for Fort Pierce Inlet and arced the dinghy toward Boot Toe Point. Several boats drifted in the inlet, tall trolling outriggers bent by the motion. The Zodiac passed into the mangroves and civilization was lost from view. The dorsal fins of two dolphins appeared to port, and he slowed the outboard, searching for calves. Nothing pissed Splinter off more than boats running over animals.

The outdoors center was coming up fast, and Splinter jerked the control arm left, and the boat arced right, screaming toward shore. The mid-day sun baked everything, heat washing over the white Florida sand. Sand was big business, and he'd heard sand was being shipped in from Cuba to restore the erosion caused by the tsunami, but not everyone wanted the beach fixed. The fishermen argued that nature caused the problem, and nature should be given time to fix it. Never did any of these soldiers of the rod and reel speak of their real fears; fixing the beach might scare away their treasure trove of fish.

Splinter killed the Johnson, tilted it up and clicked it in place as the Zodiac pushed onto shore with the sound of rubber scraping on sand and shells. He put his disposable camera in a shorts pocket, pulled the boat into the mangroves, kicked his flip-flops into the dinghy, and headed for the path that led to the ocean.

It was a gorgeous day, and Splinter sighed when he felt the sand between his toes. As he approached the beach parking lot, the faint sound of reggae music carried on the breeze. He didn't see anyone, and when the dune loomed up before him, he stopped to listen.

Waves lapped gently on shore, a faint breeze whistled, and a crowd of people talked. He couldn't hear what they said, so he inched his way to the top of the dune.

Twenty or so people surrounded a whale carcass. They were mostly beach goers, but Splinter spotted Will in the crowd, speaking to someone dressed in the blue work uniform of the Coast Guard.

His anxiety fled at the sight of Will. He always had Splinter's back.

He walked confidently over the dune, striding up to the dead animal like he had every right to be there, which he did. He'd learned in his military days that all you needed to do was look like you belong, and nobody questions you.

The stench of rot and decay overwhelmed Splinter as he approached the fallen beast, and anger rose in him. The creature's large curved mouth hung open, revealing two hundred-plus baleen hairs that helped the beast eat. Blood dripped down the whale's side from its two rectangular blowholes, and as Splinter came around the corpse his mouth fell open.

"Hey, Will, what the hell happened here?" Splinter said.

Will seemed surprised to see him. "Where you been laying your head?"

"Old boat out on the bay." He stepped forward, hand outstretched, as if he was going to caress the dead animal. "This don't look good."

It was a right whale, and it hadn't been dead long, but the cause of death was obvious. Its slick gray skin glistened in the sunlight, and white patches randomly covered the corpse like clouds. The beast's tail fin had been completely severed, and red meat and gristle hung from the end of the torpedo shaped torso. One of the whale's flippers was gone, and the other was half missing. It looked to Splinter like the tail and flipper had been bitten off, because the jagged edges of the wound looked like a shark's work.

The beast's dark eyes had gone pasty, and its white beard of lice was already turning brown from air exposure. Bloody gashes covered the carcass, as if something had bitten the animal multiple times during their fight, but a shark wouldn't attack a large whale. Sometimes they went after calves, but unless there were multiple sharks and the whale had been on its own, the attack didn't make sense. He didn't want to think about what did make sense.

Even in its state of repose, blood covering the sand beneath it, the majestic creature looked peaceful. A tear slipped down Splinter's face, and he made no move to wipe it away. There weren't many of these creatures left, and every whale lost was a tragic waste.

"You thinking what I'm thinking?" Will said.

Splinter nodded, but said nothing.

5

"So you told Lenah where I was?" Splinter said.

Jessie laughed. "She's a persuasive woman," the bartender said. "And I thought you could use the dough. What with your outstanding tab and all."

"Yeah," Splinter said. He took a long pull of his pint.

He sat on a stool at Seaside Sam's, a restaurant bar on the walkway that ran along the beach. The front doors that allowed the restaurant to be open air when desired hadn't been replaced, and wind pushed sand across the floor and tables. Most of the interior had been renovated, but here and there signs of the tsunami remained. A staircase missing its handrail. The bar itself no longer had shelves behind it and all the liquor bottles were lined up on a folding table. The kitchen was fixed, but Jessie was still waiting for the Board of Health to complete their inspection. With all the renovations and repairs they were two months behind on commercial properties. Thankfully his liquor license didn't require any further inspections.

"Hey, what am I? Dirt?" It was Kyle Grape, a local shithead Splinter couldn't stand. The guy always tried to get him to talk about his military days.

"I'll have a Bud. Tap."

"Comin' right up."

Splinter drained his pint and pushed the empty glass across the bar. A TV mounted in the corner played a Marlins game, but nobody was paying attention to it. Splinter gazed out at the Atlantic Ocean, then closed his eyes, enjoying the warm sea breeze and the fresh air.

"Another one?" Jessie said.

"Sure," Splinter said.

"I'll get that one," Kyle said. "And set up two shots of scotch. Shit. Make it three. One for you too, Jessie."

Splinter said nothing.

"Yes, sir," Jessie said, a little too exuberantly.

"What the hell are you so happy about?" Kyle asked.

"Life man. L-i-v-i-n," Jessie said, doing his best Wooderson imitation.

"That movie sucked," Kyle said.

"Bite your tongue. Dazed and Confused is a classic," Jessie said.

"Maybe for you hippies," he said. "Don't you agree, Splinter?"

"You have no idea what you're talking about," Splinter said. His beer had arrived, and he took a long pull.

Kyle made a face and buried his nose in his bud.

Splinter stared at himself in the cracked mirror behind the bar. His graying black hair was pulled-back in a ponytail, and it shined with five days grease. His fishhook scar was deep red, and his eyes burned like cinders. He looked older than his forty-two years. He'd upgraded his t-shirt, but it was smudged with dirt, obscuring the University of Texas logo.

Disgusted with his appearance, Splinter spun on his stool and stared out at Main Street through a window with no glass. Cars and work trucks snaked around piles of debris, and a thick coating of sand covered most of the blacktop. The stone buildings still stood, though they had to be completely gutted before they could be used again. Smaller, less stable structures had been swept away, and the town looked like a mouth missing several teeth. It would take years for Sailfish Haven to get back to full strength, if it ever did. Splinter felt the town's fate fell squarely on the back of the fish. If they kept coming, the town might make it, if they didn't it wouldn't, and recently fishermen had been seeing a decline in their bounty.

Nine days had slipped away since the right whale had washed-up on the beach, and in that time the fish seemed to have left.

"Any word from the big heads?" Splinter asked.

"Not that I've heard," Jessie said. "But all the fishermen have been bitching. They're starting to lose charters. Word's getting around that our fish rush might be over."

Jessie held up his shot. "Cheers." The three men touched glasses and drank.

"Splinter, you saw Lenah?" Kyle asked.

He spun back around on his stool and looked the annoying man in the eye. "Don't you worry about Lenah. She can take care of herself. Trust me."

"Sure. Just wondering if she's brought anything in the last few days."

"No idea," Splinter said. "Haven't seen her in a while."

"What is it with you? You know how hot she is, right? Every guy from here to Ocala wants a piece of her, but you, no. You've got better things to do," Kyle said.

Heat flushed over Splinter's face as anger rose in him. He closed his eyes and breathed. In and out. In and out. Splinter said nothing. He watched a homeless person digging through the garbage can on the walkway.

It was an old woman. Her gray hair fell in slimy strands over her face, and her red flannel shirt was dirty and timeworn. Her cart was parked behind her and was filled with an assortment of objects that had no apparent use.

Without warning the woman teetered and grabbed the side of the pail she was rummaging through.

Splinter moved fast and sure. He slipped from his stool, crossed the walkway, and put his hand on the woman's shoulder. "Do you need help?"

The woman's head whipped around, but when she saw Splinter, her eyes widened but her expression softened. "Just a little dizzy." Her knees gave out and she collapsed.

Splinter caught her and eased her to the ground and propped her against the trashcan. "Are you alright?" he asked.

"Yes, now I am. Thank you so much. God bless you," the woman said.

"God? You believe in God?"

"Of course. You don't?"

"Why does he let you live on the street if he loves you?" Splinter asked, though he knew what her response would be.

"Who am I but a simple servant, and I don't know God's plan, but I know he has one."

"Does it involve you sleeping on the street?" Splinter was getting frustrated.

"Son, find God and all will become clear."

Splinter nodded and headed back to his beer.

When he arrived, Kyle said, "What are you doing? You probably got fleas from being so close."

Splinter passed his stool, his beer dripping perspiration on the bar, and stood before Kyle. "Listen you moron, don't talk to me again or I'll…" The TV had caught Splinter's attention. "Turn that up," he said to Jessie, who was helping a customer.

On screen the baseball game had been interrupted for a special news bulletin from the local affiliate. The tagline at the bottom of the screen said 'Teen Missing in Indian River'. Splinter went behind the bar and turned up the volume.

"Just minutes ago the Coast Guard informed local police that Adam Darnald, a local ten-year-old boy, is missing, and was swimming in the shallows off Dynamite Point. He was last seen riding his boogie board in the light surf."

The picture shifted to a live image of two coastie boats and three smaller police cruisers moving back-and-forth across the inlet, searching. "The child's board was found broken in two, and a small scrap of his blue rash guard was found floating in the water. Investigators don't expect foul play and aren't ruling out a gator or shark attack. Great whites have been seen recently entering the bay, and with the sea still littered with corpses it may be that the bigger fish are coming in to feed. More tonight on the six o'clock news. Back to you Linda."

Splinter went back to his stool. The bar had gone silent, and the distant sound of waves lapping on the shore and the push of the wind filled the silence.

He finished his beer and tossed a five-dollar bill on the bar. He got up and hung his backpack over a shoulder.

Jessie said, "Don't go yet. Let me buy you one." The bartender took the glass and placed it under the tap.

Splinter took a seat at the end of the bar, away from Kyle.

Jesse came with the beer, and in a low tone said, "Whatcha think? A shark get that kid?"

Splinter's stomach turned to ice, the giant shark head filling his mind. "Don't know. What are the fishermen really saying?" Splinter looked down the bar at Kyle. He stared at the Marlin's game.

Jessie slid the chilly pint of Pabst Blue Ribbon across the bar to him. "They're mighty pissed. Something's scaring away the fish and they think it's all the dredging and clean-up work that's being done, but I don't know."

"What do you mean?"

"What I mean is I've been running this dive for fourteen years, and they dredge parts of the inner bay and the inlet regularly. Maybe five times in the last ten years, and it's never had any impact on the fish."

"It doesn't make sense anyway. Fish patterns are what the sea throws at them. I don't think it has anything to do with the clean-up. But if it isn't that, what then?" Splinter said.

"Got to be a shark. With the kid, the whale. Got to be a shark," Jessie said.

6

Poseidon hissed at Galatia, and Nereus whimpered like an infant.

Splinter sat with his feet dangling off the bow of his half-sunken home, his cane pole draped over the railing. Nereus was a midsized mutt with curly salt-and-pepper hair. Splinter had found him swimming in the flotsam after the tsunami, and the dog was still afraid of his own shadow.

Sunning themselves on the forward deck was Galatia and Poseidon. Poseidon was a gray and black tabby bitch who constantly bullied the calmer and more intelligent Galatia. The stray cats had smelled his cooking fish and sought him out. The animals cost minimal money, and Splinter liked having them around. They made him feel like he wasn't alone, especially in the deep of night when the sweats came on, and memories of Kabul sucked him toward the abyss.

Splinter's love of the sea had prompted his new friends' names. Nereus was the old man of the sea, and the Greek god of the sea's rich bounty of fish. Seemed right to Splinter. Poseidon was the leader of the gods of the sea, and that fit the gray-black tabby perfectly, as did Galatia's. She was the god of calm seas. The animals had their own cabin next to his, and they usually lounged there during the hottest part of the day.

Splinter had become a man of the sea despite both of his parents disliking the water and barely being able to swim. His mom, who was still alive and lived on her teacher's pension in California, despised the ocean and only went in pools when she needed to cool off. Splinter never recalled his father in the water. His seafaring genes came from further back. He was a distant relative of legendary Navy Captain Johnston Blakeley, the captain of the famous Wasp, which disappeared in the mid-Atlantic in 1814.

The fish weren't biting, but he had nothing else to eat and didn't feel like traveling into town. A week had passed, but the dead right whale and the missing child still clogged his head. His mind drifted as his red and white bobber floated away with the current. A seagull tore overhead, screeching and wailing at him. It perched itself on the roof of the cabin and stared at Splinter like he didn't belong.

In the distance the sound of a boat tearing through the inlet echoed over the water, a steady whine that rose and fell as the boat cut through the light chop. He pulled his line from the water and leaned the pole against the gunnel. He got up, went to the stern, and stuck his nose into the air, sniffing. Gas, rot, and sea salt filled his nostrils… and something else. He couldn't put his finger on it. Baking meat? The seagull jerked its head toward the inlet, then dropped off the cabin's roof and took flight, soaring above the water and disappearing into the mangroves.

The outboard's whine faltered, and there was a crash, and then screams of panic, fear, and pain. The crunch of twisting metal and grinding gears made Splinter grip the handrail that ran around the gunnel. There was a tiny pop, like the backfire of a car, then more cries.

Splinter jumped through the access hatch into the cabin. He needed his binoculars. Where the hell were those things? He searched the half-flooded galley and found nothing. He eased over a pile of fishing net he'd found, and made his way aft to his living quarters.

The gun locker he'd found in an attic of a flooded mansion stared at him as he went by, its black metal door appraising him, asking where the "real" Splinter was. When he'd found the cabinet, its key hung from the lock, and what was inside brought on the rage. He hadn't fired a gun since Kabul, but the case of guns and ammo was worth too much money to leave behind. So he'd taken the gun locker, bought a new combo lock, and tossed the combination in the sea.

He found his old military field glasses stowed with his meager clothing, and he grabbed them and darted back topside.

"Anyone coming with?" Splinter said.

Nereus cried and scuttled below deck to his room. Galatia looked up from where she lay, then laid her head back down. Only Poseidon appeared interested. The cat moseyed along the deck, watching him, as if weighing her options. Cats were supposed to hate the water, but Poseidon hadn't gotten the memo. That cat swam in the ocean and the bay, something Splinter had never seen in all his travels. He guessed it had something to do with the trauma the cat suffered at the hands of the tsunami.

Poseidon finally reached him, and Splinter said, "Well let's go. I'm in a hurry."

The cat looked at him the way cats do, with an air of superiority and nonchalance. She jumped in the boat, sat on the forward seat, and curled her tail around her back. When Splinter didn't start the engine right away, the cat turned its head and looked back at him and Splinter was certain he saw impatience there.

On this day his old 15HP beater started on the first pull. Splinter dropped the lead line and set course for the inlet. The inner bay was a blown-out mess, steep two-foot whitecaps that sent splashes of water into the Zodiac. Three inches of water already sloshed in the bottom of the boat, and Splinter was only halfway to the inlet.

Poseidon had her nose pushed out, head thrust into the spray, a light coating of mist covering the cat's sleek hair. She barely moved with the bump and jerks of the boat and sat like a statue.

Fort Pierce inlet opened to his right, and the deep channel was blocked by a large fishing trawler that was going down. The ship's alarm bellowed, and sirens pierced the day. Splinter checked the throttle. He was going as fast as he could. What could he do anyway?

Poseidon hissed, and the damp hair on the cat's back and tail rose as if with static electricity. The cat hissed again, and Splinter slowed.

The sun emerged from behind a cloud and something dark and huge passed beneath the dinghy. Splinter killed the engine, trying not to draw attention to himself as he searched the water. His disposable camera hung from the dinghy's gunnel, and he grabbed it, pointing it at the sea, but the large dark shape was gone.

A Coast Guard SAFE boat arrived, orange pontoons pounding the water, white pilothouse glistening in the sunlight. Splinter restarted the outboard and pushed on toward the sinking fishing boat. It was hard to see what was happening, but the trawler was going down fast.

"Please stay away. Do not interfere." The Coast Guard boat gave orders over their enunciation system.

They were right. If he was too close to the trawler when it went down, his little craft would be sucked under. He killed the motor again and pulled out his binoculars.

The old fiberglass hull had a huge hole just above the waterline, as if it had hit a rock or been torpedoed. Seawater poured through the main rip, and Splinter saw several other, smaller holes.

Fishermen and deckhands jumped from the vessel, splashing into the sea all around the sinking ship, and frantically swimming away from the doomed boat. The sight of the people in the water made Splinter think of the shadow.

He was floating dangerously close to the wreck when the Coast Guard vessel said, "You are interfering with a rescue. Leave the area at once." The wind and current were taking him into the inlet, and toward the fracas. Birds circled overhead, but no shiners jumped from the water. Apparently, they were smarter than him.

Splinter cranked the Johnson but it only sputtered. The current pulled him into the inlet, toward the sinking fishing vessel. He rewound the pull cord and pulled again. Nothing. Third time was the charm, and Splinter spun the boat around, racing from the coastie boat.

He looked back as he sped away. The tip of the fishing boat's bow disappeared beneath the green sea. The people in the water were being collected by the Coast Guard. Harbor Patrol cruised through the inlet from the ocean, but to Splinter it looked like they weren't moving fast enough. They'd move a lot faster if they knew what he did.

Shit was getting real.

7

Splinter sat alone in the dark, a bottle of vodka between his legs. The galley reeked of the sea and dead fish, but he barely noticed. Outside the wind whispered and sighed, and the mangrove leaves rattled. He took a pull off the bottle and wiped his mouth with the back of his hand. Stray beams of moonlight cut across the compartment, the small porthole on the starboard bulkhead providing the only light.

He heard screaming in the depths of his mind. Men yelling and children crying. He smelt gun powder, felt the pounding of the concussion bombs decimating Kabul. Strobes of light flashed, and to Splinter the porthole filled with orange-white light. If only he'd waited. Not tried to push the issue. But he had to be the big man. The hero that had to save the day.

Pale moonlight filled the porthole again. Splinter shook his head, trying to shake himself from the fog. He knew his PTSD was working on him, trying to drag him into a pit of self-pity and never let him out. What happened was his fault. No one else. The docs had said not to fight this realization. Don't let it dominate your destiny, but that wasn't easy advice to follow when your brain wouldn't cooperate.

The moon went behind a cloud and the cabin grew dark. He took a pull of vodka, the sharp bite and sweet tang soothing his jumping nerves. He savored the burn as the booze slid down his throat, momentarily easing the pain. The shifting memories. The changing scene. Where was he? Why was he here?

His hands shook, and he held them out and tried to steady them. He gripped the vodka bottle so tight his knuckles hurt. Nereus whined and started to cry. Splinter dropped his hand onto the animal's back and stroked his curly hair. Poseidon took a seat on the bench beside the galley table and rested her head on her paws.

Crickets chirped, seagulls cried, frogs bleated, and occasionally Poseidon would hiss as her dreams tormented her. Nereus sat beside him, his head on Splinter's foot, eyes wide open. The dog always had trouble sleeping when Splinter was in the fog, like the two were connected. The dog knew how he felt, shared his depression, his anger, and his rare moments of joy. Splinter knew that with a certainty he couldn't explain.

Galatia was nowhere to be seen and was mostly likely already curled up on her bundle of rags that served as her bed.

Poseidon's head snapped up, the cat's green eyes glowing in the darkness. The feline turned its head aft, staring into the blackness. Nereus started to cry, halting bursts like he was spooked. Poseidon stood up, still staring into the darkness.

The fog over Splinter's mind thinned, a ray of reality breaking through. He took a pull of vodka. Then he heard it. The distant sound of an approaching boat. Splinter shifted in his seat. His back ached, and his right knee where he'd taken shrapnel nine years prior stung like the damage was new. There were still flecks of metal in the cartilage around the knee, but the Navy docs said it wasn't worth risking further damage to remove them. Splinter lived with the pain every day, but it was nothing compared to the pain he inflicted on himself.

The boat was getting closer. A deep moan echoed over the water, and every few moments it would falter and fart. Splinter chuckled. He knew the sound of those motors. He knew it very well. Splinter drained the vodka and tossed the bottle across the cabin. He leaned forward, pulled open a Styrofoam cooler, grabbed a beer and opened it. Splinter downed the entire beer in one pull, crunched the can, and grabbed another.

The sound of the engines was all he could hear, then they ceased, and Lenah's boat bumped against his half sunken home.

"Splinter? You there?" she shouted.

He said nothing. Anger rose in him, the fog returning, the alcohol telling him he had every right to be pissed-off at the world and who the hell was this bitch anyway? She'd tossed him aside like garbage because he was damaged.

"Splinter? I know you're here. I see your boat," she said.

Splinter sat in the dark, comfortable in the blackness where he couldn't see the world and the world couldn't see him. He opened his mouth to call out to her, but didn't.

He heard her pick up her lead line, then faint scraping as she tied off on an aft cleat. "Splinter? Come on. I need to talk to you."

Footfalls on the deck above, moving toward the hatch. The snap of a flashlight coming on. A beam of light cut the darkness from above. "Splinter?"

He grabbed his sixty-inch AB Biller Mahogany Special sling speargun that fired double-barbed stainless-steel arrows with such force they could take out the biggest of fish, or so he'd thought. He held the weapon across his chest and stared into the darkness.

She came down the ladder and panned the flashlight around the galley until it came to rest on his face. "Oh, Splinter." She panned the light around. "Nice place you've got here."

"What are you doing here?"

"Hello to you too," she said. Then she noticed the spear gun and her eyes went wide. "What's that for?"

"Trespassers."

"This is private property?"

"What is it you want?" He shifted position and disengaged the silent safety on the spear gun, making a show of it, making sure she knew what he'd done. He pointed its tip at her, then rested the gun on his raised knee.

"Your help."

She panned the light around, examining his life, pity splashing across her face. A plastic bin filled with cups, dishes and bent silverware sat in a sink that Splinter had never seen run. The garbage was overflowing, and one corner waders, a tackle box, and two fishing poles rested against the bulkhead.

The flashlight settled on the locked gun cabinet. "What's in there?"

"The last person who came here asking for help," Splinter said.

"What's the combo to the lock? In case you get hit by a bus."

"I threw it in the ocean," Splinter said.

"Stellar."

"Why are you here?"

"You got plans?"

"Why are you here?" He yelled so loud he surprised himself.

Lenah jumped and took a step back. She had that look in her eyes. The look that said despite how well she knew him, he still scared her. It made Splinter feel shitty and powerful at the same time. His stomach ached, and somewhere in the back of his mind he felt shame, but the fog pushed it away. He pointed the spear gun at her. "What do you want?"

"What the hell is wrong with you?"

Splinter knew the routine well. She'd moved on from fear to anger, but he said nothing.

"Whatever."

Nereus got up and went to her, nudging her with his snout, as if to say, "Don't mind this ass."

"Nereus, get over here."

The dog hesitated for an instant, but then went to Splinter, tail between his legs. Splinter's eyes burned. He was losing it.

"Listen, you hear about the kid?"

Splinter laughed. "You mean what was the kid?"

"You heard?"

Splinter sat up, leaning forward and almost dropping the long spear gun. "What? I knew the kid was gone, but…"

"He's still mostly gone."

"Mostly?"

"Coast Guard found his right hand, severed clean at the wrist and missing three fingers," she said. "They saw a mound of crabs ripping at something on the beach over at Hook Point."

Splinter swayed in his seat, patches of black fading in and out with the moving flashlight beam. Pain lanced his back and perspiration dripped down his forehead. "Can you turn that light off?"

She stared at him, her eyebrows knitted, lips pursed. She didn't turn the light off.

"Please. Hurts my eyes."

She sighed and thumbed off the flashlight. "How long have you been sitting here? You smell three days dead."

He grunted.

"Fine." She sat down and grabbed a beer from the cooler.

"Help yourself."

She opened the Pabst and took a pull. "There's no doubt now."

"There ain't nothing but doubt," he said.

"For shits-sake. You know what I mean."

"I do?"

"Whatever we saw is hunting in our waters. First the shark, the whale, then the boat, then the kid."

"Yeah."

"Yeah, what? This kid was attacked, and it wasn't a shark and you know it," she said.

Splinter said nothing.

"You got nothing to say? We saw the damn thing."

"We saw a shadow. A dark shape beneath the water. After a long day under the sun."

"People are dying Splinter, and maybe you can fool yourself, but I can't," she said.

"What do you know of it?"

"I know we have to tell the coasties."

"We've been through this," he said. He finished his beer, crunched the can, and tossed it across the galley.

"Things have changed," she said.

"No they haven't. It's not my problem."

"Not your problem?"

As if a switch had been flipped, the real Splinter peeked through the fog. "I think I saw it. When I went out to see the wreck in the inlet. Thing swam right beneath me."

"So it's in Indian River? Not good. The water gets deep in spots."

"It's a fish, Lenah, who the hell knows where it is. And who the hell cares." He fired the spear gun, and the stainless-steel dart streaked through the air with a hiss and lodged in the bulkhead over Lenah's shoulder. It wasn't close, but even in his current state he knew it was beyond an asshole move.

She jumped and flicked on the light. "Screw you, Splinter. I'm gone."

"What else is new."

"And whose fault is that?"

"Nobody asked you to come."

"No, you didn't, but I thought I owed you an explanation. I know going to the authorities might cause problems for you."

"Problems? Problems? When they find out where and who I am, I'll have to leave Florida."

"Splinter," she knelt before him and took his hand. He pulled it from her grasp and looked away. "I know you did some shitty things in the war, but nobody blames you. It was war, whatever you did you had to do."

"How do you know? Huh? You're just talking out your ass like everyone else."

"You're not the only one in pain. Not the only one hurting. Parents have lost a son, and I'm not going to let that happen again."

"Oh, and how do you plan to stop this thing? Let's say I agree, and there's some apex out there lurking in the bay. What of it? The Coast Guard can't stop boatloads of illegals coming from every damn place, and you think they'll be able to find this thing? They'll make it worse."

"Worse? For them or for you?"

"Get out. Leave me alone." He drained his beer, but when he went to fish out another, he almost fell off his chair. Nereus cried and put his head on Splinter's knee, but Poseidon got up, flicked her tail side-to-side and pranced off.

"I'll go, but I'm telling everything I know tomorrow, whether you like it or not and they're going to want to talk to you," Lenah said.

"Let them try," Splinter said. He let the empty spear gun fall to the floor.

Lenah glanced at the gun case and got up. "See you around, Splinter." She hauled herself up through the hatch and he heard her retreat across the deck and step onto her boat. Engines rumbled to life, and Splinter heard Galatia crying in her room.

Lenah's boat pulled away, and Splinter cried, thick tears rolling down his face and dripping onto his chest. Lenah was the only woman he'd ever loved. She deserved better than him. Everyone deserved better than him. The rumble of the Parker's outboards faded, and the night deepened. Splinter leaned back in his chair, opened another beer, and waited for the dawn.

8

Seagulls wheeled overhead, their constant squawking making Splinter's head throb. The sun was brutal, and heat rolled across the park in waves, pushing over the picnic area. Splinter sat at a stone table with a chess board painted on its top, a tall bottle of water at his elbow. He didn't drink every day, but when he did he went all in, and his body didn't appreciate it. Despite being over forty, he was still in excellent shape, and his diet of fish and water served him well, and foreign contaminants threw off the delicate balance.

He was waiting for Will. They met every Thursday for a game of chess, and Splinter was eager to see his friend. Hopefully he'd have news. He heard a car door slam and looked toward the lot. Will was getting out of his white Ford Taurus, an old rusting piece of metal the retired cop refused to get rid of. When asked, his friend would say, "Who the hell do I have to impress?"

He watched Will lock up his car and make his way to him, the leather satchel containing the chess pieces under his arm. He held two cups of coffee in a cardboard holder, and he placed it on the table when he arrived.

"Have some joe. From what I hear, you need it," Will said. He sat down, took a sip of coffee, and started setting up the board.

Splinter said nothing as he sipped his coffee and gazed out at the ocean.

"Saw Lenah this morning. She told me about last night," Will said.

He didn't remember much about the prior evening, other than he'd been an ass and treated the one woman he cared for like shit. Why she even bothered with him he didn't know.

"Gonna say anything?" Will said. "You've got to shake out of this funk, buddy. You're destroying yourself. You're black."

"I know, but..." There were still some things he couldn't talk about with anyone, not even Will.

"No buts. Your move, smoke before fire," Will said.

Splinter slid a pawn forward two squares and Will matched the move. They played in silence for several minutes, and in that time Will took a rook, a bishop, three pawns, and a knight. Splinter took two pawns. He hadn't beaten Will in weeks.

As they played Will said, "So I've got a bit of news. Lenah said she mentioned the boy's hand."

Splinter nodded but said nothing. The coffee tasted good, but his head still pounded.

"There was a sighting Sunday. Right in Snake River. Two kids out on a sailboat. They got a picture." Will slid the photo across the table and Splinter picked it up.

It was a color shot of the sea, green-blue water with tiny white ripples on the surface. Beneath, a dark shape contrasted against the emerald water. To Splinter it looked like the shadow of a cloud. He slid the photo back to Will and said, "That could be anything."

"Yup, but the kid's description sounded close to what we saw," Will said.

Splinter moved his queen and said, "Check." He sipped his coffee.

"And? You got anything?"

Splinter sighed, and Will moved his king out of check. "I think I saw it again. The day the boat went down in the inlet."

"Lenah said. About that. You should see the hull. I went down to the boatyard and checked it out."

"And?"

"And it looks like just what you thought. Something bit the damn thing, but nobody downtown wants to admit that. It can't be proven, of course, but get this." He paused and took Splinter's second rook. "I talked to one of the coasties, a young kid who hasn't learned to shut his pie-hole yet. He told me when they hauled the boat a tooth was found stuck in the fiberglass."

"A tooth? How big?"

"Kid said about eight inches, and it could have been bigger," Will said.

"The boat was reinforced fiberglass, and you're telling me something bit a hole in it? I mean, I never really believed that to be possible, but a tooth? Damn, that doesn't leave much to the imagination."

"No and..." Will trailed off because Splinter got up without warning and bolted through the park onto the beach.

A young boy had lost his kite and was chasing his spool of string as it hopped and jerked across the sand. Splinter turned on the burners. He passed the kid and dove onto the sand and grabbed the kite line just as it was lifting off the ground. Splinter got on his knees and reeled in the giant red dragon modeled after Drogon on Game of Thrones. The kite's large wings bellowed in the wind and it started to fall. Splinter vaulted to his feet and ran. The dragon soared, and when the kid caught up Splinter handed the boy the spool of twine.

"Thanks, mister," the kid said.

Splinter tussled the boy's hair and smiled.

When he got back to Will the retired cop said, "You never fail to surprise me."

"What?" said Splinter, feigning innocence. As much as he didn't want to admit it, he cared for people. He couldn't help it. The more downtrodden and innocent, the more he cared. But when the fog took him…

"You…" Will switched gears. "You can show such kindness."

"Navy shrink used to say that's what…" Splinter faltered, and he looked away.

Will had known Splinter long enough to let it be. Will sipped his coffee and took one of Splinter's pawns. A long row of Splinter's black pieces ran along the right side of the board, and only four white pieces sat at Splinter's elbow.

"There's more. Talked to my old partner, Gus. He says a scuba diver fishing for lobster in the channel saw something huge. He described a huge crocodile-type beast with rows of razor-sharp teeth and pale skin. Said the thing passed beneath him and was at least thirty feet long," Will said.

Splinter snickered. "What'd they say? They call the special ambulance?"

"No, but they didn't believe the guy. Told him how the water can distort and magnify things. How there's no such thing as a thirty-foot crocodile. They told him it was a shadow. His imagination. Anything but consider he may have seen something because then they'd have to deal with it, and I think that scares them more than anything."

"What do you think? You think Lenah is right? We have to come forward?"

"Well, it doesn't really matter. Our boy—"

Splinter cut him off. "They might listen to you. You're one of them. But you're retired and they'll probably just patronize you. And me? I'm a crazy homeless person to them. No credibility whatsoever, so what's the point?"

"Harbor Patrol and the Coast Guard have their hands full, Splinter. Bodies are still washing up on shore and there is still a lot of debris in the water. They don't have time for mythical beasts, real or imagined. Plus, the town is half deserted and the fishermen don't care. If things were normal, the inner bay would be clogged with police and coasties."

"My point exactly," Splinter said.

"And that's not the least of it," Will said.

Splinter lifted his chin. "What?" He made his move. The board was looking very white, and Splinter only had a few pieces left.

Will pulled out his cellphone and tapped the screen. "This isn't going to be easy to watch, but I think you have to."

Will cued-up a news report on the local affiliate website, WPTV. A picture of Brownie Keato surrounded by reporters and cameras filled the small screen and Will rotated the phone to make the picture bigger.

Splinter took the phone with a trembling hand. Cellphones scared him. He used to love technology, but now anything beyond a radio set his nerves on edge. The wind picked up, and sand cut into his face.

The field reporter stood with the Miami skyline in the background, her long black hair falling over one shoulder. "Terror in the deep? Or terror in our bay? Mr. Keato claims to have seen a giant sea monster off the coast and he says that's what killed Adam Darnald."

The camera pulled out and Brownie stood next to the reporter, his stupid smirk bigger than normal. He wore a t-shirt that read Palmitari Trucking, and when the camera went to him, he smiled. The reporter stuck her microphone in his face and said, "Please tell Miami what you told me just moments ago."

"Sure thing, Linda," said Brownie. "Me and my bro Sal went on a fishing charter, on the Evenstar. We were pulling them in left and right because we're good fishermen. We're from up north where the big boys do it. Anyway, I'm reeling in this monster sailfish, when a shark bigger than any fish I've ever seen comes by the boat. I wanted to try and catch it, Linda, but the others were wimps."

"Others?"

"Yeah, a retired cop named William Dodge, a guy named Splinter Woods, Captain Brisbee, and my buddy. They all saw what I saw."

"What did you see?"

"You're not gonna believe it, Linda."

Splinter harrumphed as Brownie bent in close to the reporter and she leaned away, the left side of her head disappearing from the frame. "Try me," said the reporter.

Brownie laughed, and said, "We need to save that for later."

The reporter said nothing and waited patiently with the mike poised in front of Brownie's face.

"The shark circled us, like it was playing with us, waiting to attack. I wanted to throw some chum in the water and take a few shots with the spear guns, but Captain Brisbee said no. A real buzzkill Captain Brisbee is. So we waited and did nothing. The shark made a run at the boat, and his nose struck the hull hard. Shook me where I stood."

"You must have been scared."

"Naw. It's a fish, right? One with fifty razor-sharp teeth six inches long, but still a fish and we were on the boat."

Will said, "Here's where it gets interesting."

Brownie said, "The shark dove. We couldn't see it. Then the water starts bubbling like the sea was boiling. The shark's head bursts from the water, and I ran for a gaff and I was gonna poke the mother. The captain and this Woods guy wanted to take off, but Sal and I wanted to catch this thing. Then something strange happened. There was no shark. Its body was gone."

"What are you saying? Something killed the shark?"

"Severed its head right off," Brownie said.

The reporter waited, and when Brownie didn't continue, she said, "And then?"

"Oh, right, the most important part. Then we saw this huge monster glide beneath the boat. Thing had to be fifty feet long if it was ten."

"What did this leviathan look like?"

"We only saw its shadow, but like I said, it was big."

The camera focused on the reporter, and she said, "Mr. Keato came forward as a concerned citizen when Adam Darnald's hand turned up in the bay." The scene shifted to B-roll of the Indian River. "Is there a creature bigger than a great white shark prowling our waters?" she continued. "If so, what can be done about it? And by who? WPTV has discovered that Splinter Woods is none other than The Butcher of Kabul, Ex-Navy SEAL Matthew Woods."

Splinter tapped the phone and let it fall on the table. His head was spinning. How did they find out so fast? That shit Sal. Splinter shook his head. He shouldn't have antagonized the delicate Italian snowflake. The sun stared down like an accusing eye, and heat rose in him. He rubbed his temples and moved his queen.

"The little shit probably got paid by WPTV," Will said. His friend looked at the ground. "You might not want to watch anymore." He reached over and moved his remaining rook.

Splinter stared at the board and said nothing.

Will said, "Checkmate."

9

Splinter didn't want to watch the helmet-cam footage. He'd seen the eight-second clip that had defined his life many times. He knew what it showed. He tapped the phone anyway, because the tender embrace of the pain was all he knew.

The video jerked into motion and showed shadows dancing on a hallway wall. A soldier stalked a dark passage, and there was yelling and screaming in Arabic. A blast of static made Splinter jump, and he was back there. Like it was yesterday.

He got low, fanning his M4 carbine side-to-side, the fog in control, the fever blinding. He'd lost six men, and all he saw was blood.

The camera's POV showed a door being kicked in, the nose of a gun panning across the screen. Then… then…

Splinter reacted. He didn't think. He didn't reason. He didn't consider anyone's feelings or where they came from or what they stood for. He fired, and shot a woman standing beneath an archway. A man stepped into the room and yelled, followed by a thirteen-year-old boy. Splinter fired again. And again.

The woman was holding a baby and Splinter's shot went through both woman and child. The video staggered and swayed, and so did Splinter.

The video cut out and the small cellphone screen filled with the reporter's face. "Captain Brisbee and Mr. Woods are wanted for questioning, and the Coast Guard has asked anyone with any information pertaining to—"

Splinter tapped the phone and handed it to Will. "I have to disappear. Meet you in two days at the spot at sunset?"

Will nodded. "Sorry about this, Splinter."

This man had dug him out of the shit pile. He owed Will an explanation. Problem was Splinter didn't have one that he could live with. "I'll tell you about—"

Will cut him off. "That's all I needed. When you're ready."

Splinter nodded. "There's more. A lot more. You sure?"

"When you are, I will be," Will said.

"Find out what you can. Wait a few hours, but then you can give them where I live. An act of good faith."

Will's forehead wrinkled, and his eyes narrowed. It was his WTF face.

"I know. Sneaky, but I need you, Will. I need to find out what the hell this thing is and stop it. If they pull me in…"

"Yeah," Will said.

"Two days?"

Will nodded.

***

Lenah never asked him about Kabul. She knew it was bad, and Splinter understood that on some level she didn't want to know. It was easier that way. Like the cop on the beach, Splinter didn't add up on their cookie-cutter list of roles he was supposed to fill. It was much easier to pretend he didn't exist, collateral damage of their freedom that they'd rather not face.

Splinter and Lenah went to the mattresses aboard the Evenstar. Lenah stocked up on food and Splinter managed to get the pets onboard. Poseidon prowled the deck, but Galatia and Nereus huddled below, Nereus shaking like a leaf.

Wind tore across the bow, and the Parker lifted and fell with the roll of the waves. Sea spray fell across the windshield, and auto sensor wipers pushed it away.

Splinter felt Lenah's eyes on him. Watching, but not looking like she was watching. He chuckled. They knew each other that well.

"You OK?" she said.

"Lenah, about the other night. I…" he stammered, and this was when she usually said something like, "I understand", or "when you're ready" and let him off the hook. This time she stayed silent. So did he. The engines hummed, and sea spray carved a path of white over the ocean. He said, "I'm sorry. It's just when I get like that…"

"Maybe less vodka?" She was pissed and Splinter didn't blame her.

"It's worse most nights without it," he said.

Lenah looked away, then her head snapped back. Her eyes narrowed and her full lips became a thin red line. "Saw the news," she said.

"You stop in for questioning?"

"No."

"Why not?"

She said nothing and looked away, but he knew why. She would lead them to him, and she knew Splinter didn't want that.

"Thanks. For the boat. All the food. Helping me out," Splinter said. "Don't know what I'd do without you."

"Yell at Nereus." She met his eye, then looked away. "Don't go thinking this means I give a shit about you."

"Who? Me?"

"We're gonna catch the thing. Drag its dead body into port and make everything right. My charters will be booked for months," she said.

"Don't know about that. If—" Splinter grabbed the dash as a large set rolled through and the twenty-eight-foot Parker dipped forward into a wave valley. Water splashed the windshield and he shifted his weight to maintain balance. "You think people will want to come out here if they see what's swimming in the depths?"

"I do. Same reason half the population under thirty is looking forward to the zombie apocalypse."

Splinter said nothing. She had a point. She always had a point. She was looking at him again, and Splinter said, "What happened in Kabul that night. I don't remember pieces of it, Lenah. But if you need to hear the version I beat myself up with, I'll tell it."

Lenah pulled back on the throttle. The Parker settled in the water and their rooster tail and wake smashed against the transom.

"Let's get a slick going. See if we can draw this thing in," she said. The wind and current pushed them back toward the mouth of the inlet.

"Chum out here? This thing was last seen in the bay," Splinter said.

"Tide's coming in. The slick will get pulled into the bay and we'll follow it in."

Splinter nodded. He knew the sea, but she knew how to catch fish.

They went out on deck and Lenah opened the bucket of three-week-old chum and began ladling it into the sea. Splinter covered his nose. The smell made his stomach gurgle, and he coughed. He'd smelled corpses that had baked in the desert heat for days, but that was nothing compared to her concoction of fermented fish heads, rotten squirrel, and tuna blood, all mixed and aged to perfection like a nasty wine. She called it her "secret sauce."

The oily nastiness spread-out like an oil spill, drifting toward the inlet as it undulated on the rippling sea. When the bucket was half empty she sealed it and secured it to the gunnel with a bungee cord.

Splinter's eyes watered, and he dry heaved.

Lenah laughed. "Hope you didn't have eggs benedict for breakfast."

Dried sailfish, bread and water was hardly eggs benedict, but his stomach heaved anyway as bile crept up his throat. The scent stuck in his nostrils, and he rolled his shoulders and tried to crack his neck.

Lenah went into the pilothouse and spun the wheel to port and the Parker's bow pointed with the wind, the back of the pilothouse serving as a sail. Back out on deck, she said, "Now we wait."

Splinter thought that was all fishermen did.

They didn't speak for a long time as the ocean breeze pushed the Parker behind the slick. Seagulls moaned, an occasional sailfish streaked by. A pair of dolphins floated off to port, examining them, looking like they wanted to play. Splinter knew that wasn't a good sign.

"So this story you beat yourself up with. It's not that I want to hear it. Really. I think I know you and you're a good person."

Splinter laughed.

"Hard to see maybe because you do your best to hide it, but whatever you did I'm sure you have an explanation."

"What if I don't?"

She looked away.

The wind kicked up, and the Atlantic reminded them she was there. A large set of waves swelled beneath the boat, crashing over the bow and rocking the Parker. Splinter lost his footing and fell as Lenah clung to the gunnel.

"You OK?" she said.

Splinter got up, staring at the horizon, but there weren't any more large waves.

"You can thank that gust of wind for that. We should have been paying attention," Lenah said.

"Story of my life."

Silence again. Waves slapped the hull, wind whistled around the pilothouse and snapped their flag, and the Parker's marine antenna swayed back and forth.

"I guess what bothered me most was when they court-martialed me. They let me off with an honorable discharge in the end, but it still felt like punishment. Worst part is, I deserved worse."

Lenah sat on the gunnel, her gaze shifting every few seconds to the surface of the sea. The sun had passed noon, and the afternoon was waning as the inlet drew closer. Another hour and they'd be in Indian River.

"We went in to get a corporate asshole who'd partied too hard in the hash bars in Kabul. The war was in full swing, so it was supposed to be an easy crash and grab. In and out in half-an-hour. But they were waiting for us. Knew exactly where we'd hit them."

Lenah's head jerked up. "How?"

"They're not as stupid as we like to pretend. They study our tactics, and they covered all three of our potential entry points. Drew us in and ambushed us. I lost three men in a fire fight. Head shots."

Lenah gazed out at the sea and wouldn't look at him.

"They called me back. Said I was to retreat to the extraction point. I ordered us forward and that was ultimately the excuse they used to kick me out. Disobeying a direct command from a senior tactical officer," he said.

"Why didn't you follow orders?"

"I don't know," Splinter said. He let out a long breath and closed his eyes. "I was in a rage. I pressed forward, chasing down the guys who'd killed my men. They led us straight into another trap and I lost four more. Right there in front of me. I pushed on, command chattering in my head, my remaining men trying to get me to see reason. But I was gone. Snapped. Lost it. I don't remember much after that. The Navy jag said I went on a rampage through two buildings, and killed seven people, no combatants."

Splinter searched the ocean, but saw nothing but whitecaps and the shimmer of the sun. "And you saw the ending on the news. Haven't fired a gun since and I jump every time something bangs. In the dark the fog comes on and I'm not sure if I can control myself."

"Was that you on the video?" Lenah said.

Splinter nodded. She didn't look away or appear disgusted as he'd expected. Her face instead filled with pity, and somehow that was worse. That look that told him he was a lost cause. There was no hope.

"You don't remember anything about the other people they say you killed?"

Splinter shook his head no. "I have a memory gap of about eight minutes. The docs said it was blindness and mental blocking brought on by the extreme battle conditions and my PTSD. One doctor said it was like I was a metal railing that's been painted too many times. Layer upon layer of trauma, until there's nothing else there."

The Evenstar was almost to the inlet and the sun was starting its descent to the horizon. They'd seen no sign of the beast. No waste. Fish parts. No blood in the water, and the local fish didn't appear spooked.

They floated a few more hours, through the inlet and into the bay, and as the sun set and the tide shifted, Lenah started the motors. "I'm gonna head over to Jennings Cove and anchor up inside the hook for the night so we can eat and catch some sleep. Work for you?"

Splinter nodded in the twilight.

10

After two days of searching they'd seen no sign of the creature and Splinter was starting to wonder if the huge fish had gone back out to sea. Fishing is a solitary and frustrating business, and Lenah and Splinter were already getting on each other's nerves, living on the boat with no other human contact. The animals helped, though they favored Lenah and that pissed Splinter off. The three in-greats. He'd pulled them from the garbage, and they abandoned him for the first pretty face. Splinter smiled. When this was all over he thought it best the three of them stay with Lenah. They'd be better off away from him.

The day had been hot and humid, a sparrow fart breeze doing nothing to stir the air. They'd caught a few sailfish and tarpon for dinner, but there was no sign of the leviathan. The Parker rocked in the gentle swell as it cut through the water at a steady twenty knots, sea spray raining down around the boat, a fifteen-foot rooster tail jetting out behind them. Splinter hardly noticed the motion. He had his Navy legs back, and his body adjusted with every shift in the boat's position.

"Before we anchor up for the evening we have a stop to make," Splinter said.

Lenah drew back on the throttle and the engines eased and the boat slowed.

"Will's meeting us down on Middle Point at sunset."

"Do tell," Lenah said.

"Don't know. He was going to dig in and we're... gonna tell him we didn't see shit," Splinter said.

Lenah tapped her NAV screen and set a southern course down Indian River to Middle Point. "Eighteen minutes, but figure twenty. There's two boats on the NAV and I'm going to steer clear of them."

Splinter nodded. They weren't wanted, but if those vessels were coastie, police or harbor patrol, and they were stopped, it would be game over.

"Can you get the Zodiac ready?" Lenah asked.

"Aye aye, Captain."

Splinter fetched the deflated dinghy from the cabin and brought it out on deck. He unsnapped the hasps on the bag and unrolled the boat. It was Splinter's twelve-footer, and it was covered with yellowed patches and dirt and the hull numbers were half-smudged off. He took out the air pump and connected it to the port pontoon, and ass-inched across deck to the battery compartment. He opened the battery cabinet and connected the pump's negative and positive leads to the battery. The pump rumbled to life and Splinter went to get the outboard.

Lenah cut the motors and the Parker eased through the dark bay. Splinter finished filling the Zodiac then put it in the water and tethered it to an aft cleat. He mounted the new 15HP Merc Lenah had bought and placed his sixty-inch speargun in the bow. To the west the calm waters of the inner bay of Snake River stretched into the distance, and off the bow to the east, Vitolo Preserve was edged in rocks and mangroves.

A flashlight blinked on in the darkness. Then off. On. Off.

"Dropping anchor," Lenah yelled. She spun the wheel, turning the Parker into the wind as the anchor released from its holding clamps. Chain rattled over the bow and the anchor splashed into the water. Its line rubbed and squeaked as it ran out fast, then eased when the anchor hit bottom.

The Parker drifted for another twenty seconds then jerked to a stop when Lenah locked the line and the twenty-two-pound fluke anchor sunk its teeth into the soft bottom. She switched off the red/green bow light, turned on the white NAV light mounted atop the pilothouse, then turned off the electronics and the cabin light.

Headlights spilled across the mangroves as cars raced along A1A. The scent of the sea mixed with rot and tainted with gas fumes reminded Splinter of San Francisco Bay. Pipers and herons chirped and sang, frogs bleeped, and seagulls squawked at the sparrows who fought for dead crabs along the shoreline. The water was still, and the dinghy hardly moved as Splinter and Lenah positioned themselves in the small craft. Lenah sat by the transom on the starboard pontoon, and Splinter sat forward, half on the wooden bench seat and half on the port pontoon.

The Merc screamed to life with one pull. Lenah adjusted the throttle control and put the motor in gear. She pushed the control arm left, and turned toward shore, the whine of the outboard pushing the Zodiac like a brick.

Will stood on a rock looking out on the bay. The shoreline was stacked with stones except for a patch of sand just big enough to beach the dinghy. Lenah cut the motor and the Zodiac crunched onto shore.

"Hope you brought beer," Splinter said. "Warden here doesn't allow the devil's juice on her ship." Splinter hadn't had anything to drink in three days, and he felt like shit. His muscles and joints hurt, he had a headache, his knee screamed, and the slightest thing irritated him. But he felt better than he had the prior day, so that was something.

"I did. A six for us to split," Will said.

"I'll take what I can get," he said. Inwardly the anger rose in him, and the fog covered his eyes. Another person trying to control what he did. He could drink whenever… He rolled his shoulders and tried to crack his neck, a blood vessel in his forehead pounding like a bass guitar.

Will broke off a beer and handed it to Splinter, who opened it and took a long pull. "It's like that first sip of wine after you've crossed the desert."

"Scent of a Woman," Lenah said.

"Ding ding. We have a winner," Splinter said.

No one spoke, and an awkward silence stretched on. Will knew Splinter and Lenah had been together, and he also knew Splinter threw film quotes at her. It was a thing they did. Had done.

"You want to walk to the ocean? Cooler out there," Lenah said.

"Sure is. I was out there before you came. Wind's light." Will climbed down from his stone and headed for the deer path that ran through the mangroves. Mosquitos and flies attacked as soon as the friends passed into the mangroves, and Will ran. With light winds the insects set up camp in the vegetation and feasted on any blood that came their way, including birds.

They exited the forest and climbed over the dunes, being careful not to step on the beach grass. The Atlantic lapped gently over rocks and crushed stones. A gibbous moon hung on the horizon, and thin clouds drifted like streamers across an otherwise clear sky. The beach was deserted.

"What did they think of my place? They freak about the gun cabinet?" Splinter said.

"I didn't tell them where you live yet," Will said.

"Ah, dude, you've got to—"

Will put up a hand. "You were right. So far they're patronizing me, being nice to grandpa because they really don't have anything anyway. I'm saving it for when they do."

Splinter smiled and nodded.

"You guys OK? Need anything?" Splinter opened his mouth and Will cut him off. "Do you need anything, Lenah?"

"We're good for now, but I may need to meet you for a food drop in a couple of days." Lenah jerked a thumb toward Splinter. "This clown can't fish for shit."

"And you've been hauling them in?" Splinter said.

Lenah looked to Will, and said, "We haven't hauled in much."

"You're not alone. Every charter in the marina is complaining. Saying they're below pre-tsunami levels," Will said. "They're bitching all the way up to St. Augustine. Flights being canceled. Hotel no shows."

"Is the irony lost on anyone that the very thing that brought the fish might have also brought what's chasing them away?"

"What's irony?" Splinter said, but he couldn't say it with a straight face.

"In other fun news, there's a dog missing. Owner claims it was running on the beach. No corpse. Yet," Will said.

"You think it's our boy?" Lenah said.

"Why do you assume it's male? Bit sexist, isn't it?" Splinter said.

"No."

"Can you two do this someplace else? As much as it might surprise you, this old white man doesn't like his ass getting chewed off by flies," Will said.

"What do you think about the dog?" Splinter said.

"Normally, I'd think nothing of it. But I walk the beach down by South Beach Park. Knew that dog. I don't think Kissenger drowned. The seas were calm, and Kiss could swim like a dolphin. Would always come out of the ocean to say hi to me."

"So you think this thing came into the wave break? That close?" Lenah said.

"No, but I can see Kiss sensing the thing, swimming out and going after it," Will said.

The sea breeze rattled the beach grass, and the ocean sucked pebbles and shells back into the Atlantic.

"There's a little more. Another boat got busted up off South Beach Park. Man missing," Will said.

"What are the coasties saying?" Splinter said.

"Nothing. Total silence. Three rescued boaters were guests at the infirmary on the Coast Guard base on Seaway. Took them out on a MH-60 Jayhawk yesterday morning to Miami," Will said. "The orange-strips took the hull also, pulled it out of the bay that night. I asked to see it and they sat me in a waiting room for four hours before they told me to come back tomorrow."

Splinter sat on the sand. "At least we know where to look," he said.

"Off South Beach Park. Oh, only a search grid of a hundred square miles," Lenah said.

"What's the range on your fancy sonar and radar?" Splinter said.

"Less than that, but we'll cover it. Start close to shore and work our way out. From the inlet all the way south to Surfside," Lenah said.

"We can drift most of it? Otherwise, we'll need gas," Splinter said.

Lenah nodded. Yet another complication of their exile. "I'll gas up over at Lenny's at night. Bring a bone for Buster."

Plans laid, and business settled, Splinter got up and brushed himself off. He and Lenah needed to anchor-up and cook some fish and get to sleep. "Thanks for everything, Will. I don't know what I'd do without you."

Will put his hand on Splinter's shoulder. "Don't be seen on shore unless you're going to the coasties, my friend. There's some nasty shit going around about you, and people saw the news. The cops really want to talk to you, and you should consider going in. You've broken no laws, and you're being painted as a criminal."

"A criminal?" Splinter said. Homeless dirtbag. Yeah. Inconsiderate asshole to those he cared about most. Yeah. But a criminal?

"They don't say that," Will said. "But it's clear they weren't surprised you were out on a boat with a known mobster."

"Sal. A pox on that asshole." Splinter bit his lip. If he ever saw the Pacino wannabe again he didn't know if he'd be able to keep the fog away. "Lenah, can you give Will and I a few minutes? I need to fill Will in."

"Sure thing," she said. "Oh, can you watch Splinter's menagerie? Having them out at sea is difficult."

Daggers shot from Splinter's eyes.

"No problem," Will said.

"Thanks."

When she was gone, Splinter said, "You ready to listen?"

Will nodded.

11

At dusk on the third day of scouring the Atlantic off South Beach Park, the creature showed itself.

The sun had set, leaving a rainbow sherbet sky, and the inky sea pitched and heaved against the boat. Two eight-foot whaling harpoons leaned against the gunnel, and each had a lead line running from it connected to a sealed plastic twenty-gallon drum. Splinter had his sixty-inch and pistol spearguns at the ready, and Lenah had her rifle. They were prepared, or at least they thought they were.

Poseidon had refused to leave the Evenstar with the other animals and hid below deck in the cabin. Splinter was happy for it, but the cat pissed Lenah off. She didn't like when her orders were disobeyed.

A wake approached the Parker through the dusk, like a sub rising from the depths, rolling white water carving the ocean like a boat propeller. Lenah tried to take pictures, but in the poor light the animal blended into the surge of whitewater.

Then the beast was gone, leaving only a swirling vortex that reminded Splinter of the whirlpools made by whales as they feed. Lenah went to the SONAR and whistled. "See that there," she said as she pointed at the screen. "That purple blob? It's right under us."

"How much water we got?" Splinter asked.

"We're at forty-two feet. The thing is running along the bottom."

"Let's drop some chum and see if we can get it to come up."

Lenah turned up the gain and volume on the SONAR and followed Splinter from the pilothouse. She ladled some of her secret sauce into the water while Splinter hefted a harpoon and checked its lead line.

"You sure about going after it with that? Might piss the thing off," Lenah said.

"Let it come," Splinter said. He was wedged into the crux of the bow, legs braced against the gunnel, staring out at the ocean with harpoon at the ready.

Waves lapped against the hull, wind gusted and pulled, and the salty air tickled Splinter's nose. He stood in the bow for several minutes, the rank stench of the chum slick spreading out around the boat. "If that shit don't bring it I don't know what will."

The boat rocked hard and Lenah fell, slamming into the pilothouse. Splinter stayed on his feet, but dropped the harpoon, and it slid across the deck away from him. "We taking on water?" Splinter asked.

Lenah got to her knees and pulled up the access hatch, revealing the bilge. A thin river of water sloshed around, but it wasn't enough to kick on the bilge pump. Lenah closed the hatch, and said, "Look's good so far. You think it nudged us?"

"I think it rammed us," Splinter said.

The two companions searched the ocean with spotlights, but saw nothing.

The radio crackled, then a man's voice, but Splinter couldn't hear what it said. "You hear that?"

"Yeah. Thunderstorm's rolling in from the south. Won't be here for an hour or so," she said.

It was full dark, and the sea looked like oil in the moonlight. Off the port bow, water splashed as something large broke the surface. Splinter panned his light in that direction.

A fist of whitewater with a long narrow mouth full of teeth sticking from it torpedoed toward the boat. A low humming sound like deformed whale song rose to a buzz, and the scent of rot and decay filled the air. The creature was white, its gray eyes the size of baseballs. Jaws snapped closed as the whitewater dispersed and the beast slammed into the Parker.

The boat rocked backward, the transom momentarily submerged. Fiberglass cracked and Lenah squealed. "Splinter, we have to do something, or this thing is gonna take us down." Water spat from the bilge pump exit, hitting the water like a giant peeing.

"Get to the helm. Start the motors and come about."

Lenah started for the pilothouse, but stopped. "Why?"

"Bring us lateral so I can prick this bastard."

The deck drained, and Splinter sloshed through the seawater and retrieved his harpoon, checked its lead line to ensure it wasn't tangled, and propped the spear on his shoulder.

"There!" Lenah said.

The creature's caudal fin snaked through the water, the top of the leviathan's head skimming the surface like a gator. It was moving fast, side flippers pushing the water aside like it weighed nothing, its sleek body cutting through the Atlantic like a dolphin.

Splinter lifted the harpoon from his shoulder and drew it back. Lenah shined her light on the beast as it charged. It was twenty feet away. Ten.

"Splinter!"

Splinter was gone, frozen in the fog, fear and anger taking control, his mind spinning to that irrational place where nothing mattered. He stood still as stone, Lenah screaming at him, the wind tearing at his shirt, spear poised and ready to throw.

The beast hit the Parker, but it was a glancing blow and there was no sound of fiberglass cracking. Lenah brought her rifle to her shoulder and fired at the knot of water that was dissipating off the port side as the creature dove.

Lenah went back into the pilothouse and scanned the SONAR. A large purple oval ran along the bottom and started to rise. Poseidon peeked her head into the pilothouse.

Lenah cranked the motors and dropped the boat in gear. "Scat," she yelled at the cat, and Poseidon disappeared.

Splinter still hadn't moved. He watched the scene play out as if encased in ice, heart pounding in his chest, the burn of worry stinging his stomach.

"Splinter!"

The beast surfaced and came on fast, flippers pounding the water, its long crocodilian mouth opening as it prepared to take a bite of the Evenstar.

Lenah put the Parker on auto, ran from the pilothouse and got in Splinter's face, yelling and punching him on the arm, but he refused to hear her. Splinter was in Kabul, gun smoke filling his nostrils, screams of pain and death paralyzing him.

Lenah grabbed the harpoon and pulled Splinter toward her. "Listen up, soldier. What's wrong with you, wimp? You a fighter or a little baby?"

Splinter heard soldier, wimp, baby, but said nothing. There was a break in the fog and he saw himself there, staring through a gap in his reality.

"You gutless piece of shit. Coward. You're a cow..."

Splinter's hand shot out and he grabbed Lenah's neck. Her hands came up, clawing at his fingers. "Sp..l...int..er." Anger rose in him. Frustration. Hatred. Then the comfortable embrace of fear. "Just tr...ng to shake y..o o..."

Lenah kicked Splinter in the balls and he released her as he doubled-over and hit the deck, whimpering like Nereus.

The creature was back. It was alongside the Parker, its tail thrumming the side of the boat and causing vibration.

Lenah knelt, and tried to help Splinter as he got to his feet.

"Lenah, I—"

The creature breached, its head and torso spearing from the water in a geyser of whitewater. Its massive body fell backward into the sea, just missing the boat. A surge of seawater rocked the Evenstar and the harpoons and spear guns slid across the deck.

Another blast of static streaked from the radio, and this time Splinter heard it perfectly. He was back. For now.

"Lenah, I'm so sorry. I don't know—"

"Not now Splinter," she headed for the pilothouse. "We need to get the hell out of here before this thing sinks us."

Back at the helm she dropped the hammer and spun the wheel, pointing the bow toward shore.

"It's on us," Splinter said. Just beyond their rooster tail the beast's head glided within the whitewater. The Parker bowled over the building swell, and the shoreline appeared and disappeared with the roll of the ocean.

Splinter retrieved his sixty-inch and sighted the beast's head. The rubber band twanged as the spear shot from its holding channel and whistled through the air. Splinter didn't hear the thump of an impact, and the beast didn't let up. The Parker was doing thirty knots and the monster was keeping pace.

The creature was out of harpoon range, so Splinter went to the pilothouse. "Lenah, what if you go full stop and I try and put a barrel on the bitch as it comes at us?"

"You nuts? That thing hits us again and we might go down. The bilge has been running full tilt. We're taking on water. Not critical at this point, but we're two miles out and if we end up in the water..."

Splinter rubbed his eyes and rolled his shoulders. "I only need a second. As soon as I loose the spear you can gun it. The thing won't have enough time to reach us."

Lenah looked back over her shoulder at the mound of water trailing after them, then back at Splinter. "If you think you can do it, I'll try. To be safe I'll turn sharply to port as soon as I gun the engines."

"10-4. Wait for my signal," he said.

Back on deck, Splinter positioned himself against the transom, harpoon at the ready. He breathed deep. In, out.

He pressed against the gunnel and raised his hand. The boat eased to an awkward stop, their wake almost bubbling over the transom. Splinter threw the harpoon, aiming for the beast's head. Line snaked off the boat and the keg leapt over the gunnel and smacked on the surface, but didn't move. The barrel sat there like a bobber floating on a windblown pond.

Lenah gunned the engines and the Parker arced to port.

Splinter almost fell. "The hell with this," he said. All thought of getting a picture, proof for the coasties, fled from his mind. He wanted to kill.

Splinter slid open the pilothouse door and got two of the depth charges he'd made. They were comprised of gunpowder and round shot sealed in coffee cans. The short fuse was wax coated twine, and when lit he'd have seconds to seal the devices and drop them in the water. He had to wait until the fish was close to the surface, otherwise the explosion and underwater soundwave would have little effect.

The beast came at them, its huge torpedo-shaped body bearing down on the Evenstar.

Splinter ran back out on deck and then realized he had no way to light the devices. "Lenah, there a lighter on board?"

"The drawer on the command consol. I keep one there for cigar smokers. Always gets me an extra tip."

Splinter headed back into the pilothouse to retrieve the lighter. The deck was slippery with mist, and the boat rolled as the monster brushed past on the port side. Splinter slid across the deck but managed to keep his footing.

The beast circled the boat, then turned, coming in on the port side for another attack run. Lighter in hand, Splinter opened the charges and braced himself against the gunnel. He flicked the lighter and it sparked, then blew out. The wind wasn't strong, but it was enough to make lighting the fuses difficult.

The leviathan rose from the sea twenty yards out.

There was no way he'd be able to light and drop both charges, so he put one on deck and held the other in a trembling hand. He tilted the charge away from the wind and dipped the lighter inside, holding it against the wick.

The creature was ten yards away.

He flicked the lighter and it sparked. The charge didn't light.

The beast was on them.

He thumbed the lighter again and the fuse sparked and lit. Splinter sealed the can, threw the charge in the water, and dove behind the gunnel.

A deafening explosion blew a surge of water at the Parker.

Splinter got up. The beast was gone, but there was no blood in the water. There was no sign of the creature at all.

"Time to go break that lock off my footlocker," Splinter said.

Lenah smiled. "You're gonna need a bigger boat," she said.

"Too easy. Don't insult me," Splinter said.

12

The skyline in the east was gray, and soon the sun would be up. The late thunderstorms of the prior night had blown through, and thin mist hung over Indian River, but it would bake-off within an hour of sunrise. They'd raced back to Splinter's half-sunken home and pounded the lock off the gun chest with the Parker's anchor.

They now had a 90's era M16, with two clips of ammo, single and double barreled shotguns with four boxes of shells, and the prize of the bunch, a Marlin high-powered rifle with two boxes of thirty-five caliber hollow point bullets. The no frills depth charges he'd made had done nothing but scare the beast off. There'd been no blood in the water, or any sign the bombs had harmed the animal. He'd have to get his hands on something better.

Splinter felt like shit. Lenah had been quiet and reserved since their encounter with the leviathan, and he didn't blame her. She said he choked her, though he didn't remember doing it. The fog had been thick, the abyss deep and dark, and the last thing he remembered before snapping out of his panic attack was rows of needle sharp teeth coming at him in the darkness.

Will's advice to go to the cops rattled around in his head. They'd put him in Southport VA psych ward, but maybe that's what he needed. What he'd done to Lenah, despite what she described as a major provocation as she attempted to snap him from his trance, was inexcusable, and now he trusted himself even less.

"Any ideas?" Lenah said. She had dark bags beneath her eyes, which were bloodshot, and her hair was greasy and matted to her head.

They needed to beach the boat and see how bad the damage was before they went back out into the ocean—if they went back out on the ocean. The debate wasn't over, only tabled. Lenah said if the boat can't go out there was no point arguing if it should.

"There's a maze of tight channels over in Avalon State Park. There's several fine silt beaches along them. I think we could beach the Evenstar there," Splinter said.

"I know where you mean. Good idea," Lenah said.

Sea spray blew across the windshield, an odd east wind pushing the mist over their path. They were cruising at thirty-three knots, the Parker skimming over the top of the six-inch ripples. Boats of all shapes and sizes dotted the bay, but they hadn't encountered any coastie or harbor patrol vessels.

Poseidon lay on the pilothouse floor, staring into oblivion and curled in a ball.

The *womp womp* of an approaching helicopter echoed over the water, and Poseidon lifted her head and started to cry. Lenah pulled up on the throttle and brought the Evenstar to a stop under a mangrove tree that hung over the water.

Splinter pet the cat, and said, "Go down below." Splinter wanted the animal out of the way. As if she understood English, the cat looked sheepishly at Splinter, then disappeared into the back of the pilothouse.

The HH65 Dolphin flew low, and the window in the Parker's pilothouse door rattled in its frame. The Coast Guard helicopter moved slowly along the Indian River, and it glided by overhead, wind tearing the mangrove leaves, small branches bending and cracking.

"Good to see the patrols," Lenah said. "Maybe they'll handle this for us. Save us the trouble of getting proof."

"Sure. You keep telling yourself that," Splinter said.

The coasties ran drills and did patrols all along the sea shore, but fuel was expensive, so they only did a run or two a day unless there was an emergency. Splinter said, "We need to find out what this thing's habits are. Does it feed at night? Is there a pattern for day and night?"

"And how do you propose we do that?"

"We need to be less conspicuous. Whatever this thing is, it's an alpha, and most likely it can sense vibrations in the water from far off."

"You're suggesting we get a row boat?"

The copter had become a spec on the northern horizon, and Lenah pushed the throttle down and maneuvered out from under the tree. She brought the twin Yamahas back up to speed, slowing only to make turns. As the channel narrowed, a small cove opened up to starboard.

Two fifteen-foot crocodiles lounged on a sandy beach, their dark eyes staring across the cove as they sunned themselves. As the Parker approached, the crocs slipped into the estuary, which was almost fresh water this far in.

Lenah drew back on the throttle and angled up the motors with the level controls. The whine of the outboards increased, and water exploded from the propellers. The boat slipped onto the beach with a faint scraping sound, and Lenah dropped the anchor and killed the engines.

Splinter grabbed some line and he and Lenah jumped into the knee-deep water. Poseidon allowed herself to be lifted from the bow and placed on the sand, where she proceeded to trot off into the mangroves to take care of her business.

Using the anchor tied to the bow, Splinter pulled the boat to port, revealing most of the starboard underside. Splinter wrapped the rope around a thick scrub palmetto tree and went to help Lenah feel along the bottom.

They found nothing, so Splinter repeated the process on the starboard side, and he didn't even have a chance to join Lenah in the search before she yelled, "Got it."

The hole wasn't bad, but the damage to the fiberglass around the hole didn't look good. Cracks in the hull spidered out from where the beast had rammed them, and clear resin peeled off revealing torn fiberglass fabric. They needed to repair a three-square-foot area, giving extra attention to the hole itself.

"Shit," Splinter said.

"I can fix this," Lenah said. "Easy."

"Will it be able to take a hit?"

"I haven't agreed to go back out, but yeah, it'll be as strong or stronger than the rest of the hull."

"What do you need, though? Resin, fabric, hardener, adhesive filler. Where are we going to get all that?"

"They sell fiberglass repair kits. I can get one at Lenny's. It'll cost me another bone for Buster, though."

"Alright. Let's get out of here. We'll come back after dark and take care of it," Splinter said. Boat traffic was high, but any passing coastie or harbor patrol boat would surely run the Parker's numbers if they spotted her.

Lenah whistled for Poseidon, who trotted from the foliage, and they all got back onboard the Evenstar.

"I know the perfect spot. We can do some fishing," she said.

Lenah cranked the outboards and pulled back gently on the throttle. The outboards clawed at the shallow water, kicking up sand and mud, pulling debris into the cooling system.

The Parker lurched off the beach just as the engine warning klaxon sounded. Lenah cut the motors. "I'm going to restart for a second. Tell me if you see the water pump stream jetting from the bottom of the powerhead."

"Yup. We probably sucked-in some crap," Splinter said. "Clogged the intakes."

The motors cranked, and Splinter yelled, "Off."

Lenah killed the engines.

"Engine one isn't spitting water. Bring her up," Splinter said.

Lenah hit the tilt control and Splinter went out on deck. The sound of hydraulics and crying seagulls were an odd combination.

"Yep. I got it." Splinter cleaned the in-takes on the lower unit and the Parker was back in motion.

Lenah pushed down on the throttle and turned the Parker in a gentle arc north, heading up the Indian River bay along with the traffic. They were doing a steady twenty knots, blending in, green walls of mangroves boxing the bay in on both sides. They cruised that way for several minutes, enjoying the sun and sea breeze.

She spun the wheel and the boat turned sharply to port, and Splinter gripped the control consol. He didn't see the tiny gap in the mangroves until they were right on it, and Lenah pressed the throttle down further and the Parker leapt from the water.

The Evenstar passed into the mangroves, and the waterway widened. Lenah pulled back on the throttle and turned to Splinter. "Sped up because it's shallow there. Wanted to be on plane."

Splinter nodded. "Here I am thinking you're trying to get choked again." The second he said it he wished he could have the words back.

Lenah looked at him and smiled.

Relief washed over him.

"Trust me, I don't want to see that Splinter ever again," she said.

Herons flew in a tight flock overhead, their mournful cries echoing over the mangroves. Flies and clouds of gnats littered the air, the sun's heat baking the sea shore, bringing out the bugs. A large tree with oval leaves rose above the mangroves, and Lenah turned the boat down another byway when she saw it.

"I think when this is done and we have our picture, or the thing's head, you need to do something about your trauma, Splinter. You and I may be done, but that doesn't mean you won't meet someone else. Fall in love, and I'd hate for that woman to meet evil Splinter."

That hurt. He still hoped on some level that bordered on fantasy that he and Lenah would get back together someday when he settled his shit. She talked like they were dead as dirt. "Nothing they can do. Counseling is bullshit," he said.

"There are drugs, other ways—"

"To what? Turn me into R.P. McMurphy from One Flew Over the Cuckoo's Nest?" He did his best Jack Nicholson impression. "Is that crazy enough for ya'? Want me to take a shit on the floor?"

"Sorry I brought it up."

"No, it's OK, but when people say stuff like that it implies, at least to me, that I haven't tried anything and don't know my own head." Yup, he'd just said that. "Guess that sounds pretty stupid. 'Cause I don't know my own head sometimes."

"And that's not you, Splinter. You will win, but you have to have a battle plan."

They'd arrived at the end of a thin channel. Lenah turned the boat into the wind and dropped anchor.

"You have a black marker on board? Like the ones used to label the packed fish?" Splinter said.

"I do. Same drawer as the lighter. Why?"

Splinter laughed. "I'm gonna change the five in your hull numbers to an eight, and the four to a nine. Might fool them if they're in a hurry."

"Nothing to lose," she said.

Splinter got the marker and hung over the bow and colored his numbers while Lenah prepared some food, and soon the ex-lovers were lounging in deck chairs, baited lines in the water.

"So we'll hit Lenny's after dark?"

Lenah nodded and took a bite of her sandwich.

"We have to break in?"

"Naw. He always forgets to lock the side door, and even if he doesn't the lock is so worn I can push it open. I'll grab gas while I'm there as well."

"Lenny can be trusted?"

"I think so, but I didn't leave a note last time and I won't this time either. I'm keeping track of what we take, and we'll pay him down the road. He'll understand. No point taking the risk."

Splinter nodded. "So assuming we can get the boat fixed, we'll head out tomorrow?"

Lenah said nothing. She leaned her head way back, trying to catch the sun on her face. "I think we should go see the cops."

Splinter had known this was coming, and he was prepared. "Lenah, if we do that, we're off the case."

"Why? They'll never admit they believe us, and they can't hold you for telling a crazy story and you've broken no laws."

"They can hold us. Are you worried about what the creature can do to the boat?"

"Of course. The thing almost sank us."

"It was beauty killed the beast," Splinter said.

"Hmmmm. A hard one. Ah, the beast. King Kong."

"Yes, but which one?"

"The original, of course."

13

Splinter and Lenah sat in silence for a time, water lapping gently against the hull. Birds tittered, the sea breeze rattled the mangrove leaves, and a low static emanated from the marine radio, which they heard via an open pilothouse window. The emergency channel was quiet, and the fish stations buzzed with bitchy fishermen whose charters weren't catching any fish.

"All kidding aside, I am concerned about going out deep and having this thing crunch the Parker," she said.

"If I could get a barrel on the thing we can track it and call in help," Splinter said.

"What we really need is a tracking dart, so we can tag the thing and monitor its movements," Lenah said.

"That would work better than the barrel. You think Will can get what we need?" Splinter said.

"Yeah, I'm sure he knows someone. They tag sharks, seals, all kinds of marine life in Florida's waters, so I'm sure he can find something," she said.

"And you'll go out again, so I can tag the beast?"

"I think so. If done right we don't need to get near the creature," Lenah said.

"OK, we'll get in touch with Will. He'll be monitoring our station this evening at the normal time," he said.

"I have one more condition," Lenah said.

Splinter sighed.

"Successful or not, after we try and tag the beast, we go to the coasties. Deal?"

"Deal."

As the sun went down, they cleaned up and set out for Lenny's. The boat supply/bait house/fuel depot was nestled on Main Canal, which led to Sailfish Haven's main marina.

On route Lenah said, "You see that news piece a couple weeks ago about the Bermuda Triangle? The one about the waves?"

"No."

"You know ships have disappeared in the area for over a hundred years, with an estimated one thousand people lost. Now scientists believe the losses were the result of rogue waves up to a hundred feet tall. Much more powerful than our tsunami."

"What do the eggheads base that on?"

"The triangle lies in the Atlantic Ocean and stretches 270,271 square miles between Florida, Bermuda and Puerto Rico. Using satellite imagery, scientists observed these rogue waves, which they say are caused by focused wave energy. Storms create waves that go against the normal wave direction, shortening the wave frequency. This can cause waves to join up and create larger waves, but that's just speculation. They really don't know," she said.

"You're thinking, why wasn't our beastie disturbed by one of these in the past?"

"I was, but these are rare occurrences, and I'd figure the odds of one hitting while the beast was on the surface would be slim. It also made me think the creature might be the cause of some of the disappearances," Lenah said.

"Like the odds of this thing being discovered before now?"

"I didn't say it explained all the mysteries of the oceans. The Atlantic Ocean covers forty-one million square miles and has an average depth of twelve thousand feet. The Atlantic Rift Valley isn't that far from here, and it's deep in spots. Seas cover seventy percent of the Earth, and it's believed there are countless species in the depths we haven't discovered. Our monster is most likely part of a tiny family. A long-lost hybrid of a creature that survived and adapted for life in the depths."

"These rouge waves get all the planes that have gone down in the triangle too?" Splinter said.

Lenah chuckled. "Good point. Who knows? We have no idea what this thing is, so speculation is useless," she said.

"But fun. It's obviously some form of rogue mutant gator," Splinter said, and he half believed it.

Moonlight and starlight beamed through the thin cloud cover, lighting their way. Lenah drew back on the throttle and the boat slowed. Nothing moved at Lenny's, and a single light that illuminated the gas pump marked its location. There was a camera on a pole at the end of the dock, so Lenah cruised past and worked the Parker into a narrow gap between Lenny's and Zeke's Shipyard.

Buster bounded down the dock and barked, but when he saw Lenah he bounced up and down, whining and crying like he wanted his mother. Lenah gave him a bone and stepped off the Parker onto a floating dock that served as a maintenance platform.

"You need help?"

"Nope. Sit tight and I'll be back."

Splinter leaned against the gunnel and stared at the stars. The rank scent of oil and rotten eggs pervaded the air, and somewhere a lead line dinged against its aluminum mast.

A cloud passed over the moon and the darkness thickened. The burp-bark of crocodiles and the buzz of insects soothed Splinter's nerves. A warm breeze pushed across the marina, and a door closed.

Lenah made her way down the dock and jumped onto the boat. "Good to go." She tossed the fiberglass repair kit on the dash in the pilothouse. "Covers ten square feet. We'll do two patches of five. Overlay them for extra strength."

Over the next two hours the duo beached the Parker, and Lenah was applying the second patch when 11PM rolled around and it was time for Splinter to call Will.

Lenah's cellphone was dead, and she'd forgotten her charger, but Splinter and Will had their regular system. He called his friend on channel 119 every night at 11PM.

Splinter got a bowed mangrove branch and wedged it into the ground, then propped the flashlight on it so it lit the bottom of the boat. Lenah applied the resin and hardener mixture over the second coat of fabric, spreading it thin and even like icing a cake.

"I'm gonna call Will. Get him going on the dart," Splinter said.

"10-4." Lenah didn't look up from her work.

"Umm. You need to take a break," Splinter said.

"What?" She stopped working and looked up. "Why?"

"I need to go on the boat and if it sinks or shifts it could roll on you."

She looked around and sighed, then moved away from the boat.

Splinter climbed onto the Evenstar, being careful not to shift the boat's position. He slid open the door to the pilothouse and went to the marine radio. It was on, and he tuned it to channel 119.

"Rogue One this is Finnick. Do you copy?"

Crackling static, then nothing.

Splinter waited a minute, then opened the channel. "Rogue One do you copy? This is Finnick."

Nothing.

Splinter tried several times before he gave up and made his way back to Lenah. She'd commenced work and was finishing up.

"Will didn't answer," Splinter said.

"That's odd."

"Sure is. I can set my watch by that guy's habits. When he says he's going to do something, he does it."

"You worried?"

"A little, but it could be anything. Maybe he fell asleep."

"Maybe," Lenah said, but to Splinter it didn't sound like she believed it.

"Wish your cell wasn't dead. Lenny's doesn't have a phone accessory rack?"

She shook her head.

"He should," he said. "Now what do we do? We need that dart."

"Maybe Guppy?" Lenah said.

Splinter grunted.

"If you've got another idea I'd love to hear it," Lenah said.

Brett "Guppy" Reynolds was the owner of a chain of Florida based tourist adventure companies called Oceanic Memories. Guppy's infatuation with Lenah annoyed the shit out of Splinter, but the bowling pine of a man would do anything for Lenah, and that was useful.

"We'll see. I'll try Will later. Head to our cove and we'll shut it down 'til morning."

"Aye, aye."

Lenah dropped the hammer and the newly repaired Parker sliced through the still water, the twin 150HP Yamahas singing. The breeze died away, the night clear and humid. The wakes of crocodiles snaked across the channel, but there were no other boats. It was late, and even Harbor Patrol had packed it in for the night.

The sound of the engines changed. One of the motors faltered, choking and struggling. Its rooster tail lessoned from twenty feet to ten.

"Engine two is losing RPMs," Lenah said. "And I didn't touch the throttle."

Splinter said, "Slowly back them both down. Then—"

There was a screech, and a pop, and black smoke bellowed from engine two's exhaust port.

Lenah pulled the throttle back into neutral, then killed the motors. A thin trail of smoke rose above engine two.

The good news was the bilge pump hadn't come on, so the patches had worked, and the Parker was watertight. The bad news was that without two fully functioning outboards they couldn't go out on the Atlantic Ocean.

"Now you can hold the light for me," Splinter said with great pleasure. He'd held the light for three hours as he watched Lenah patch the boat, but he was the better outboard mechanic. "If it's a blown cylinder we're screwed, or the linkage."

She clicked on the flashlight and Splinter undid the hasps on engine two's cover. He lifted it off, being careful not to hit the powerhead. He placed the cover on the deck and clicked on a penlight.

Visual inspection showed nothing. There were no odd smells, no oil spray. "Can you get the tool box?"

"Yup," she said.

Splinter checked the fuel filter, and it looked clear. The water intakes were clear, everything was clean.

Lenah put the tool box on the deck and Splinter took out a socket wrench. One by one he checked the sparkplugs. Nothing looked gummed or burned. He did compression tests on each cylinder and they all read full compression.

"Turn the ignition on, but don't crank the motors," he said.

Lenah did as instructed and the buzz of power cycling into the engines sounded like a swarm of bees. Using the voltage tester Splinter checked various components of the engine, slowly narrowing the possible problems. When he checked the fuel pump he said, "I think I've got it. Fuel pump is dead. That's why it was choking for fuel. Plus, the smoke and a pop. Fuel pump. I can replace it in an hour. I just have to peel off the pollution controls."

"So we need to go see Lenny," Lenah said.

"You can't steal a fuel pump?"

"No way. The stockroom is a puzzle beyond rational thought," she said.

Splinter said nothing.

He cleaned all the plugs and put the cover back on engine two and unplugged the control cables. The engine would remain up and decommissioned and engine one would power the Evenstar alone.

When they reached their sheltered cove, the sun was coming up, and purple-black sky gave way to a blue horizon. The Coast Guard weather report said it was going to be a nice day, and with luck they'd sleep through a chunk of it. Lenah went down into the cabin and Splinter called Will. He tried eight times, but got no response.

Splinter's stomach went cold. He was worried for his friend.

14

When Splinter woke, Indian River was the Sahara. The noon sun was intense and unyielding, and the Parker's cabin was like an oven. Splinter's t-shirt was soaked through, and the scent of piss and fish overpowered the sea breeze sneaking through the open portholes.

Splinter heard Lenah moving around on deck. He needed to decide what was best before he and Lenah talked about what to do. She would argue they should trust Lenny, because she thought he was a good guy and was her friend.

Lenny was like most of the men Lenah met. They put on their best show as they tried their best to get in her pants, and this blind spot amazed Splinter, though he knew Lenah wasn't as blind as she sometimes pretended to be. Splinter had no substantive reason to distrust Lenny, nor did he have a reason to trust him.

The fuel pump. That was the reason.

Splinter didn't have another plan. They needed the part, and Lenny was their best chance to keep a low profile. He got up and went to the head and splashed water on his face. He hadn't bathed in two days and he smelt like rotting fish.

His knee ached and his head pounded, but not as bad as the day before. Not drinking was taking its toll, and mild nausea dogged him most of the day, except after eating when he felt really bad. The fog hadn't come on in the last couple of days, and Splinter wondered if there was a correlation. Maybe Lenah was right. Maybe the alcohol fueled the fog rather than cleared it.

He looked in the mirror. His eyes were red cinders, and dark black bags hung beneath his eye sockets. The scar that ran up the side of his face and hooked around his right eye was deep red. Strands of gray and black hair had escaped his ponytail and fell across his face, and his beard was unruly and matted. He decided a change was in order.

***

Splinter headed into the pilothouse. "Morning."

Lenah turned from the command console and said, "Good…" She paused when she saw him. "You trimmed your beard."

"It's a bit uneven. Had to use a fish knife, but it's better."

"You look so different," she said.

"That's the idea."

"And is that soap I smell?" She stepped close to him and sniffed.

He felt an uncomfortable stirring and he sidestepped her and headed for deck. "Let's get over to Lenny's and get this thing done. I'll grab the lines."

Out on deck Splinter felt like the twelve-year-old boy he'd been at his first dance, when Cindy Dumers tried to kiss him, and he'd shrunk away like a scared child. He chuckled at himself. She was just sniffing the soap dipshit.

Motor one rumbled to life, and engine two was tilted up out of the water and silent. Splinter coiled the lead lines and Lenah brought up the anchor. The winch whined, and chain rattled over the bow as the anchor set in place.

Lenah spun the Evenstar around and kicked-up the throttle. Splinter went back into the pilothouse and sat down so he couldn't be seen by other boaters.

There was an increased Coast Guard presence in the inlet, but they weren't seen as they passed. It was a beautiful day and a line of crafts fed through the inlet like ants leaving their hill, but the charters looked half empty. Word about the lack of fish was getting around. Sea spray coated everything as a breeze out of the south pushed a crosswind over Indian River. The tide was going out and the muddy banks smelt like rotten eggs and dead fish. Crabs scuttled through the mangroves, and pelicans divebombed the bay, catching shiners.

Lenah maneuvered the boat into her spot on the side of Lenny's away from main canal and killed the engine. Splinter tied off the bow while Lenah took care of the stern.

"How we going to handle this? Best if I'm not seen, but I want to hear this," Splinter said.

"Splinter, I can handle it alone. Wait here."

"Not happening. What's your plan? You going in the back entrance?"

"Yeah."

"I'll stay in the stockroom. That way he won't see me, but I'll be right there if you need me."

She sighed and rolled her eyes. "Whatever."

Splinter hated that word. The "screw you" of the new generation.

The docks were quiet. Most of the charters were out for the day, and the shipyard was at lunch. Splinter heard the men laughing in the warehouse, music playing in the background. Every minute or so there'd be an outburst of yelling and laughter, and Splinter figured they were playing dice.

The back door to Lenny's was open and Lenah went in first, peering around to ensure Lenny wasn't back there. When he wasn't, she entered and called out his name.

"Out here," came Lenny's voice from the front of the store.

Lenah eased through the dimly lit supply room and Splinter took up position behind the swinging door that opened to the work area behind the main service counter.

"Hi," Lenah said.

"Well, hey. People looking for you," Lenny said.

"About that. I came to you because I know I can trust you," she said.

"Trust me to what?"

Silence. Splinter's heart pounded in his chest and sweat dripped down his forehead.

"To keep our meeting between us?"

"Sure. Sure thing. What is it you need?"

"This." The rustle of paper as she handed Lenny the model and part number.

"Blew the fuel pump. Dang. You need it put in? Terry'll be back tomorrow and—"

"Nope. I'm gonna put it in today. You have it?"

"Let me check."

It took a second for Splinter to realize Lenny was coming to check in the back room. He darted down an aisle just as the swinging door squeaked on its hinges.

"Should have that one," Lenny called back.

He walked down the center aisle toward the back of the storage room. Splinter got low and watched through the shelving. Lenny stopped in front of a wall of boxes and counted. Then he rubbed his chin and said, "Shit."

Lenny headed back out front and Splinter positioned himself behind the door again.

"I don't have it, Lenah. Take forty-eight hours to get it here," Lenny said.

"Forty-eight hours? No way to do it faster?"

Lenny laughed. "You could drive to Miami."

Beeping blasted from the wall mounted TV playing I Love Lucy reruns.

"What the hell is this now," Lenny said. The volume on the TV rose.

Splinter eased the door open a crack so he could see the TV.

A middle-aged reporter stood before the Atlantic Ocean, the wind tousling his hair. "We interrupt your regularly scheduled programing to bring you this local special report."

The scene shifted to an aerial shot that showed a sinking sailboat, its tall mast tilted at a thirty-degree angle. "Just moments ago, the Coast Guard responded to a distress call off South Beach Park. Two sailors are missing, and two others are confirmed rescued by the Coast Guard cutter Valiant." The scene cut to a close-up of the sailboat's cracked hull. "Authorities are unsure what caused the boat to capsize, but speculate that the vessel was hit by a whale or other large marine animal. More on this breaking story as information becomes available. Now back to your regularly scheduled programming."

Splinter stepped back, his heart pounding in his chest. They had to find the creature before it hurt anyone else and tag the beast and prove it existed. Despite his personal situation, he still believed this to be the best course of action. After he told the coasties what he knew, they'd tell him to stay away, go home, then continue with their routine patrols, which clearly weren't working.

"Damn. Must be a big shark out there," Lenny said.

"That what you think is doing all the damage?" Lenah said.

"What else could it be, a rogue orca?"

"What are the fishermen saying?"

"Between bitching about there being no fish anymore and the price of gas, not much. Rumors, but nothing worth talking about."

"Rumors? What rumors?"

Lenny's voice dropped an octave. "Some of the guys are saying something bigger is out there. That the tsunami dragged in something big from out in the rift valley and it's scaring everything away."

Splinter pressed his face against the door, listening.

"Something bigger? Like what?" Lenah said.

"Who knows. Most sea stories don't hold much truth. Fishermen and hunters, they can spin a tale about nothing. About a way a fish swims, or where a deer chooses to take a dump."

"Lovely."

"Oh, I'm sorry. What are you going to do about this part? You want me to order it?"

"Yeah, I suppose. I'll be back in a couple of days."

"Where you been? Sheriff Bankton stopped to ask if I'd seen you."

"I saw him. They just wanted to ask me if I'd seen anything unusual when I was out the last couple of weeks."

Lenny said nothing, waiting for Lenah's report.

"I haven't seen anything unusual, except for the fish deciding to split."

Lenny laughed. "Yeah, there's that."

"OK, I'm out. I've got a charter on the inner bay," she lied.

"Call me if you need me," Lenny said.

"10-4."

"OK, hey can we have dinner one night? One of these days I'm gonna stop asking," Lenny said.

Splinter almost laughed out loud when he heard Lenah cough.

"We'll see Lenny. You know us tomboys," she said. Her voice was steady and somewhere between playful and stern. "You forget you saw me an' we'll talk when I come get the part. 'K?"

"You deserve better than that burnout Splinter," Lenny said. "Where is he? Made you come in alone? He's with you, right?"

Splinter's vision went a little red, and he stepped forward, the fog rolling in as he pressed his hands against the door. He heard a thump as Lenah put her hand on the opposite side of the swinging door, keeping it closed.

"Don't you worry about Splinter," she said and pushed on through the door.

Splinter shrank back and let her pass and then fell in behind her. "I might have to hit that ass," Splinter whispered.

"Build a bridge and get over it," Lenah said.

"Hannah Montana? Really?"

Outside the day had gotten hotter and steam rose off the dock, which was wet with morning dew. As they headed back to the Evenstar, Splinter said, "Notice you didn't settle up with him for the stuff we've taken."

"Timing is everything Splinter, you should know that," she said. "I didn't want to piss him off. We still might need him."

"Yeah, we can't wait two days for the part."

"I've got an idea. Another one of your favorite people," Lenah said.

"Guppy?"

Lenah nodded.

"Crap. No other options?"

"He can get the part and the tag gun and darts. He has a boat and can meet us on the water. Don't get any easier than that."

"Why would Guppy do all that?"

"I'll make him an offer he can't refuse," she said.

"Wow. You're on a roll, Fredo," Splinter said. Lenah smiled and started to say something, but Splinter put up a hand. "I know, I know. He'll do anything for you."

"Don't call me Fredo. It was the Godfather said it, as you well know."

Splinter tried to call Will again on the marine radio and got no response.

"Look what I borrowed when he was in the backroom looking for the part," Lenah said. She held-up a slender white cord.

Splinter took the cord and examined it. Where you going to plug this thing in?"

"Cigarette lighter."

"This is a USB. You need an adapter."

"Shoot. How am I going to call Guppy?"

"Don't know."

The sun was climbing toward noon when Lenah tucked the Parker away in a secluded cove off Indian River. Shiners leapt in ordered rows from the still water, sending tiny ripples across the surface.

Splinter tried to relax, the sun giving him the stink eye from its place in the clear blue sky. Lenah baited a line, dropped it in the water, and sat in the fighting chair.

She didn't get a nibble.

15

Back out on the bay, the single 150HP Yamaha screaming, the Parker sliced through the afternoon boat chop that slapped the shoreline and tore at the mangroves. Vessels moved south and north, a traffic jam of boats coming in from a day's fishing, and charters leaving to catch the gray haze of dusk. When the weather cooled, fish came up from the depths to feed.

This was the hour Splinter worried about the most.

Lenah had gone back into Lenny's and he let her use his cell phone to call Guppy.

"Guppy bitched and moaned a little, asked me out again, but he said he'd meet us at Hell's Rip with the part. Said the tracking dart and gun is harder, but he knows a guy. I think we're good," Lenah said. She had one hand on the wheel, and with her other she fingered the knot of hair on her head.

Splinter could tell she was uncomfortable. Lenah was an independent woman and asking for help wasn't easy for her. Especially asking Guppy. Splinter knew she was doing it all for him. She cared for him, even if he'd destroyed their relationship.

Lenah brought the boat on plane and sat back in the captain's chair. The Parker threw spray off the bow, and the sea breeze blew the mist across the deck onto the windshield. Indian River narrowed, and estuaries branched off like spider's legs. Lenah eased back the throttle and the boat slowed to twenty-five knots at 3400RPM.

"SONAR is showing nothing. RADAR looks clean," Splinter said. "What time are we meeting Guppy?"

"Twenty-one hundred," she said.

"You hungry?"

"Yeah, but I've had enough fish for a lifetime," she said.

"I'd kill for a burger from the diner," Splinter said.

"Doesn't Scales deliver?" Lenah said.

"Out on the bay? Don't think so."

"Don't be dense. We'll hang out over by Pier Twenty-one and when we see the delivery car come over the causeway will dock for a second. Doubt the high school delivery boy will recognize us."

Splinter nodded.

Third time was the charm at Lenny's, where Lenah used his phone, but he didn't have a cigarette light adapter, so Lenah bribed the girl taking their burger order into telling the delivery boy what she needed and promised a big tip if he could make it happen.

They coasted into the marina, paid the kid, and were back out at sea in sixty seconds, the boat reeking of onions and charred beef, Lenah's cellphone charging atop the command console. As soon as it would turn on, Splinter intended to find out where Will was.

Lenah dropped anchor within a knot of boats fishing the inlet and she and Splinter ate in silence, the gentle roll of the water slapping against the boat, the sweet sea breeze and the occasional cry of a seagull breaking the peace.

Splinter called Will, and the call went right to voicemail. "Where the hell is he?" Splinter said.

"I'm getting worried," Lenah said.

"If I don't hear from him soon I'm gonna have to go on land and find out what's happening."

"But you're only allowed on land for one day every ten years," she said.

"Very funny."

When the sun set, Lenah pulled anchor and headed south for Hell's Rip, which was a thin river that ran from the Atlantic Ocean through to the bay. A hurricane in the 1800s had caused a breach in the barrier island, pushing over the dirt road that would one day become the famous highway A1A. The rip in the barrier island was a favorite fishing spot when the tide was going out because the sea got sucked through the thin gap like a straw, pulling the fish with it.

Lenah sparked the NAV lights, and Splinter went out on deck and sat in the fish fighting chair, staring up at the black-and-blue sky. No stars were visible yet in the growing darkness, and the paper-thin clouds stretched to the horizon like a blanket.

Fifteen minutes later Lenah arced the Parker east. She pulled back on the throttle and the boat slowed, kicking up brown and green seaweed. "Dang." Seventeen boats were parked side-by-side across the rip, lines out.

"Wonder if they're hitting?" Splinter said.

"You see Guppy's Whaler?" Lenah said. Guppy's runaround boat was a twenty-four-foot Boston Whaler, with twin 200HP Johnsons. He flew a flag showing a setting sun with a smiling face at his center. It was the logo of his company, Oceanic Memories, a chain of tourist adventure companies that had branches along Florida's coasts.

"That it there in the middle?"

Lenah grabbed the binoculars and put them to her eyes. "Yup. Let me hail him," Lenah said, but before she could, Guppy must have seen her approaching because the Whaler backed away from the throng of boats and headed her way.

"Splinter, hate to do this to you again, but I think it's best you hide in the cabin," she said.

"Yes, me lady." Splinter bowed and headed down the short set of steps that led from the pilothouse to the cabin and small galley.

Splinter locked the cabin door and sat at the galley table, positioning himself so he could hear everything that was said.

Static crackled from the radio. "Evenstar this is the Double Zero, do you copy?"

"10-4 Double Zero."

Minutes passed before the Double Zero bumped into the Parker. Guppy was big, and the boat rolled to port when he stepped aboard.

"How are you, honey? How do you get yourself into these messes?"

"Just lucky, I guess."

"Now if you'd take me up on my offer, you'd never need to worry about any of this stupid shit again," he said.

"That's sweet, but you know me."

"People looking for you. Cops even called me. They're worried about you. They think that nut Splinter has you."

"I can trust you, Gup. Splinter has nothing to do with this. He helped me on a charter and I haven't seen him since."

Silence.

"You think you can forget you saw me?"

"I think so. You didn't kill anybody or anything, did you? This pretty face wouldn't look good in jail doing time for aiding and abetting."

Lenah did her school girl chuckle. Splinter hated it. Lenah was one of the toughest people he knew and when she laughed like that his stomach knotted.

"Of course not, silly. What you got for me?"

"One Xls pump for a 2014 150HP Yamaha."

"Great. I really appreciate it," Lenah said.

"Want me to put it in?" Guppy said.

Long silence. The tinkle and pop of the sea against the hull echoed in the cabin.

Guppy, apparently realizing his poor choice of words, attempted a recovery. "Installing the pump would be no problem."

"That's OK. I'll do it in the morning," Lenah said.

Guppy chuckled, then nothing.

"Did you bring the darts and gun?" she said.

"Sure did. Ready to go," Guppy said. Splinter could hear the pride in his voice.

Poseidon leapt on Splinter's lap and he jumped and let out a squeal.

Everything went quiet on the deck outside as Splinter lifted Poseidon close to his face, scolding him with gentle headbutts.

Two metal clasps snapped open, and Splinter sighed.

"This here is a TelroDart RD719 Injection Gun. It shoots XK23 tracker darts." Guppy eased back the slide and it locked in place with a clang. "It has a range of eighty yards, but depending on the thickness of the hide, you might want to be closer."

"How close for a croc?" Lenah asked.

"Say fifty yards."

"And the darts?"

"They snap in here like this."

A clink of metal, and the bolt rammed home and locked in place. "It has a five-mile range and should be easily detectable up to one hundred fathoms. Closer you are, the deeper you'll see."

"Trackable on my GPS screen?"

"Yes, Ma'am. Just program your GPS into the dart, and let the Bluetooth find it. It will show up as a large yellow dot regardless of what the SONAR shows."

"Alright. You hitting anything over there?"

"Naw. They're all bitching like passed-over prom queens," Guppy said. "Where you headin'?"

"Got a charter tomorrow."

"Need a hand?"

Lenah said nothing.

Splinter pressed his ear to the cabin door.

"So, what you up to the rest of the evening?" Guppy said.

"You want to go get a drink?" Lenah said.

Splinter's head jerked back.

"Sounds great. But I thought you were keeping a low profile?"

"We can hit the back room at Tilly's. Nobody should know me there. My face hasn't been all over TV."

"Yeah, you ain't that killer Splinter."

Splinter rolled his shoulders and cracked his neck.

Lenah did the chuckle. "Let's go."

Shuffling feet, the thump of Guppy's fat frame landing on the deck of his boat. Engines roared to life. Splinter came up from the cabin into the pilothouse, keeping low.

"What the hell was that?" he said. "Why do all these moon-eyed babes have it in for me?"

Lenah smiled. "Had to get rid of him somehow." She pushed down on the throttle and the Parker plowed through the chop and jumped in Guppy's wake.

Splinter said nothing.

"We're gonna ditch him at south bend," she said.

Splinter smiled.

The Parker cut through the darkness, Guppy's white NAV light on the transom marking his progress before them. The channel widened, and the chop doubled in size and strength.

"Double zero, do you copy?"

"Go ahead, Lenah."

"Guppy, I hate to be a woman, but I don't feel so great. Can I get that drink another night?"

"Not feeling well? You OK?"

"Yeah, just shot to the sea. You know how it is. Now that you helped me solve tomorrow's problem I feel exhausted."

Blast of static. Nothing.

"We can do diner next week. I'll make it up to you."

"Promise?"

"As much as that means in this crazy world, yes, I promise."

"Sleep tight, darling."

Lenah closed the channel, turned to Splinter, and said, "I didn't say I'd be alone."

***

Next morning Splinter got up in the predawn hours and installed the new fuel pump, and when he was about half done, Lenah emerged from the galley with coffee.

"You rule," he said.

"You didn't even taste it."

"Doesn't matter." Splinter sipped his coffee and held up the metal mug in salute.

"What's the plan today?" she asked.

"Get back out on the ocean and tag this bitch. End of plan."

Lenah sighed. "Location is off South Beach Park?"

"For starters unless you have something better? This is your turf."

"This thing isn't acting like any fish I've every tracked. I think it will move on to a new feeding area. The seas of South Beach Park are going to be packed with coasties and law. I'd be surprised if the thing was still hanging around there."

Splinter finished putting the outboard back together and snapped on the cover. Engine two hummed to life, and Evenstar was once again in full readiness.

The inlet was jammed, and it took Lenah two hours to navigate the Indian River, pass through the inlet, and get out into the Atlantic. Six-foot rollers cut across the inlet, and the Parker heaved and pitched as it launched over the swells, the Yamahas wailing in protest on each drop as the back of the boat lifted from the water.

Lenah spun the wheel and the Evenstar arced south, hugging the coast. Splinter searched the horizon and they hadn't gone far south before the gaggle of boats appeared out of the haze.

A hundred-foot boat with a huge gantry crane hauled the sunken sailboat from its watery grave.

Lenah checked the Parker to a stop with a rapid burst of reverse, then dropped it in neutral. Splinter brought up the binoculars and said, "Holy shit."

A Coast Guard cutter, four marine patrol boats with lights flashing, and a dark gray Navy Zodiac formed a tight knot around the salvage ship. Another layer of smaller boats surrounded the rescue vessels, and a whirly-bird circled overhead.

"Lenah, as usual, I think you're right."

16

"What now?" Lenah said.

Splinter rubbed his chin and pulled on his ponytail. "As we figured, it's probably fled the area. Question is, where will it go feed now?"

"Up or down the coast I'd wager," Lenah said.

"With that copter in the air the thing probably went deep. We might not see it again for a while."

"I don't know. If it's some type of mutant croc it won't have gills," she said.

Splinter hadn't thought of that. Without gills how could the creature stay in the depths for so long? "I don't know, but right now it doesn't matter. All that matters is north or south? Let's take the path of least resistance and go north," Splinter said.

"50-50 shot," Lenah said.

She nudged the throttle forward an inch, and the Evenstar pushed through the five-foot swell. To the west a line of dark storm clouds paraded across the horizon, and by mid-day it would be raining. Two herons flew overhead, the pair in sync like an airshow. They dipped and rolled, plucking small fish from the ocean and staying clear of boats.

Lenah turned on the fish finder and plotted a jagged course that would take them two miles out into water that was over a hundred feet deep. She spun-up the motors and brought the Parker to twenty knots as they patrolled the sea.

The hours slipped away, and they saw nothing, not so much as a garbage fish. The rollers slapping against the hull grew as a stiff wind from the west stood the waves up, doubling their size. The Parker dipped and rolled in the valleys and peaks of the swell; Splinter perched on the bow staring through the binoculars while Lenah monitored the SONAR.

At around 3PM Splinter screamed, "Hard to port. I think I've got its caudal fin."

Lenah banked hard and slowed the boat, not wanting to make noise. Not that it mattered. Splinter figured if the creature was anything like other deep-sea dwellers it could sense the slightest vibrations in the water miles away.

As they closed in, it become clear Splinter had spotted a dolphin pod. Four of the intelligent creatures played together on the surface, jumping out of the water, nudging each other, and frolicking like human children. They eyed the boat, but didn't pay the Parker much attention. They squeaked and bleated, trying to talk. Splinter had seen a documentary about a scientist who'd learned to talk to the creatures, and some believed that dolphins were smarter than humans given the relative size of their brain.

The dolphins took off so fast Splinter didn't know what direction they'd gone in.

"Wonder what spooked them?" Lenah said as Splinter entered the pilothouse.

"That." Splinter pointed to the western horizon by the entrance to the inlet.

"Oh shit," Lenah said.

A dorsal fin knifed through the sea, heading for the inner bay. The gray fin protruded three feet from the water, its triangle resembling a small sail. "That's a great white. Judging by the size of the dorsal fin it's at least fifteen feet long."

"Double oh shit," Lenah said.

A hundred yards behind the shark was the tip of a gray three-foot caudal fin, swishing back-and-forth as the leviathan moved silently through the water stalking its prey.

"Fall in behind them. Keep your distance, though," Splinter said. "What's the SONAR showing?"

"Nothing yet, we're not in range," Lenah.

"Let's cut the angle and see if we can get to the inlet mouth before them," Splinter said.

She drew an imaginary line on the NAV screen with her finger as she assessed their position. "Coming around to 31 degrees. We might make it." She pushed down on the throttle and brought the boat up to half speed. With the waves rolling in, full speed wasn't an option, and she was pushing it at twenty knots. Sea spray pounded the windshield, and the bilge pump kicked on as waves broke over the bow.

Splinter took the TelroDart RD719 Injection Gun from its case and jacked a dart into the firing chamber. He brought the weapon to his shoulder and sighted the beast through the windshield. It was still a half mile distant. When he was satisfied the dart gun was ready, he retrieved the M16 from the gun stock and snapped in a full cartridge.

"What are you planning to do with that?" Lenah asked as he passed through the pilothouse.

"Just insurance," he said.

Splinter slid the pilothouse door closed behind him and leaned against the bulkhead. He felt dizzy, as if the sea was finally eroding his resolve and urging him to find land. He braced himself in the bow and waited.

Poseidon leapt on the dash above the command counsel, and Splinter saw the cat watching him through the windshield.

"Still nothing on the SONAR. Closing to within 1,000 yards," Lenah yelled.

The Parker bounced and rolled as it pushed through the sea, and Splinter closed his eyes, letting the breeze ease his nerves.

"Got them. Changing course to 324 degrees southwest," Lenah said. "Our big purple blob is back, and it looks like it brought a friend."

"Or dinner," Splinter said. "Is that a boat?" A white shape bobbed through the haze.

"Yup," Lenah said.

In the distance a large pleasure yacht was anchored, and people jumped off the rear dive platform.

"Hail them. Hurry!" Splinter said.

With trembling hands Lenah pulled the handset from the radio. "What's the boat's name?"

"I can't tell." Splinter peered through the binoculars. "Wait. The Eighth Day."

Lenah opened the emergency channel. "To the Eighth Day, this is the Evenstar. A shark is approaching your vessel. Get out of the water. I repeat, to The Eighth Day, shark in water. Do you copy?"

Nothing.

"Screw this," Splinter said.

He pulled the M16 strap from his shoulder and stepped away from the pilothouse window. He fired six times into the air, the pop of the gunpowder expanding echoing over the water.

Lenah said, "They didn't hear that. The kids aren't getting out of the water. They're body surfing the waves."

Splinter ground his teeth and went back into the pilothouse.

"Bogeys haven't changed course. The shark will be on that boat in a minute. It's two-hundred yards away and closing fast," Lenah said.

"Get us over there."

Lenah dropped the throttle and the Parker launched off a wave as the engines whined. The deck tilted at a thirty-degree angle as the twenty-eight-foot boat went down the face of a wave.

"Call for help?" Splinter said.

"We have to."

"Agreed."

Splinter picked up the radio and hailed the Coast Guard on the emergency channel. They said their ETA was twelve minutes.

"This is going to be over in twelve minutes," Lenah said. "Go get ready to tag the big boy, and I'll try and use the boat to force the shark away from the yacht."

"Got it." Splinter went back out onto deck and wedged himself in the bow, M16 over one shoulder, the dart rifle pressed against his other. He couldn't see the beast.

"Four-hundred yards," came Lenah's voice from the exterior speaker. "ETA thirty seconds."

The people on the yacht still hadn't taken notice, and the children splashed in the water. Splinter rolled his shoulders. He knew sharks could sense vibrations in the sea, and the apex predator's dorsal fin knifed directly at the swimmers.

Commotion erupted on the yacht. They'd seen the fish. Children paddled wildly toward the yacht's swim platform, but one smaller boy had fallen behind and struggled through the swell, getting pushed backward as he tired.

Splinter put down the dart gun and brought up the M16. He sighted the dorsal fin and opened fire, spraying the fish with bullets.

The people on the boat looked panicked, and as the Parker closed in, Splinter saw a man waving a gun. He pointed it at the Evenstar and squeezed off two shots. The bullets went high and wide, but Splinter heard them whizz past and slap into the ocean.

"What the?" yelled Lenah.

"They think I'm shooting at them."

The shark launched from the sea, its sleek gray body glistening, powerful jaws extended. It bit down on the boy as he struggled through the surf, and fish and boy disappeared within a mound of red foam.

The caudal fin of the larger creature emerged off the port side, its giant crocodilian head floating on the surface.

Crying and screams of terror came from the yacht as the shark dove, its dorsal fin disappearing beneath the waves.

The yacht shook, and a man standing on deck flipped over the gunnel and fell into the sea. He was pulled under and didn't come up.

The big boat rocked again, bow sinking into a wave, unable to recover as the transom lifted in the air.

"They're going down," Lenah yelled.

"The shark didn't do that," Splinter said.

Gunshots. The man on the yacht was firing at the Parker again.

"They think this is our fault," Lenah said.

The yacht was going down, but both beasts had left the scene.

In the distance a Coast Guard cutter pushed through the growing swell. The clouds on the western horizon were close, and forks of lightning lit the gray sky like a camera flash.

"Splinter!"

Splinter turned to see the leviathan surfacing behind the Parker, its caudal fin at the end of its tail flicking back and forth. Its flat head broke the surface, gray eyes staring up at the Parker through the swirling water, jaws opening.

He dropped the M16, shouldered the dart rifle, and fired.

The dart hissed from the gun barrel and hit the beast square on its head. It bounced off and floated listlessly on the water, appearing and vanishing in the roll of the ocean.

"Shit!" Splinter went to get a second dart, but the creature dove, disappearing into the depths.

The shark was back, and it circled the sinking yacht. The Coast Guard cutter was almost on scene, its main stack billowing white smoke as engines strained to push through the swell at top speed. An orange Zodiac dropped off the cutter's starboard side, and the rescue boat darted toward the sinking vessel.

"What should I do?" Lenah asked.

The Coast Guard boat hadn't hailed them as they focused on the rescue.

"Looks like the coasties got this under control. You have anything on the SONAR?"

"The larger creature is moving away to the south. Fast."

Splinter was unsure what to do. If they stayed, they'd get caught up in the investigation, and they'd be back where they started: out of the race, with no proof, and the beast would get away. Add to that the crazy ass on the yacht, who based on the shots he'd fired at the Evenstar, felt they were somehow responsible for the arrival of the shark. Clearly nobody aboard The Eighth Day had seen the second creature pursuing the shark. All that added up to Splinter and Lenah being screwed.

"Track the creature. Try and slip away slowly," Splinter said.

"People have died here, Splinter," Lenah said.

Anger rose in him. "And more will die if we don't get this bitch," Splinter said. "Can we bring them back? Can we help in any better way than staying on this thing's ass?"

Lenah said nothing. She nudged the throttle and slowly eased away from the chaos.

17

They hadn't gone far when the marine radio crackled to life.

"Evenstar, this is the USG cutter Valiant. Please hold your position. Do you copy?"

"Do I answer?" Lenah asked Splinter.

Splinter turned off the radio and said, "Bring us up to thirty knots."

Lenah looked at him, but said nothing.

"Too fast for these swells?"

"Yeah, a little. We're running from the coasties? I don't know, Splinter."

"We have to stay on that thing's tail. I need another shot with the dart gun. I've got to tag that thing, so it can be stopped for good. I'll take responsibility. We can say I forced you."

Lenah sighed. "What the hell can we do anyway. Everyone's out of the water."

"That's the spirit."

"But we saw what happened. We have to tell them."

"We will. Let's go tag this thing and we'll come right back here and give them the tracking frequency and explain everything."

Lenah sighed, but depressed the throttle and the Parker picked up speed, kicking up seaweed and churning the ocean into whitewater. Thunder cracked, and a light rain fell, layering the boat with water and making everything slick.

"SONAR shows the creature heading two, one, four, closing in on Seagull Island," Lenah said.

"Keep pace. What depth is it at?"

"Hard to tell. At least fifty feet based on what I'm seeing," she said.

"It just ate, so it might be chilling out until it gets hungry again. Stay on it."

Splinter went to the dart gun case and removed the other tracker dart. Made from stainless steel, the point was a barbed needle that could penetrate a thick hide. Splinter activated the transmitter in the dart, and a red light came on. It had a small battery and was also equipped with a drug chamber. Unfortunately, Splinter had nothing to put in it. The dart's orange flight stabilizer was wrapped with a rubber band, and he took it off and pushed the dart into the rifle's firing chamber and jacked it closed. Then he retrieved the M16 and slung it over his shoulder.

Lenah said, "It's coming up. Thirty feet. Twenty. Ten. Off to starboard."

Splinter went out on deck, headed to the stern, and peered through the binoculars. He let them fall to his chest on their lanyard and brought up the dart rifle. He sighted the beast, but it was still too far off.

"Get me closer," he yelled.

Lenah cycled the motors up and the Parker increased speed to thirty knots, and the twenty-eight-foot fishing boat pushed up waves and fell into valleys. Seawater pummeled the Parker, crashing over the bow and soaking the windshield, but Lenah didn't falter. She'd been out in ten-foot swells, and this was nothing more than ripples in her bathwater.

Poseidon joined Splinter aft, the cat sticking its head into the wind, spray leaving tiny droplets of water on her slick hair.

"You hold on buddy," Splinter said.

"It's picking up speed, Splinter. It must know we're here." Lenah's voice boomed from the exterior speaker.

They were playing a dangerous game with the animal. Once it figured out it was bigger than the Parker, their advantage would be lost.

"Splinter, come look at this," Lenah said.

Splinter went to the pilothouse and found Lenah staring at the SONAR screen. "What is it?"

"See these here, all those small blue blobs running along the bottom?"

"I do."

"I think that's a school of American shads, a species of anadromous clupeid fish that roam Florida's coasts and swim up rivers to spawn. The creature appears to be heading toward them."

"New source of food?"

"I'd think. Much smaller vibrations, but the beast probably sees them as easy prey."

"OK, reduce speed and let's see what it does. How far are we from Seagull Island?"

"Mile or so."

"Shoot. We're ten miles out already?" Splinter asked.

"Yup. Look there," Lenah said. She pointed off the port bow.

Seagull Island was justly named because it was a barren, mangrove covered tidal island that thousands of gulls called home. There was no fresh water. No game. No beaches. No good reason to go there unless you were a bird.

"The beast going deep?"

"Not yet."

"Any signs of pursuit from the Coast Guard?"

"Naw. Maybe the folks on the boat realized we were trying to help them?"

Splinter said nothing.

The rain came hard and cold, and Splinter and Poseidon stayed in the pilothouse. Lightning flashed, and thunder reverberated over the water like concussion bombs. The sea kicked-up and the Parker fought through the growing swell, the waves peaking at seven feet. The Evenstar's bilge pump snapped on, sending a torrent of water jetting from the hull.

Eyes locked on the SONAR, Splinter watched the purple blob of the creature dive deeper, heading straight for the school of shads that moved fifty feet above the ocean floor.

The cabin was cold, and Lenah clicked on the heater, the rain still pounding them. "Looks like the creature is slowing," Lenah said.

The beast turned south, moving around its prey, positioning itself to knife through the school like a whale devouring krill.

"That shark showing up is the worst possible thing that could have happened," Lenah said. She gripped the wheel so tight her fingers were red, and she stared intently through the rain-soaked windshield.

Splinter didn't know what she meant. "Why's that? It might have helped. If the sea monster had attacked the boat, it might have gotten everyone."

"True. But now the authorities will think the shark has been causing all the problems."

"Not entirely bad. They'll still be searching for the shark."

"Assuming it's not already gaffed," she said.

To that Splinter had no response.

Fifty-eight feet below the surface the mystery animal gobbled shads in his huge flat jaws. On the surface, rolling waves pounded the Parker, tossing it back and forth like a leaf.

"Would we still be in range if used Seagull Island to block some of these waves?"

"No, and there'll be no place to hide there. The natural flow of the waves is east to west, but this storm is standing everything up and turning the ocean into a choppy mess." She minimized the SONAR and brought up the long-range weather report, which had an accompanying satellite photo taken four minutes prior. "This stuff should blow out in the next hour, and it should ease up."

Splinter said nothing.

"What do you figure the creature will do when it's done feeding and the sun comes out?"

"If it's what we think, some kind of mutated reptile, then I'd think it would come up and sun itself."

"Soon as the storm passes, it's secret sauce time. The thing seemed to like it."

"It did indeed."

The mystery creature didn't go far, spending the next two hours eating shads. The sun started its descent to the horizon, leaving streaks of orange and white through the thinning clouds. The storm had moved out, and it was hot and humid.

The two-foot chop was like a kiddie pool compared to the last twenty-four hours, and the Evenstar cut through the still water, the Yamahas barely audible as they rotated at 2300RPM.

Lenah slowed the Parker because the monster had slowed. It was moseying upward and west, slowly coming to the surface and heading back toward the mainland. Seagull Island was ten clicks to starboard, and several boats dotted the horizon.

Lenah ladled some of her chum into the sea, its rank smell making Splinter cough. Lenah laughed and so did Splinter, spittle dripping from his mouth.

"Why don't you cover your nose?"

"Wow. Never thought of that."

"Why are you such a wiseass?"

"It's all I know," Splinter said. "You see anything?"

Lenah said, "It's on the SONAR. Should be here soon."

"Camera ready?"

"Right here. Dart?"

"Check."

Banter and business completed, Splinter prepared for his shot. If everything went perfectly the creature would come up behind the Evenstar, following the chum slick, and Splinter would wait until the monster was fifty yards out before he fired. Then Lenah would gun the motors, and it would be a chase.

He laid the M16 flat on the deck within reach and put the dart rifle to his shoulder. Small whitecaps dotted the ocean, and patches of seaweed and dirty foam from the storm formed a patchwork across the undulating sea. He felt salt in his nose and eyes and his skin had tightened like piano strings. He was afraid to laugh for fear of ripping his face.

Both spotlights were on, and in the fading light Splinter saw one hundred yards out.

"It's coming in on the port side, Splinter. Shit, it's not going after the slick. Something's wrong," Lenah said. She backed down the throttle and the boat slowed to fifteen knots.

Splinter strained to see in the gray of twilight, the spotlights blackening everything beyond their glow. A splash brought Splinter's head around and a giant white torso rolled in the ocean. It looked like a whale, and an eye the size of a baseball examined them. With a flick of its caudal fin the creature was gone.

"It's under us, Splinter. The thing is huge. Thirty-feet." She put the motors in neutral.

The sea tumbled over the Parker, bubbling and snapping against the hull. A cacophony of seagulls floated over the black ocean, their chirping and screeching a welcome sound in the stillness. The glow of the control screen lit the pilothouse with a faux neon that mixed with the white gauge lights creating a kaleidoscope of color that reminded Splinter of light shining through a diamond.

"Anything?" Splinter said.

"It's cruising at around twenty feet. Steadily spiraling up. Chum?" she said.

"Naw. We've been wasting it. The thing wants our asses, not some nasty fish possum stew."

"Splinter, what are we doing out here?"

He said nothing.

"I get you're damaged and obsessed, but why are you doing this? How did this become your fight? My fight?"

Splinter said, "You know that answer better than me."

"I do. I'm here for you and you're here because you're obsessed."

"Obsessed?"

"You know we should go to the coasties, tell them what we've seen."

"We're about to tag this thing and get proof for the cops and you're preaching at me? We've been through this," he said.

"I know, I just keep getting this nagging feeling that we made the wrong decision, like we're crying wolf, and when we need the coasties they're not going to be there for us."

"Stay with me for a few more hours. Sunset tomorrow, and if—"

"Port bow. Twenty yards," Lenah said.

The ocean erupted, and Splinter went out on deck and sighted the dart gun on the mountain of whitewater. He saw no white skin, no teeth. He waited for any sign, anything to shoot at, but as the water flattened and cleared, the creature dove sharply to starboard and cut beneath the boat. A surge of water pushed the Parker up and it jumped from the sea and landed with a splat.

A roar sounded in the darkness. A great braying that made Splinter think of dinosaurs. The monster surfaced, snapping its saw-like jaws, chomping on seawater as it disappeared beneath a fist of whitewater.

"It's moving southeast toward Seagull Island. Fast." Lenah's voice boomed through the exterior speakers.

Splinter sighed the dart gun, but the creature had already disappeared into the gray of oncoming night, leaving only its wake behind.

"Get on it, Lenah. Full speed," he yelled.

The Yamahas purred, and the Parker sprang from the water with a spray of seawater.

A knot of water came at the Evenstar as if an invisible boat steamed across the ocean intent on colliding with the Parker. It was a hundred yards out and closing.

18

Lenah brought the Parker to a full stop. Splinter braced against the gunnel as the boat tossed side-to-side as their wake smashed into the transom. The creature's flat head and long mouth broke the surface, jaws opening.

Splinter took his finger off the trigger guard and placed it on the trigger. The beast was sixty yards out.

"Be ready to drop the hammer as soon as I fire," Splinter yelled.

"10-4," Lenah said. She watched from the rear pilothouse window, her hand poised over the throttle controls.

The creature opened its massive crocodilian mouth, revealing a row of sharp teeth. Its caudal fin smacked the water as it flicked back and forth, its two forward flippers pounding the sea.

Fifty yards.

The wind picked up and Splinter adjusted his aim. His hand and arm hurt from staying still for so long. The creature's torso surged from the water and in that brief instant, Splinter thought he saw gills along the creature's front flank.

Crocs didn't have gills. They needed air to breath.

Splinter fired, and the dart streaked from the holding tube, whizzing through the air as its flight stabilizer expanded and guided the dart. The wind pushed it off course, but the dart struck home above the beast's right flipper.

"Hit it!"

The Parker leapt from the water, the twin 150HP Yamahas clawing at the sea. Splinter got tossed against the transom and he dropped the dart rifle into the water and it sank below the churning ocean.

"Shhhhiiittttttttt," he yelled, but then he remembered it didn't really matter. He had no darts left, and he'd tagged the beast. Mission accomplished.

If it didn't take them down.

The creature breached from the sea in its fury, launching itself at the fleeing Parker. The dart had stirred the animal into a frenzy, and it landed feet away from the Evenstar. A torrent of seawater poured over the gunnel, and Splinter swam across the deck. The bilge pump kicked on the boat started draining, but the Parker was swamped.

Lenah reduced speed due to the floodwater, and the Parker moved sluggishly as she changed direction, moving away from the thrashing creature.

The giant mutant-croc surfaced in the Parker's wake, head pointed forward like an arrow, its rear fin and mid-flippers digging at the sea like boat propellers. The Yamahas shrieked and moaned with the crest of each wave.

The creature was gaining on them.

"I think I pissed it off," Splinter said.

"You're good at that," she said.

The creature chomped at the boat, jaws snapping closed with a terrible *crack*.

Lenah jerked the wheel right and the Parker arced away from the beast. Splinter retrieved the M16 and ran to the stern. A thin mist from the churning propellers hung over the water at the back of the boat, but Splinter saw the beast's massive frame disappear beneath the waves.

He sighted the swirl of water where the animal had submerged and squeezed off eight shots, each *pop* echoing over the ocean. The sea calmed, and the whitewater dissipated. Splinter's heart hammered in his chest, his lower back screeching with pain. "Where is it?" he yelled.

"It's coming up beneath us," came Lenah's voice from the pilothouse.

"How long?"

"Sixty-feet and rising," she said.

The Parker lumbered through the sea at ten knots. The hull rocked and heaved as it cut through the chop, and several fishing poles fell from where they hung along the gunnel.

Splinter worked his way around the pilothouse to the bow, peering into the dark water. It was fully dark, and it was impossible to see more than a few feet into the churning sea.

"It's right under us. Splinter!"

The front of the Parker rose from the water as the creature pushed the vessel upward, the force of its massive body shaking the Parker and driving the bow from the ocean. The engines screamed and sucked for water.

The creature dove, and the Evenstar fell back into the water with a bone rattling crash. Seawater pounded Splinter, and he got washed across the deck like a dead fish. His arm shot out and grabbed the corner of the pilothouse, stopping his slide toward the transom.

There'd been no crunch of fiberglass, but Splinter knew from past encounters the Parker couldn't take many more hits like that. He got to his knees and pulled himself to his feet. He'd lost the M16 and it sat wedged between the gunnel and transom, tangled in a gill net. It was useless until he had the opportunity to fully clean it, and the ammo was most likely water damaged.

"It's circling now, Splinter," Lenah yelled above the din.

Splinter pushed through the water, working his way to the pilothouse. If he could get the rifle maybe he'd find it in him to put a bullet between this thing's eyes.

The beast bellowed again and headed right at the Evenstar.

It struck the boat on the port side, and Splinter saw Lenah's head disappear behind the command console as she went down.

Anger built in him, the fog coming on, his mind racing back to Kabul, all the old fears and hatreds rushing back. He slid open the pilothouse door and jumped down the steps into the cabin. He grabbed the rifle and searched for the box of bullets. When he found it on the galley table, he tore it open and jacked a round into the firing chamber, and put a handful of shells in his pocket.

Splinter didn't hear Lenah as he ran through the pilothouse back out onto deck. She was trying to tell him something, he could see her mouth moving, tears leaking from her eyes, but Splinter was gone, back in Kabul, and all that mattered was killing the beast.

The creature smashed into the port side, driving the Parker across the water at an odd angle, and the Yamahas coughed and struggled to draw the water necessary to cool the engines. The boat spun and before Lenah could kill the motors the propellers dug in and pushed the Evenstar toward the creature's open maw.

The Parker slammed into the side of the beast's head and the sound of crunching fiberglass made Splinter wince. The creature's slate-gray eyes bulged from recessed eye sockets, its slick white skin covered in seaweed as it surfaced.

Lenah dropped the boat into reverse, and the Parker's bow pulled away from the leviathan. The beast appeared stunned from the impact and floated listlessly, waves breaking over it in the darkness.

Splinter turned the floodlights on the beast, and that seemed to rouse the animal. It tossed and rolled, throwing water and turning the ocean into a boiling mess. He killed the lights.

Lenah put the boat in neutral and spun the wheel, pointing the bow away from the creature. The engines coughed and stalled as Lenah depressed the throttle. She put the boat in neutral and turned the key and spun-up the motors. They restarted, and she dropped the hammer and the propellers dug in, pushing the boat forward. The bilge pump was going full tilt, but the water above deck wasn't lessening.

Splinter sloshed his way to the bow and let loose with a primal scream of anger. He brought up the rifle, fired, and heard the smack of the bullet as it hit home. His legs shook, and pain lanced his back. Deep in the fog he pulled a thirty-five-caliber hollow point bullet from his pocket, loaded it into the high-powered Marlin, and fired.

Again.

And again.

He didn't hear the slap of the bullets striking home. All he heard was his own savage scream.

The beast roared and launched from the water, its right flipper landing on the transom and pushing the Parker beneath the waves. The bow rose from the water and Splinter grabbed hold of the lead line that was tied to the bow cleat. He hung on as his feet washed out from under him and the Evenstar yawed and almost tipped over.

The Parker's hull was filled with Styrofoam-like material, so unless the craft was broken into multiple pieces it couldn't sink, but it could be turned up-side-down.

The creature opened its jaws and the rows of teeth bit down on the port side gunnel and tore a six-foot section from the side of the boat. Water surged through the hole, the Yamahas pushing the bow downward into the waves.

Lenah cut the engines. The boat stopped and bobbed up, but tipped sharply to port.

"Here! Splinter!"

Splinter heard the echoes of Lenah's voice in the back of his head, a distant call behind the fog. She shook him, her beautiful face suddenly in front of him.

"Splinter! Put this on."

She thrust a yellow deflated lifejacket at him and ran back to the pilothouse.

Seawater reached the top of the gunnel as the creature chomped on the Parker, fiberglass, wood, and metal spewing from the beast's mouth. The leviathan eased back into the sea, its jaws smacking, massive flat head thrashing like a shark.

Splinter shook his head, the fog fading, the fear draining away like sewage. "Lenah," he said, and pushed through the rising water toward the pilothouse.

The sea calmed. Debris floated all around the Parker, which was totally swamped. There was a foot of water in the pilothouse and the cabin below was totally submerged. All the bridge electronics were out. The battery compartment was sealed, but wasn't water tight and it was currently underwater.

"Do you see it out there?" Lenah said. Her dark silhouette reflected off the pilothouse window, and in that moment, Splinter realized he loved her. Who else would stay with a crazy bastard like him?

"Yeah, off the stern. It's circling us. Hopefully it didn't like the taste of fiberglass," Splinter said.

Three-foot waves rolled into the Parker's windshield, the pilothouse the only part of the boat above water. The vessel rolled and yawed with each set of waves, but the layered foam in the hull was keeping the Parker afloat.

"Meow. Meow."

"Oh god. Poseidon," Splinter said. He dove into the water and swam into the galley without thinking. If he were to get trapped or disorientated, or if the fog returned...

The cat was on top of the storage cabinet in the far corner of the galley, curled up in an air pocket.

Splinter's head burst through the water right next to the cat and Poseidon hissed at him.

"I don't blame you for being pissed, but you wanted to stay. You're gonna need to go under pal, and fast."

The air pocket was getting smaller as the swamped Parker shifted.

Poseidon seemed to understand, and she let Splinter take her in his arms. He stroked her and kissed her on the top of the head. Then he shoved the cat under his arm like a football, covered her nose and mouth as best he could, like he was holding the nose of the football the way he had in high school.

Splinter dove, swimming with one arm, pushing himself toward the galley exit. It was only six feet, but it was the longest swim of his life. Poseidon struggled and fought to breathe. Splinter's arm felt like lead, his legs slowing with pain and weariness, his knee screaming, the adrenaline draining away.

Lenah gasped when Splinter emerged into the pilothouse. He released the cat, and Poseidon screeched and swam, pulling in air. Lenah picked her up and put her over her shoulder like an infant, slapping her back and forcing out any water. The cat sputtered and coughed, but appeared fine.

They'd survived.

The creature circled.

19

Water sloshed around the inside of the pilothouse, slapping against the bulkhead. The Parker's engines and cabin were submerged, and the boat rocked with the ocean swell. Darkness blanketed the water, and moonbeams cut through the cloud cover and sent errant rays across the undulating sea. The air smelt of resin, dead fish, and fear.

Lenah snapped an emergency glowstick and the pilothouse filled with pale yellow-green light. She and Splinter peered through the windshield, and every few seconds the creature's caudal fin passed close to the boat and disappeared into the blackness, its wake rocking the Parker.

"What's it waiting for?" Lenah said.

"It's confused. It thought the boat was food, but now it's debating how hungry it really is. It just fed, so maybe it will move on."

"What are we going to do if it doesn't? The wind is picking-up out of the west, which means these rollers are going to get bigger as they stand up."

Splinter said nothing. He didn't know what they'd do if they ended up in the drink with the creature. "Do you have a life raft?" They'd lost the Zodiac in the first attack when it was thrown from the deck. Splinter was sure it was floating out there somewhere, but in the darkness, there was no way to see it even if it was close enough.

"I took it off to make room because we had the Zodiac," she said. "You think it would matter? I'm not bouncing around on the open ocean in a blow-up toy with that thing around."

"If you see another choice, I'm open to suggestions."

"You want a suggestion? Shut up, Splinter. Look at my boat. My life."

Splinter's eyes shifted to the brackish water rolling over the pilothouse deck. She had a point. This was his fault. She'd wanted to go to the coasties from the beginning, but it had been his insecurities, obsession, and fears that led them to their current dire situation. His inability to seek help. To want help.

"I'm sorry, Splinter. It's just…"

"Don't you dare apologize. I'm the one who's sorry. You didn't want to be out here. You shouldn't be out here. This is all my fault. You're right."

Water gurgled and snapped as it hit the hull. A thick patch of clouds passed overhead, cutting off the moonlight and turning the ocean into deep space. Waves pushed against the half-submerged pilothouse, and the whistle of the wind rose and fell with each set of waves. Yellow-green shadows danced on the bulkhead, and the dot of a red light in the distance made Splinter think of something.

"You have an emergency beacon?"

"I did. No idea where it is. Underwater somewhere."

"Great."

Lenah gasped, and Splinter jerked back from the command console.

The beast floated over the Parker's submerged bow, its massive white body filling the windshield. Luminescent eyes protruded like giant warts from the side of the creature's flat head, steel gray baseballs rolling their way. Its flippers were still, but the creature's long crocodilian mouth was slowly opening, revealing its razor-sharp teeth. It wasn't coming forward. It hung still, waves breaking over its exposed back and tail.

"What's it doing?" Lenah said.

"I think looking for us."

"It's huge. Its torso looks bigger than a whale."

"Be quiet and don't make any sudden movements. Stay still," Splinter said.

"Mmmm. OK. You think that will help?" she whispered.

Splinter said nothing.

"Because I don't think staying quiet is going to help at all when those jaws come through the windshield."

A large red tongue lay in the long mouth behind the teeth. Splinter thought the thing was smiling at him. With two sharp pushes of its flippers the beast inched forward, its nose touching the glass of the Parker's windshield.

The creature closed its jaws and eased backward. Time slowed, and Splinter realized he knew nothing. He was an insignificant piece of sand on a never-ending beach. The beast backed away, slate-gray eyes blinking as it disappeared in the inky water.

"Did that just happen?" Lenah said.

"Did you get a picture?"

"Camera is underwater somewhere," she said.

"You get any pictures before it got dark?"

"A bunch. Don't know how good they were. We'll never know now, but I probably got something," Lenah said. "You hit it with the dart though, right?"

"I saw the dart hit and penetrate next to its flipper. We should be good." If they lived to tell anyone the frequency of the tracker dart.

Lenah said nothing.

To the south, the dark outline of Seagull Island was like a distant black rock on the horizon. If they had the Zodiac they could've made a run for it, but the island was at least five miles away and there was no way they could swim it with an apex croc on their asses.

Splinter didn't know what to say. Expressing his feelings to others had never been a problem, until Kabul. His stomach heaved. He had to say something, break the silence that threatened to pull them under.

"I ever tell you I love the name of your boat?" he said.

She chuckled. "Ironic it's going down." Arwen Undómiel, daughter of Elrond, was called the Evenstar because she was the most beautiful of the last generation of elves to live in Middle Earth.

Splinter said nothing.

"My father used to call me the Evenstar. He wanted to name me Arwen, but mom wouldn't let him. Said it would mark me a geek."

"That so bad?"

"To her it was. I think she was afraid we wouldn't be able to relate. That she'd lose me. She wanted me to listen to country music. Not worry about life so much."

"Dad was the task master?"

"Kind of. He was always preaching about making decisions that affect your future. He wanted me to be happy more than anything else, I think. Don't get me wrong, he pushed me to reach my potential. Both my parents loved the sea, so it makes sense that I'd end up out here."

"You speak of your father in the past tense."

"He died last year. Cancer."

Splinter had no idea. She'd never said anything. "I'm sorry for not being there. I—"

The Parker was thumped on its starboard side and the half-sunken boat was driven into the sea. Poseidon screeched as she got tossed across the cabin, arms and legs fanned out. Splinter lost his footing and sailed across the pilothouse. He twisted in the air like a receiver diving for a ball in the end zone and snatched the cat from the air as he crashed into the bulkhead, cradling Poseidon in his arms. Splinter landed in the rising floodwater as the creature continued to drive the Evenstar beneath the waves.

Lenah gripped the command console and managed to stay on her feet, but she dropped the glowstick and it sank beneath the water.

The pilothouse door window shattered, and Lenah screamed. Splinter tried to get to his feet, but the deck tilted at a forty-degree angle and was half filled with water. Something snapped, and the sound of cracking fiberglass filled the cabin as water poured through the broken window.

"We need to get out of here," Lenah yelled.

Splinter was fading. Water poured over him, and he floated toward the pilothouse ceiling. Anger rose in him. Fear. Fear of dying out here in the wet barren nothingness, where nobody would know or care. He'd given his life, and it had been taken, and he didn't see how he would ever get it back. So why not die here?

Splinter fell into the embrace of his abyss, the other Splinter rising through the PTSD fog.

The young girl wore a tattered yellow dress, and long strands of greasy black hair fell across her face. Her eyes were brown pools of fear, and she looked at him with a pleading face. Gunshots rang out, and firelight danced in the ruins of a brick building.

Splinter fired.

Then Jasmine was there, the bullet striking her in the head and blowing her brains out the back of her skull. He just shot his sister. She looked so much like that girl in Kabul. The yellow dress and dark hair. He hadn't shot his sister. But the little girl…

Jasmine rattled around in his head. "They were the enemy. Sometimes there are casualties of war," his sister said.

"You weren't there. You didn't do it."

"Why did you do it?"

The fog thickened, and his hands shook. The water rose, and the ceiling came to meet him. He'd just close his eyes, force all of this from his head, but the faces wouldn't leave him alone. The memories of those killed, and those he couldn't recall. Those were the worst, because when a lost memory did come through it was like killing all over again, and it tore him apart.

Lenah floated beside him. She had his shirt in her coiled fists. She was screaming, water rising around her, but Splinter couldn't hear her. He was lost in the fog. Give up, he told himself. Let go.

Splinter blinked, his head pounding in rhythm with his heart.

"Splinter!"

He said nothing.

"Swim. Swim as if your life depends on it because it does."

"I love you," Splinter said. "I'm so sorry."

Lenah froze for an instant, her beautiful brown eyes filling with tears.

Fiberglass cracked and snapped, water filled the cabin, and the beast bellowed as its powerful jaws crushed the Parker.

"Then follow me. As soon as you're clear of the boat, inflate your vest. Let's go soldier!" She pecked him on the lips and dove into the floodwater.

"One more time, buddy," Splinter said.

Poseidon meowed and didn't fight as Splinter took the cat beneath his arm and covered her mouth and nose as he had before. Pushing off the bulkhead, he dove for the broken pilothouse window. Below the dark water the green-yellow light of the glowstick Lenah had dropped lit the way. The sinking boat yawed, the broken window moving away from Splinter as he was sucked upward with the surging sea.

He stroked with one arm, fighting his way to the window. The glowstick faded. Something rushed past him in the darkness, a large fish running from the leviathan. Bubbles streamed through the pilothouse window as Splinter crashed against the windshield, and white foam sizzled on the glass.

The Parker rocked as the beast rammed it again, and Splinter tumbled through the water like dirty underwear in a washing machine. Food wrappers, supplies, everything they had with them churned in the deluge, the light from the glowstick dying out.

Poseidon struggled, and Splinter's lungs burned and his eyes stung. He found the pilothouse window and pushed off the bulkhead, stroking hard, legs kicking, putting out one last effort. Bubbles escaped his lips as he let out the last of his air. Tiny pinpricks of light danced before his eyes.

The Parker finally gave up the ghost and split in half, fiberglass shattered, wood snapped, and metal bent as the twenty-eight-foot Parker broke apart. A torrent of seawater pushed Splinter into the ceiling of the pilothouse as it tore from the deck and sank into the Atlantic.

Splinter pulled the red clasp on his lifejacket and closed his eyes.

20

The life vest inflated, and Splinter was thrust upward in a swirling cloud of bubbles. The water was cold and dark, and he couldn't see beyond the surging whitewater as he was sucked toward the surface. His shoulder hit something hard, and for a moment he was held up. He wiggled and shifted his position and continued upward through the darkness.

Splinter broke the surface, gasping for air, lungs burning. Blackness covered the ocean, and debris from the Evenstar littered the surface, rolling with the waves.

Poseidon scrambled from Splinter's grasp and perched herself on his shoulders, coughing and choking up water.

"Easy, buddy. You made it." The cat looked like a drowned rat, but she was alive.

Splinter remembered Lenah and yelled her name, then stopped. The creature was about, so he felt it best to keep quiet. He searched the flotsam; pieces of broken fiberglass, seat cushions, papers, everything they had was either floating in the drink or on the bottom of the ocean in what was left of the Parker.

"Here! I'm here."

Splinter's heart ached, and relief swam through him. If she'd died on his watch that would've been the end for him. "You OK?"

She laughed. "All things considered."

The larger parts of the Parker were sinking and disappearing beneath the dark waves, but Splinter grabbed a seat cushion and used it to help support his weight. His lifejacket was working, but he was at the weight limit. He gently stroked through the water, trying not to disturb the debris field.

Lenah clung to a chunk of fiberglass that had once been part of the Evenstar's bow. Her lifejacket was punctured and lay across her chest like a deflated balloon. When Splinter reached her, she threw her arms around him and they started to sink.

"Easy, there. Here." Splinter thrust the seat cushion in her direction and she pounced on it.

The wind out of the west picked up and wave heights increased from three to five feet and crashed over the remains of the sunken boat, driving the debris into the depths.

"Quiet," Splinter hissed.

To his right, thirty yards off, a white caudal fin swished back and forth as the beast circled the debris field. The ocean surged when the beast swam past, but it was hard to see the creature in the darkness.

It was hours until sun-up. A big wave crested and closed out on them, pushing Splinter underwater. Poseidon squealed, and positioned herself on Splinter's head as he tried in vain to stay above the waves.

"Here." Lenah slid Splinter a chunk of the Parker and he placed the wet cat atop it. Poseidon did her best to stay balanced on the piece of fiberglass as it shifted in the turbulent sea, but Splinter had to help her or she would have slipped off.

The wind howled, and Splinter's fingers and toes were getting cold. The sea was temperate, but with the wind picking up the water felt icy. Splinter and Lenah huddled together, Poseidon on her float between them.

"What now?" Lenah said. "We're pretty far out and by morning I doubt the debris field will be easily seen."

"Yeah, we're screwed, blued and tattooed."

"My dad used to say that."

"Mine too."

Poseidon meowed twice as if to say can we move on to more important things? Like where I'm getting my next meal, and how do you plan to stop me from becoming one.

"Easy, sweetie," Lenah said. She stroked the cat's wet hair and Poseidon closed her green eyes.

"I've got an idea, but you're not gonna like it."

"What? Swim down to the Parker and retrieve a fork to fight the thing with?"

"I was thinking butter knife."

No laugh.

"We swim for Seagull Island."

Lenah let out an exasperated sigh. "It's at least three miles off, Splinter. I can't see it anymore, can you?"

Splinter twisted his hips and spun in the water, holding onto the collar of his lifejacket. He searched for the island in the darkness, but he couldn't find it. "We know what direction it's in. We go southeast and as we get closer, we'll see it."

"I don't think—"

A shriek of anger and pain rose above the crashing waves as the beast wailed. Lenah jumped, and Poseidon hissed. Splinter searched for the creature's head, but couldn't find it in the darkness. The creature's labored breathing and grunting sounded like an out-of-tune car engine, and it was getting closer.

The beast's right flipper brushed Splinter as the creature snaked through the debris, long mouth closed, searching. Splinter stayed still, holding his breath. The beast's massive body disappeared beneath the surface. Splinter let out his breath.

"You think it's best to stay in the debris field?" Lenah's voice was shaky, and her teeth chattered.

"For now. I think it doesn't know the difference between us and the pieces of the Parker. If we can keep it confused it might move on."

"It can't smell us? Thought you said it probably could sense vibrations in the water from miles away?"

"It probably can, but with all the debris, it's getting mixed signals. As to the smell, I don't know. A weak scent, we are in salt water. There's no blood or other food floating around that I can see, but I can't see far at all."

The night dragged on, and the sea got colder. They drifted with the debris northeast away from Seagull Island, each wave taking them further from dry land and out into the vastness of the mid-Atlantic Ocean. An hour had passed since they'd last seen the sea monster, but Splinter knew it was out there. He could feel its presence like an enemy on the battlefield. The unease that something stronger and smarter was stalking you, looking for weaknesses in your armor, forming an attack plan.

Splinter and Lenah shivered, having been in the drink for over four hours. They pumped their legs to keep the blood flowing, but they were afraid to make noise or disturb the water.

"Splinter, what are we going to do? This thing's gonna get us at some point."

"What if we run a little test?" he said.

"Like?"

"I take my shirt off, fill it with some debris, and toss it as far as I can and see if the thing attacks it."

"That's pretty thin."

"Paper."

"But I got nothing," Lenah said. "Can't you just build us a new boat with spit and all the broken pieces?"

"Alright, I'll make our decoy while you look around. See if you can find something to use as weapons."

"You shitting me? Use a glass shard against this thing?"

"Maybe we can make a spear or two using cracked fiberglass as a point. At least then we could go for the thing's eyes. Again, you got something better, I'm all ears."

Lenah harrumphed and pushed off into the debris field, being careful not to disturb anything. Splinter pulled off his shirt and stuffed it with the innards of a seat cushion. Then he tied it off and tossed it as far as he could. It landed with a faint splash and floated southwest with the roll to the sea, separate from the debris field.

Nothing happened.

Lenah joined him. "This work?" She held two triangles of cracked fiberglass and a broken piece of wood covered in cracked fiberglass that looked to have been one of the hull's interior ribs.

"That'll work just fine. All we need is some twine."

"What's that?"

A fist of water rose from the Atlantic, moving toward the decoy. A tail flicked back-and-forth, the beast's massive torso torpedoing through the water, jaws opening. The creature's mouth closed on the stuffed t-shirt, and the beast dove, sending waves and sea spray across the debris field.

"That's not good," Lenah said.

"No. No it's not."

The debris thinned as pieces of the Parker sank or floated away, and dawn was still several hours off.

"Let's go. Now while its down deep."

"You sure? It took our decoy pretty fast. And won't it notice us going against the wind?" Lenah said.

Splinter jerked his head side to side. She was right. So was he. "The current is taking us away from the island, and we need to get there or it won't matter if this thing is after us. We'll be dead. As we drift, the debris will sink and spread out and we'll be left. Let's break away and hope for the best. Make for the island," he said.

"I guess you're right. We can't wait here any longer." Lenah stroked through the waves, moving away from the remains of the Evenstar, and striking a line to where they thought Seagull Island should be.

Splinter plucked Poseidon off her fiberglass float and put her on his neck. "Hang on now," he said to the cat. Splinter followed Lenah, looking back over his shoulder every few moments, expecting to see a tunnel of rectangular teeth coming at him.

Instead waves pounded him, and he and Lenah swam the valleys and faces of waves as a westerly wind kicked-up the Atlantic. They'd been in the water seven hours when Splinter yelled, "I see it. There. Look, Lenah."

No response. Splinter thought she was ahead of him in the darkness. "Lenah!" No response. He'd seen her only a moment before when she crested a wave and rode its face, disappearing under the water.

A dorsal fin knifed through the ocean, cutting across the grain and heading right at Splinter. He held out his spear, the fiberglass point brittle, but sharp. The beast was almost on him when he saw the creature's long conical snout and blowhole. The dolphin eased toward Splinter, its human eyes staring at him in the moonlight.

"Where is she?" Splinter asked.

He reached out to stroke the animals slick gray flank, but the dolphin rolled away and disappeared into the depths.

Splinter didn't see or hear from Lenah for an hour as he backtracked, panic filling him with worry and despair. If she died out here it would be his fault, and he wouldn't be able to deal with that. He called out to her, no longer caring if he attracted the beast.

They found each other by sheer luck with a little help from a fish. Lenah realized Splinter had fallen behind, so she'd turned around and headed back toward him, but they swam past each other in the darkness. Only after the dolphin had returned, squeaking and braying, did they find each other.

All the commotion was most likely what brought the creature.

The beast announced itself with a roar that echoed over the ocean like thunder. Splinter and Lenah clutched each other, Poseidon hissing and crying as she balanced on Splinter's shoulders. To their left the beast surfaced in a mound of whitewater like a submarine. Its luminescent gray eyes shined in the night, sleek white skin reflecting beams of moonlight.

Splinter and Lenah stayed still, floating like logs on the churning sea. Even Poseidon seemed to understand what was happening and fell silent. The creature's jaws snapped as it eased through the water, its flippers pounding, caudal fin thrashing.

In the distance the dark outline of Seagull Island beckoned, a mile separating Splinter and Lenah from the shallows and safety.

The creature swam past them, moving in an expanding arc as it searched.

Lenah coughed, the sound loud and distinct.

The creature bellowed, and a shadow slid toward them in the dark water. Twenty yards out, giant eyes poked through the blackness, then a long mouth filled with teeth rose from the sea.

Splinter held his makeshift spear out before him, but he had no real hope of survival. He closed his eyes and waited for the abyss.

21

The leviathan's head lifted from the ocean, its massive jaws opening, eyes locked on its prey.

Two dorsal fins knifed across the beast's path, and a dolphin leapt from the water in a steep arc and crashed back into the sea next to the creature's head. The pair of dolphins squeaked and clicked as the beast slowed.

The dolphins harassed the creature, and the massive animal snapped and bit at them as they swam circles around the monster. The sleek gray aquatic mammals were highly flexible, the equivalent of Ferraris. The apex croc was an eighteen-wheeler; large, bulky, and unable to change its direction quickly.

Water surged toward Splinter and Lenah as the beast thrashed and heaved, trying to bite the dolphins.

"They're buying us time. Go. Go." Lenah pushed away from Splinter and they swam for Seagull Island.

The wind died, and the sea calmed, which wasn't good. The calmer the ocean, the easier it would be for the creature to sense their movements. Splinter followed Lenah, Poseidon clinging to his neck. The cat hadn't scratched Splinter's neck up too bad, but he had a couple of thin gashes that Poseidon had given him in her moments of panic.

Splinter had already sacrificed his shirt, but he still had his lifejacket. He inched next to Lenah as she breast-stroked through the ocean, her head half submerged as she drove toward the island.

"Lenah?" She didn't hear him. He nudged her, and her head jerked from the water in panic, her head whipping around as she searched the surface.

"What is it?"

"I didn't mean to scare you," Splinter said. "What if I took my life preserver off, smeared some blood on it, and let it float away from us with the current? Might bring a few more distractions."

"You're not bleeding, they're just scratches, and I don't suggest opening the wounds, but the decoy worked last time."

"A great white can smell a drop of blood from miles away, it shouldn't take much. It might buy us a few minutes with croczilla."

Lenah peered toward the island that was still almost a mile distant. "You can swim the rest of the way?"

"You'll need to take Poseidon, but yeah, I can make it."

"Do it then."

Splinter lifted the cat from his shoulders and handed her to Lenah. Poseidon didn't protest, but the soaked feline didn't look happy. He patted his friend on the head and said, "Bet you wish you went with the other two knuckleheads, don't you?"

The cat stared at him with her glowing green eyes.

Splinter reached between his legs and undid the clasp that secured the lifejacket harness. Then he loosened the chest straps and slipped the jacket over his head.

He started to sink, and Splinter tread water to keep his head above the surface. He was tired, hungry, bruised, his knee ached, and as he rubbed the lifejacket along his neck, smearing it with small traces of blood, he felt dizzy and his vision blurred. He let the lifejacket float away, and it disappeared in the roll of the ocean.

"You OK?" Lenah asked.

"Um," he mumbled. He felt like shit, but saw no reason to tell Lenah that. She was dealing with her own survival, her own pain. "I'll be better when I feel rocks between my toes."

Several minutes passed and the sounds of the dolphins struggling with the creature died away as the companions swam on. In the darkness, Splinter heard the beast pushing across the surface, like a sailboat cutting through chop.

"Just keep swimming. Just keep swimming."

"Nooooooo. Nemo can kiss my ass."

They chuckled.

Splinter looked over his shoulder. "It's going for the bait," he said.

An orange glow hung on the horizon as the gray of daybreak seeped across the Atlantic. In the distance the beast's caudal fin cut through the sea, making a line for his blood smeared lifejacket.

"We've got to move now," Splinter said. "Second time pays for all. The decoy will only keep our alpha occupied a few minutes."

They were a half mile from Seagull Island, and the shoals were closer, another quarter mile to go. Splinter was starting to believe they might make it when he heard splashing water, tearing flesh and cracking bone reverberate over the ocean.

"Swim hard now."

"What about—"

"Swim!"

Splinter dove forward and stroked hard, his arms and legs heavy with lack of sleep and nourishment. Salt water stung his eyes, and his legs cramped from the cold—he'd been in the drink over eight hours— but he pretended he was in the Olympics, swimming the 500 meters, nothing on his mind except touching the side of the concrete pool.

He brought his head from the water and looked back. Lenah was struggling in the lifejacket while trying to hold onto Poseidon who slipped and grabbed at Lenah's hair in a vain attempt to gain purchase.

Lenah screamed as the cat scratched her face, and Splinter stopped swimming to wait for her. When Lenah caught up, he took Poseidon from her and said, "Take that jacket off. We don't have much time."

What he didn't tell her was there was a fist of water rising from the sea behind them.

Lenah pulled off her lifejacket and swam on. Splinter waited three heartbeats, then trailed after her, staying directly behind her. The ocean erupted and the beast moaned and roared as its flippers slapped the sea.

Splinter's foot touched something, and he kicked it away, only to bump up against it again. Seagull Island loomed before them a quarter mile distant, its dark outline mocking them. To come all this way only to be eaten off the island's shore would be the perfect irony.

"We made it! We made it Splinter!" Lenah stood in the ocean up to her shoulders, tiny ripples breaking over her as she waited.

Splinter tried to stand, but the water was still too deep, so he eased forward, stroking with his arms and letting his legs dangle. His toes touched the bottom, then he stood, neck high in the Atlantic, a stupid smile spreading over his face.

The creature breached in the shallow water, pushing itself up and out of the sea like a missile, jaws open. It landed with a splash that knocked Lenah and Splinter from their feet and drove them toward the island in a mass of whitewater that broke on a rocky beach.

The two companions hauled themselves from the sea as the creature used its flippers and tail to work its way back into deeper water.

The shallows grew silent, and Splinter and Lenah collapsed on the rocky shore, Poseidon shaking herself off between them, spitting up water and cleaning herself. Out at sea, the beast's caudal fin paced just outside the wave break. The sun peeked its head above the horizon and the gray of dawn gave way to bright sunlight.

It was morning.

Splinter and Lenah lay on the beach, not speaking and staring up into the clear blue sky. Splinter's stomach gurgled, and his mouth was so dry it felt like his lips were cracking.

Poseidon licked his face, and sat down, curling her tail around herself. If it wasn't for the small beads of water on her slick fur it would be impossible to tell the cat had been through any hardship at all.

"So, since we're alive, what was all that I love you stuff before?"

Splinter rolled on his side to look at her. Poseidon sat watching, her gaze flicking between Lenah and Splinter. She meowed three times, as if saying you better get this response right.

Truth was, Splinter didn't know what she was talking about. He remembered saying something. The fog clouded his memory, and sometimes he forgot things he shouldn't, but he couldn't let her know he didn't remember because whatever he'd said it appeared important to her.

He brushed sand from his face and said, "What do you mean, specifically?"

"Specifically? You told me you loved me. You don't remember?"

Splinter opened his mouth to lie, but thought better of it. "I'm sorry, but I don't, but I do love you."

"Really? Haven't we been through this?"

"Things have changed a little, no?"

"Not for me. You're still the same person I've always known. I love you too, Splinter, but I just—"

"I understand," he said, and he did.

Herons with gray and white feathers and long bright orange beaks inched from the mangroves, and seagulls shouted and circled above. There were thousands of them, and it made Splinter think of Hitchcock. He'd have had a field day with croczilla.

"Don't they ever stop migrating?" Splinter said.

Lenah laughed. "The Birds. Most people wouldn't get that one. It's pretty old."

"But you did," he said.

The Atlantic splashed and a surge of water pushed through the gentle waves, driving across the shoals like a tsunami and breaking a hundred feet off shore. Whitewater rolled across the shallows only to be sucked back into the ocean.

The seagulls stopped shouting and the herons didn't caw. Every living thing on Seagull Island had suddenly decided to be silent.

Splinter searched for the beast, but the whitewater dissipated, and the shoals went flat. "I think we should get away from the shore," he said.

"Why? You think it can get us here?" Lenah said.

"I don't know, but I don't see why we shouldn't take precautions. We've been lucky so far and that luck might run out." Splinter knew that better than most.

The seagulls resumed their arguing as Splinter searched the shoreline for a trail through the mangroves. Everything was wet with the prior night's rain, and Splinter and Lenah dropped to their knees when they saw a puddle in an indentation in a large stone. They both lay on the stone, faces pressed to the hot rock, lapping up water like puppies, Poseidon's head pushed between them.

Splinter rubbed his lips with his tongue, moistening the cracks and rinsing off the salt. He dipped his index and forefinger into the puddle and rubbed his eyes with the tips of his wet fingers. His stomach rumbled.

"Yeah, we've got to get something to eat soon," Lenah said.

Splinter said nothing.

The wind whispered across the mangroves and Splinter, Lenah and Poseidon climbed over rocks and around outcrops of mangrove. The sea was a mass of rolling waves of heat, and the air was suffocating humidity.

A growl as loud as Godzilla's screech pierced the stillness.

The creature's caudal fin knifed through the ocean, snaking through the sea as the behemoth circled the island.

Lenah and Splinter paused and looked at one another, neither needing to share what they were thinking. They were ten miles offshore, on a barren island with no food, no water, no supplies, no means of lighting a fire, or contacting the mainland.

Splinter was tired. If he didn't get sleep soon, he might fall down. "We need to rest before we even think about how to get out of this mess," he said.

Lenah nodded.

The pair worked their way through the mangroves as best they could, but it took time. The branches were a windblown tangled mess, and they were packed together tight. They'd gone about thirty feet when Splinter said, "I'll break some of these mangrove trees to make a platform to lay on. Work?"

Lenah nodded.

She looked three days dead; dark bags beneath her eyes, grease streaked across her face, her long hair dirty and slick. She was still beautiful.

The beast roared as it circled the island.

22

Seagull Island was six square miles of mangrove covered wasteland, with a tidal pool at its center surrounded by a rock beach. Gnats and flies filled the air, and rodents and snakes owned the dry ground, which there wasn't much of. Most of the mangrove trees had water stains at their bases indicating the high tide mark. There were a couple of palm trees at the center of the island that had large green coconuts hanging from them, and as soon as he got his strength back, getting a few and opening them would be his top priority.

Lenah slept beside him on the makeshift litter of bent mangrove trees. She snored gently, and a thin trail of spittle dripped from her mouth across her chin. Splinter loved watching her: the curve of her cheeks, her dark black hair, full lips. Even in her current state she was beautiful. He frowned. How had he lost her?

Poseidon sat next to Lenah, eyes open and alert. Splinter needed to find her something to eat as well.

The midday sun glided overhead, baking everything in stifling heat. He sat up, and his movement stirred Lenah.

"What is it? Everything OK?"

"Yes. Go back to sleep while I get us some coconuts. Maybe some fish."

Splinter planned to walk the shoreline, and he was bound to find tangled fishing line. The line, along with a mangrove branch, would make a good fishing rig. All he needed was bait and a hook. Shiners teemed in the shoals and catching a few would be simple. As to the hook, Splinter was confident that if he didn't find one attached to the line he found, he could use a curved sharpened fishbone.

He struggled through the mangroves toward the center of the island, making for the tallest palm tree. It took him over an hour to reach it, but when he arrived he was pleasantly surprised. All along the tidal pool, wild blueberry bushes covered in berries encroached up to the water. Small fish swam in the tidal pool, and it would be no problem catching a few.

The immediate problem was water. The rain from the prior day had dried up, so the coconut milk would have to suffice until they found another solution. Climbing the palm tree proved difficult. There were no branches to assist in the climb, and when Splinter got to the top, the inside of his legs were scraped raw. One by one he knocked the coconuts from the tree, and when he was done, eight green nuts lay at the base of the palm. Getting them open without spilling the liquid inside was the trick, but Splinter had seen Castaway. He knew how it was done.

He found a rock with a thin edge and cut off the rough green exterior of the coconut and stripped it. Once down to the more recognizable inner brown nut, Splinter used a pointed stone as a nail, and carefully tapped it into the nut using the bigger stone.

He drank the white water greedily, but it wasn't enough. Splinter started collecting the coconuts, so he could bring them to Lenah, then he figured it would be smarter to bring Lenah inland to the tidal pool, away from the shore, where she could also eat berries.

He left his haul and went searching for parts for the fishing rig. The island shore was remarkably clean. In most spots the mangroves encroached into the water. Even with this limitation, it only took a few minutes to find a ball of fishing line tangled around a decayed Styrofoam float. There was no hook, so he circumnavigated the island and ended up back at the point where he and Lenah had headed into the interior.

In his travels he hadn't seen or heard the creature, but Splinter had no illusions. It was out there. Waiting.

Lenah wanted coconut and berries and trekked to the center of the island without complaint. Splinter opened the nuts and they ate as much white coconut flesh as they could, drank all the water, and stripped the bushes of berries, but it wasn't enough. Splinter and Lenah were still thirsty and weak.

"What are we gonna do Splinter?"

"Light a signal fire? Someone will see it."

"We could try, but I've got no matches, and unless you're more skilled than I think, starting a fire with wet mangrove trees is going to be a challenge."

She had a point. A good one.

"There is no clearing big enough to make a sign in the sand, or with rocks. We have no radio, not so much as binoculars," she said.

Splinter said nothing.

Lenah got up and dusted herself off. "I'm going to look around before the tide comes in."

"There's nothing to see."

"Maybe you missed something."

"Take Poseidon with you."

"Fine."

The cat lifted her head at the sound of her name.

"Come on," Lenah said to the cat.

Poseidon glanced at Splinter, then at Lenah. The feline looked put out, then with a great exaggerated effort and stretch the cat got up and stepped forward, as if to say 'let's go then.'

Lenah left, and Splinter went about sharpening the fish bone he'd found, making it into a hook. Exercising extreme patience, he untangled the fishing line, wound it around a mangrove branch and attached his hook. When that was done, he put the rig aside and went looking for crickets. This proved difficult. Seagull Island was tidal, and during storms and full moons the entire island was covered in seawater except for its dry center by the tidal pool. The small salt water lake was what kept that section of the island dry, because when the tide crept across the island the pool took on much of the water.

High tide was coming on at 3PM and judging by the sun that was only a couple of hours away. He pushed the problem from his mind. One thing at a time, and first order of business was food and water.

He didn't find any crickets, but he did find a beetle pulling its way over a chunk of driftwood. Splinter snatched it up and headed back to the pool's edge. He hooked the insect, unraveled some fishing line from his stick, and tossed the hook into the water.

Slowly he wrapped the line around the stick, keeping the hook moving. Several fish eyed the bait as it passed, but there were no takers. Splinter repeated this process several times but got no bites, so he figured he needed different bait. He'd have to go to the shoals and get shiners like he originally planned. He was pulling the hook from the water when Lenah screamed.

"Splinter! Come see this," she yelled. She didn't sound panicked, or afraid, but Splinter hustled anyway, climbing through the mangroves like it was a jungle gym. Before he reached the shoreline, he saw the problem.

The tide was indeed coming in. The rock beach was gone, and the low branches of the outer ring of mangroves were underwater. Splinter's heart raced, then relaxed. Even if tidal waters covered most of the island, it would be shallow. The island was packed with vegetation, so there was no real cause to fear the beast attacking if they stayed at the center of the island. Then he remembered the odd way the creature inched back into the sea and worry and doubt seeped through him.

Lenah stood in thigh-high water on the rock beach, staring out at the shoals. "We're truly screwed."

"You see our friend?"

"No, but it's hard to see anything with the glare coming off the ocean," Lenah said.

It was. The heat was stifling, and the light reflecting off the ocean's surface formed a blinding glow that made it impossible to see what was going on outside the wave break.

"It could be sitting right out there, and we wouldn't know," Splinter said.

"Thanks for the info," she said.

He laughed. "Do you remember the time I took you to Disneyworld? The Magic Kingdom?"

"How could I forget. We got thrown out."

"That's their fault for having that one place that sold beer. Anyway, you remember what you said to me that day?"

Lenah looked away.

"Do you still feel that way at all? Even in the back of your mind? Ever?" Splinter said.

"I do still love you, but love isn't enough. Shit, it isn't half."

Now Splinter said nothing.

"It's not your fault or mine. I fell in love and wanted to make a life with a guy who got a raw deal and changed."

"It was my choice."

She chuckled. "I know. And I was second."

They'd been going out on and off for two years, but when he came back from his last deployment, he was different and it was no mystery why. Kabul. He was back three weeks and they broke up and Splinter's downward spiral continued from there.

"Any luck fishing?"

Splinter said nothing.

"What?"

"Need better bait."

Splinter waded out into the shoals, eyes scanning for shiners. Schools of the tiny fish darted about, but catching one with your hands was like trying to catch smoke.

Seeing him struggling, Lenah said, "I saw a piece of netting over there," she said, pointing to an outcrop of rocks on the eastern tip of the island. There was no rock beach there, and the deeper water encroached into the mangroves.

"In those rocks?"

"Yeah, about half way out."

"Wait here, be right back."

Splinter waded down the rock covered shoreline and moved into the shallow water to skirt the mangroves. When he reached the natural jetty, he started climbing, rock by rock, working his way out.

"Splinter! Splinter!"

Splinter smiled. He'd gotten used to the sound of her voice calling his name. Liked it even. He turned to see her jumping up and down, waving her arms and yelling, though he couldn't make out what she was saying. A block of ice fell into Splinter's stomach and he whipped his head around.

A knot of water rose from the ocean, and the beast launched from the sea, spearing forward, mouth open, eyes locked on him as if he were the last morsel of food on the planet and the apex croc was determined to have it.

The beast crashed back into the sea ten feet away, and the ensuing surge of whitewater knocked Splinter from the rock he stood on and he tumbled headlong into the Atlantic. He came up sputtering and coughing and got a good look at the creature.

It was thirty-feet long, and more white than gray. It had an elongated tail like a crocodile's, but instead of ending in a sharp tip, it ended in the now familiar caudal fin. Its dolphin-like torso had a diameter of twenty feet, with two large flippers protruding from each side behind the creature's head. At the end of each flipper there were half-formed claws that reminded Splinter of lizards and dinosaurs. The creature's jaws snapped as it thrashed in the heaving ocean. Behind its head on both sides ran thin cuts that opened and closed.

When the monster realized it missed its prey, the predator pushed upward with its flippers, and thrust toward Splinter, trying to catch him in its jaws as it landed in shallow water.

Splinter went under, and the beast landed next to him, its right flipper holding him in place between two rocks under the crashing waves. For the moment he was safe, so he held his breath, the flipper pinning him in, and waited for croczilla to breach or roll off.

He got sucked from his hiding place when the beast shifted position. Splinter stroked down and away, but he hit bottom. If the beast came down on him, he'd be crushed.

Splinter changed direction and headed toward the beach, swimming along the torn-up bottom. He heard the muffled mumble of the creature's wail, and the splashing water sounded like the tsunami all over again. He stroked up and broke the surface.

He hadn't swum toward shore, but away from it.

The creature struggled in the shallow water, its gills flaring, tongue lashing out as it searched for food. Lenah stood in the mangroves, waving her arms. Splinter got low, leaving only his head above the surface, the sun burning his face.

23

The tide rose and the waves that pushed across the shoals got bigger and stronger. The beast pushed backward, using its flippers to propel its huge body back into deeper water.

A rush of whitewater washed Splinter into the natural jetty, but he thrust out his arms and pulled himself onto a stone. He stared at the creature, still unable to fully process its existence. Though it looked like a huge white crocodile with flippers and a longer mouth, Splinter now knew it was no such thing. Crocs were reptiles and needed air to breathe, and whatever the beast was, and wherever it came from, its gills marked it as an underwater creature, which meant the beast couldn't live out of water long.

As a seaman who lived on the waters of Florida, Splinter knew there were more issues with the croc theory than size. They didn't like cold water, and if he was right and the creature came from the rift valley where the water was cold, he didn't see how that could work. They were dealing with something hitherto unseen.

There were reasons the mutated croc theory did make sense, however. Body structure. Facial features. Crocodiles can tolerate saltwater due to specialized salt glands for filtering out salt, and scientists believed warm water was expelled from the vents at the bottom of the world's deepest valleys and trenches. Also, crocodiles have a much higher level of aggression than other crocodilians.

A geyser of seawater jetted from the ocean like a stream from a whale's blowhole, and the beast breached. Its white hide glistened in the sunlight and hit the water like a brick.

Lenah ran down the shoreline waving her arms. A chill fell over Splinter. The creature submerged, but on the western horizon about two miles away a tuna tower shined, its stainless steel reflecting the sunlight.

Splinter worked his way over the rocks to the shoals and back to Lenah and Poseidon.

"We need to signal them," she said.

"How, exactly? I doubt they'll see you running around with your hands in the air."

"To quote you; you got a better idea?"

Splinter said nothing. With only the clothes on their backs to assist them, Splinter didn't know another way, so he joined Lenah. He ran along the shore, splashing through the tidal water that was now a foot deep, waving his arms. The boat looked like it might be coming their way, but it was hard to tell. There was still a lot of ocean between the boat and Seagull Island.

Out beyond the wave break the creature's caudal fin moved back and forth, its giant flat head floating just below the surface.

"You think it's safe on the shoreline?"

"As long as we keep an eye on it, yeah. We need to stay here anyway, signaling this boat may be our only chance."

"Wish we could make some smoke. They'd definitely see that."

Poseidon meowed from her spot atop a stone. She curled her tail around herself, and put her head down on her front paws as her green eyes watched them.

The boat on the horizon was slowly growing closer as it moved on a northeast course that would take it past the island on the northern side. This path would take the ship across the debris field, if there was anything left floating.

The boat got closer, but either the captain didn't see them, or he didn't care, because the ship got close to the island but didn't stop. Splinter and Lenah screamed, waved, but to no avail. The vessel passed the island and continued northeast, then to Splinter and Lenah's delight the boat turned around and headed straight for Seagull Island.

"Thank someone," Lenah said.

"They must have seen pieces of the Parker floating."

"Oh, shit," Lenah said.

"What?" Splinter followed her gaze, and said, "Double oh shit."

The unknown ship was sailing right toward the creature.

"We need to warn them," Lenah said.

"Great idea, wish I'd thought of it," Splinter said.

Lenah stared out at the sea and said nothing.

"They probably have some kind of SONAR. They'll see it."

"How do you know that?" Lenah said.

"The tuna-tower. It's a fishing boat, therefore it will have a fish finder, no?"

Lenah said nothing as she looked out to sea, brow furrowed, neck muscles tight.

The mystery boat was a half mile offshore when the predator surfaced like a sub rising from the depths. First the rectangular caudal fin, then the top of its head, and finally the long mouth of teeth.

Lenah grabbed Splinter's arm, and he flinched. "Damn, Lenah."

"Sorry."

The ship turned abruptly to port, presumably because the boat's skipper had seen the creature. The vessel tilted, the tuna tower leaning at a sixty-degree angle. The beast wailed, a long mournful scream that sounded like the monster was injured. It shot from the ocean, jaws spread, and slammed into the boat's starboard side. The vessel held its ground, but was rocked hard and the ship momentarily disappeared beneath a swell of whitewater as the beast crashed back into the sea.

Splinter heard the boat's engine rev, and smoke billowed from the craft as it entered the shoals and ran aground. A dinghy dropped from the boat's side and two men jumped into it. An outboard screamed to life, and the Zodiac skittered and jumped across the shallow sea, the creature still rocking the bigger boat. The apex predator nudged the vessel with its snout, trying to tip the boat over, and it tilted sharply but came back upright.

The dinghy screamed through the shoals and a smile spread across Splinter's face.

"Will!" Lenah yelled. She ran forward, then realized what she'd done and stepped back onto the rocky shore covered in a foot of tidal water. The Zodiac's outboard cut off and the inflatable nudged into the mangrove trees.

Lenah leaned over the Zodiac's gunnel and hugged Will, who said, "I can't believe I found you."

"In the nick of time too. You got any water?" Splinter said.

"Here you go," said the other man who Splinter didn't know.

Lenah did know him. "Thanks, Donny. I owe you one." She took the water bottle Donny held out to her and uncapped it. She drank half the sixteen-ounce bottle with one pull and handed it to Splinter who drank the rest greedily, water spilling down his chin.

Will said, "Splinter, this here is Donny Peso. He's a charter captain out of Vero Beach."

"Pleased to meet you," Splinter said.

"Yeah, thanks for looking for us Donny," Lenah said.

"The Parker?" Will said.

"Gone," Splinter said.

Will turned and looked out across the shoals toward Donny's boat. The beast had given up nudging the vessel and circled outside the wave break.

Splinter said, "Where you been? What happened?"

"Is this really the best time to catch up?" Donny said. "How the hell are we going to get back to the boat? And you guys are standing in the water."

The fisherman had a point. The day was fading and soon the sun would sink below the horizon. He was starving and thirsty and tired. He wanted nothing more than to get off Seagull Island and go have a steak dinner with all the trimmings, but they still had a long way to go before that could happen.

"I still don't believe my eyes. What the hell is that thing?" Donny said.

"We have no idea," Lenah said.

"What did the cops say?" Donny asked.

Nobody spoke.

"OK. What's the plan here?" Donny said.

Splinter looked out to sea. "That's a nice rig you got there, Donny. It OK to run?"

"Yup. It has a Caterpillar C-7 diesel that pushes 460HP. That thing rips. The boat's light for its size and has hydraulic steering. We can outrun the thing."

"Can we distract it somehow so we can get aboard?" Will said.

"That's how we got here. We bought time with a couple of decoys. What are you thinking?" Lenah said.

"One of us acts as bait while the other three make a run for the boat. Once we're aboard we can pick up whoever stayed behind as the decoy," Will said.

"You're saying one of us should swim out there and offer ourselves up?" Lenah said.

"Not exactly, but yeah," said Will

"And I'm the one, I presume?" Splinter said.

Wind rustled through the mangroves and seagulls cried.

"Will, give me your shirt and toss me that lifejacket," Splinter said.

"What are you going to do?" Lenah said.

Splinter said nothing. He took Will's offered shirt and stretched it over the lifejacket. Then he reached into the water and drew out a broken shell with a sharp edge and pricked his finger with it. Deep red blood dripped onto the shirt, Splinter squeezing the digit to make the blood flow.

Lenah winced, and Donny said, "Will said you were hardcore."

"You have no idea," Splinter said. A red stain was forming as the blood dripped.

"Oh, I have an idea," Donny said.

Splinter looked at Will, his face twisting.

"Don't look at me. Blame WPTV and dumb and dumber."

"No worries," Donny said. "I was a marine, myself. Two tours in Afghanistan. I know how it goes."

Splinter nodded.

Once there was a stain the size of a baseball on the shirt, Splinter tore off a small piece of fabric and tied off his wound. He said, "I'm gonna go to the east side of the island by that sandbar and swim out with the decoy. As soon as you see the thing moving, make a run for it. Be ready and we'll hope third time's the charm."

With nothing left to say Splinter headed off through the tidal water carrying the decoy.

"Splinter." Lenah sloshed up behind him, and when Splinter turned she pecked him on the lips, and whispered, "Be safe. Remember the fog. Don't let it take you."

Splinter nodded and continued on. He made as much noise as he could, lifting his feet and stomping them into the outgoing tide. Dead leaves and other debris pushed through the mangroves as the tide went out. This was the first piece of luck Splinter had had in a long time. With the tide going out he wouldn't have to go too far out to set his trap.

After ten minutes of trudging through foot high water he no longer saw his companions. He walked on until he came to a section of shoreline with a narrow shoal running almost due east like a lone tooth. The sandbar looked solid and the current flowed fast at its tip.

Splinter eased out into the water, cutting around an outcrop of mangrove trees and making his way to the sandbar. The sea rose to his waist, but his footing was solid on the hardpacked sand as he stepped onto the sandbar.

The narrow shoal extended into the Atlantic 200 yards. The water got deeper as he went, and when he reached the end of the sandbar, he could barely touch bottom with the tips of his toes. He floated out to sea, gently kicking his legs and pushing the decoy. When he'd gone fifty feet he released the bloodstained lifejacket-stuffed shirt into the current. The outgoing tide took it and Splinter swam back to the shoals.

He'd gone thirty feet when he heard the tiny outboard roar to life, and then the steady moan as the motor pushed the three adults and one cat toward Donny' boat. Splinter stroked hard, the decoy wasn't far from him. A surge of water cut through the waves, heading for the bloody decoy. The creature's head breached the surface, its mouth opening.

The dino-croc snapped down on the lifejacket and arced in Splinter's direction, chewing as it locked on him as a new target. A mound of water rose above the surface. Splinter's feet hit ground, but he kept digging with his arms and legs.

The beast roared, and a wave of whitewater lifted Splinter and pushed him toward shore.

24

Splinter sucked in air and dove, arms and legs stroking through the turbulent water, riding the wave caused by the monster's breach from the sea. He pushed air through his nose and opened his eyes, but saw only white and bubbles. He was back in his Olympic fantasy, and he'd just made a turn at the poolside, flipping over and surging up to the surface, sprinting to the finish.

The monster roared, and the sea trembled like Jell-O. Splinter lifted his head from the water and spared a glance over his shoulder.

The creature swam in the deeper water on the northern side of the sandbar, its caudal fin knifing through the sea, its massive body just below the surface.

Splinter's hand hit the sandbar as he stroked. He'd run out of water.

He pushed off and got to his feet, the water up to his waist. He sloshed forward, fighting through the ocean, his muscles burning from lack of nutrition and rest, his knee throbbing. Seagull Island was still a hundred yards off, and the beast glided on the northern side of the sandbar.

Saltwater burned his eyes, pain seized his joints, and his stomach growled. The afternoon sun was stifling, the breeze a faint fart that smelled of low tide. Scattered clouds slid across a clear sky from the west, filling in the blue. Thicker clouds marked the western horizon, and they looked fat with rain.

The water was at Splinter's knees when the creature bellowed, and the sea rose. To his right the monster swam along the edge of the sandbar. The knot of water broke the surface and a cone of teeth below two cold gray eyes launched from the sea.

Splinter dodged left and dove into deeper water. He heard the monster breach behind him, and a massive surge of whitewater and sand pushed Splinter like a feather. He tossed and tumbled, hitting the sandy bottom and bouncing back toward sunlight.

He broke the surface. The creature was hung-up on the sandbar, its flipper-claws digging into the sand, but not gaining purchase. Splinter put his head down and made one final push.

He rotated his head to breathe and heard an engine rumble to life. Not the bicycle-motor of the small outboard, but the big diesel under

Donny's main deck. Then his head was underwater, and he was swimming for his life.

Splinter surfed. He was used to getting pulled into the blackness, but the power of the fist of water that punched him in the back as he swam pushed the air from his lungs and propelled him through the ocean so fast water pushed through his sealed mouth and up his nose so hard his sinuses ached. He slammed into the seafloor and rolled like a broken shell, hitting the mangroves with a jarring crunch that sent a jolt of pain up his back. He reached out in his whitewater induced blindness and grasped the first branch he found.

The heaving water dissipated, and Splinter pulled himself to his feet with the aid of a mangrove tree. Seawater tugged at his legs as it receded, and another set of waves crashed into him. The beast was over the sandbar, and it lurched through the shallow sea, unable to swim.

A horn sounded on the horizon, and Splinter smiled. Donny's thirty-four-foot Jarred Bay cut through the fading swells. The beast ignored the horn and came on until it was in three feet of water. It lifted itself on its flipper-legs, gray head swinging side to side, eyes rolling as it searched. Water surged toward Splinter as the creature jerked in his direction, jaws snapping.

Splinter climbed through the mangroves away from the shore, the outgoing tide inches deep inland. He'd gone about a hundred feet when the ground became dried mud. He heard the distant sound of splashing, but no crunching mangrove trees. Splinter figured the beast had gone back out to sea.

He worked his way to the palm trees at the center of Seagull Island and collapsed to the ground exhausted. His heart raced, and his lungs pumped double-speed as he sucked for air and exhaled as fast as he could. White dots danced before his eyes like stars in the clear blue sky.

He didn't feel the fog seeping over him, or his nerves jumping. Hadn't felt it at all. Splinter smiled. Could all this new trauma be pushing out the old? New wounds and all that rot? He lay on the ant infested sand for several minutes, listening to the trickle of the sea push through the mangroves, the faint whistle of the wind, and the distant thrum of Donny's motors.

After fifteen minutes he sat up, rubbed his face, and got to his feet. When he first arrived on Seagull Island, he'd walked the entire shoreline. There was no other sandbar that provided such an easy and fast way to get out into deeper water than the one he'd just been on. Splinter decided to head back that way and flag down the boat.

There were three green coconuts still laying on the ground from earlier efforts and he stripped one and broke it open, drinking the water and eating some of the horrible tasting flesh. Then he plunged back into the mangroves and climbed over branches and spidery roots until he reached the shoreline. The tide was almost out, and half the sandbar stood above water. He waited within the tree break for Donny's boat to pass.

He didn't have to wait long. To Splinter, Donny didn't appear to be rushing and was doing no more than twenty knots. The engines hummed calm and steady, and the boat threw minimal spray. The tip of the beast's caudal fin trailed behind like the dorsal fin of a shark, except it wagged back and forth as the beast's tail helped propel the creature through the water.

Splinter ran out onto the sandbar. He had to wade across the section where the creature had landed, but he reached the end of the shoal in good time, and as the boat came around the island, he waved his arms and shouted. Donny shifted course slightly, making straight for the sandbar. The creature wasn't far behind the boat, and there was no way Donny could stop.

Donny killed the engines just as he cruised by the point of the sandbar where Splinter stood.

Will yelled, "We're gonna drop the Zodiac for you next time around."

The engines roared to life as Donny dropped the hammer and the thirty-four-foot luxury fishing boat leapt from the water, its prop clawing at the sea, sending seawater and sand bubbling up from below.

Splinter ran back down the sandbar and hid within the confines of the mangroves once more. Three minutes passed and the boat went by again, but this time they dropped the dinghy.

It bobbed on the water for a twenty count, then disappeared within the waiting jaws of the apex croc as the monster chomped on it like a dog snatching a rubber duck from a child's bath.

"Shit!"

The creature swam on and Splinter heard Donny kick-up the Jarred Bay's engine, and it whined as he pushed it. They were trying to get a lead, so they could stop and pick him up.

Splinter had had enough playing cat and mouse with this fish. He jumped like a long jumper when he reached the flooded gap, and just missed making it across. He landed in the waist-high water and scrambled forward onto the sandbar.

The boat came around the island, and they were moving at least thirty-five knots, which was fast for a boat that big. As they got closer, Splinter saw Lenah standing aft with a round rescue ring in her hands.

Will stood next to her holding coiled rope. They meant to throw him a life line.

Splinter ran his fingers through his hair. This was nuts. If he didn't make it to the boat fast enough he'd be left dangling in the sea like a piece of chum. He was closing in on the end of the sandbar and the boat was 300 hundred yards off. He didn't see the beast.

The engine slowed as Splinter reached the end of the sandbar. Donny didn't bring the Jarred Bay to a full stop, but close. Lenah tossed the ring as the boat slid past, and she came up thirty feet short.

Splinter looked south. There was no sign of the beast.

He dove into the deeper water and swam for the life ring. The current was taking it away from him, but not fast. He'd reach it in thirty seconds. He took his head out of the water and saw Lenah and the others watching him from the Jarred Bay, the yellow line trailing to the red life ring splaying out straight.

He reached the ring and Will and Lenah started to pull him in. Donny kicked-up the Caterpillar C-7 and the lifeline tightened, and the ring jerked through the sea.

A loud thump rolled over the ocean, and Lenah screamed.

The creature's head shot from the water, slamming into the port bow of the Jarred Bay. The boat's tuna-tower rocked and flexed, and the motor sputtered, coughed, and fell silent. The tension on the life ring eased, and Splinter came to a stop. He tread water as he watched the beast peel off the boat and head his way.

The creature had gone the opposite way around Seagull Island, surprising the Jarred Bay head-on.

It was decision time, but Splinter didn't have any good choices. He could swim for the island, which was 200 yards off, or stay where he was, and hope Donny managed to get the boat started.

The boat's motor gurgled and popped, but rumbled to life. Donny revved the engine, and Splinter heard the *thump* as he slammed it in gear. The boat spun as the bow thrusters turned the craft and the engine drove it forward. Donny got on the creature's ass, but it didn't appear to daunt the beast. It came at Splinter, head rising from the water, flippers pounding the sea, crocodilian jaws opening.

The Jarred Bay hit the creature's wake, and the pitch of the motor went up as Donny squeezed every revolution from the diesel motor. The boat was thirty yards behind the beast, and the creature was fifty yards from Splinter.

As Donny closed in, the monster rolled east, carving the sea and sending a three-foot wave rolling over the surface. The beast's caudal fin disappeared as the creature dove, and Donny eased off on the motor and brought the boat close to Splinter as Will dropped a rope ladder over the side and Splinter climbed aboard and collapsed on deck.

The creature surfaced and came at them again.

Donny pushed down on the throttle and the engine roared. The boat jerked through the waves, picking up speed. The beast dropped into the boat's wake, tracking the vessel as it bounced toward the west coast of Florida.

25

Donny's boat was called The Day After, but that didn't seem right to Splinter. The thirty-four-foot sport fisherman powered into the sunset, the tuna-tower casting a long shadow over the turbulent sea. The falling sun shone through the encroaching clouds and shimmered off the ocean, making it difficult to see. A dark line ran across the western horizon like a smudge, and distant cracks of lightning and the hollow booms of thunder echoed over the water as dusk settled over the Atlantic Ocean.

Poseidon sat in the fish fighting chair, curled in a ball, uninterested. Splinter rested with his knees pulled up to his chest, and Donny piloted the boat while Lenah paced back and forth across the deck.

The beast trailed after The Day After a hundred yards back, matching the boat's speed and course.

"What happened to you? Splinter and I were worried," Lenah said.

"Yeah, not a great time to go off the grid," Splinter said.

Will sighed and ran his hand over his balding scalp. Will glanced to stern, and dug into a cooler filled with ice where their catch was supposed to be. Instead there was twelve cans of Miller 64, the low-calorie beer that Lenah and Will liked.

"One for you guys?" Will said, popping open his can as he stood over the open cooler.

"Two for me," Splinter said.

"Yes, please," said Lenah.

Will took a long pull on his beer and dug out cans for Lenah and Splinter. He gave them their beers and for a couple of minutes nobody spoke as they focused on drinking.

Will said, "It wasn't my choice."

"Do tell," Splinter said.

"I have high blood pressure, type-two diabetes, and I'm on blood thinners because some of my veins are so clogged the thinner blood is hardly getting through. You guys know that?" Will said.

"I do. What happened?" Lenah said.

Splinter said nothing. He'd known Will for a couple of years and Splinter considered him a close friend. Will had helped him so many times, what had he ever done for Will? He wasn't even aware of his serious medical conditions.

"I take drugs to control all these things, and some of these drugs don't mix well with certain foods, or alcohol, and I had a small… incident."

"Incident?"

"I went down in my apartment. Passed out like a drunk on a three-day binge," Will said.

Now Splinter was concerned. "Are you OK? Were you hurt? I—"

Will lifted his hand. "I'm fine. I took my meds, then had a couple of drinks, not thinking that I'd just taken my pills. I got dizzy and lightheaded, and I passed out. Thankfully I didn't hit my head on anything on the way to the floor."

"How long were you out?" Splinter said.

"Overnight. My neighbor Toby found me because he heard Nereus barking. Toby said Nereus and Galatia were standing over me and wouldn't let him come near me. Toby called an ambulance and I ended up in the hospital for two days and Nereus and Galatia got to spend some time with Toby. I think he treated them pretty good because when I went to collect them, they wanted to stay with him, so I left them. Figured they'd be better off until all this craziness is settled."

"And you're sure you're alright?" Lenah said.

"Sure," Will said. "Just a nasty drug cocktail mix, which wasn't helped by the alcohol."

"Live and learn," Splinter said.

"You'd think," Will said.

"So my guys are doing well?" Splinter said. He missed his other cat and his dog. Poseidon was a good cat, but she wasn't the cuddling type.

"They're great. I got them groomed and cleaned up."

"Great," Splinter said. "Now they're gonna expect all kinds of fancy treatment."

"They came through for me when I needed them. You ever get short on food, I'll buy a few bags," Will said.

Splinter said nothing, but his gaze shifted back to the sea and the monster trailing behind them.

In the west, lightning lit the sky like a camera flash, and thunder rumbled like concussion bombs. The swell picked up, and the wind out of the west stood up the rolling waves, making them four feet tall. The Day After cut through them like they weren't there, the V-hull throwing spray fifty feet on both sides of the boat. Cables that ran along the outriggers and up the tuna-tower pinged and clanged as they tapped against the metal supports in the howling wind.

Splinter braced himself on the transom, staring out into the dusk, searching for the beast's caudal fin. It scythed back and forth, cutting through the sea, but Splinter couldn't see the beast beneath the dark surface. They planned to lead the creature closer to shore and call the Boat Scouts.

The rain came cold and hard, pelting The Day After, and forcing the group inside the cabin. Donny put on his rainslicker and stayed above deck in the pilothouse, which was enclosed on three sides.

Once seated around the galley table, Will said, "Before I took my short sabbatical, I did a little research. Didn't find anything really useful, but I did find two pieces of information that might interest you." Will dug in his pocket and brought out two sheets of paper. He unfolded them and spread them out on the table, using the palm of his hand to flatten and straighten them. "The first is an article from the Fortean Times."

"What's that?" Lenah said.

"It's a magazine that publishes stories about all kinds of strange stuff. Cryptozoology, mutants, both animal and human, conspiracy theories, UFOs, you name it. If it's strange they publish articles about it," Splinter said.

"They're out of England. It's based on the ideas of a guy named Charles Fort. He was a conspiracy-type guy long before there were conspiracies," Will said.

"What the hell did you find in there? I always thought they were like the Inquirer or the Sun Times?" Splinter said.

"Not at all. While you may not agree with what they print, they take a more scientific based approach then those you mentioned. They require some form of evidence or science, no matter how far-fetched," Will said.

The article was a blurry library printout dated March 22, 1981, titled, "Carcharodon Megalodon: Prehistoric Creature of the Sea." There were two pictures interposed with the text, one of the author standing within a huge jawbone at a museum, and an animation showing a standard fifteen-foot great white shark next to *megalodon*.

The boat rocked, and rain pounded the deck. The cabin light flickered, went out, then snapped back on as Splinter pictured a fifty-foot shark with eight-inch teeth and jaws that could crush a car. Apex predators from another time, another place. But fiction was fiction and there were no fifty-foot sharks anymore, but were there? After what he'd recently seen, it was plausible.

Splinter scanned the page and looked up at Will. "A shark? We're not dealing with a shark here, but you know that, so what's this mean?"

"The article talks about how *megalodon* could still be alive, way down in the Atlantic rift valley or the Mariana Trench. Since our theory is croczilla was dragged from the rift valley by the tsunami, I figured it might be relevant."

"But this is fiction, right? These huge sharks don't exist. Nobody has ever seen one alive, there aren't even fossils because shark skeletons are mostly made of cartilage and they deteriorate. Samples of the creature's teeth are the only reason we know they even existed," Lenah said.

"Yes and no. Some scientists feel that it's possible, however unlikely, that megs live miles below the surface, well below the thermal layer where they eat tube worms and subsist off the minerals spewed from the vents and smokers at the deepest parts of the world's oceans," Will said. "Sound like our monster?"

Splinter harrumphed.

"Didn't say I believed it, it just made sense given what we know about the creature," Will said.

"I did see gills, and crocs don't have gills," Splinter said.

"Mutant," Lenah said.

Splinter got up and stared out the forward porthole. The sun had sunk below the horizon, leaving a purple sky that was quickly fading to black. He walked to the rear of the cabin and stared out at the monster that still trailed after them, but had fallen further behind. Donny had The Day After going at thirty knots, and Splinter thought the beast might be tiring.

Splinter rejoined his friends, and said, "It's still back there. It's slowing, but showing no signs of begging off. This weather sucks."

"You think it will attack?" Will said.

"No clue at this point. It must be getting tired, though, and it hasn't eaten since it snacked on the bloody shirt and lifejacket, which I can't imagine was very filling," Splinter said.

The rain came on harder, and rivulets spilled into the cabin through the open door and slipped down the floor drain. Splinter heard the bilge pump kick on, and the cadence of the motor lessened.

"OK, you think we're dealing with a prehistoric fish that has mutated with a croc, or some shit, and has managed to stay hidden for millions of years?" Splinter said.

"Well, when you say it like that," Will said.

"Anything else?" Lenah said.

Will looked sheepish and he glanced at the deck.

"What?" Splinter said.

"I did a little research on you, Captain Woods," Will said.

Off in the back of Splinter's mind the fog rose, and his face got hot and his stomach churned. "Why would you do that?" Splinter said, his voice restrained fury.

"Nothing sinister. I was just trying to get a handle on what was out there, so we wouldn't be surprised and could do damage control," Will said.

"Annnnddddd," Splinter said.

"Nothing we don't already know, except this," he said as he slid another piece of paper across the table. "It's an article from Naval History Magazine about a guy named Captain Johnston Blakeley. Recognize the name?"

Splinter rubbed his chin, the fog fading, his anger dissipating. So much for new trauma pushing out the old.

Splinter said, "He's a distant relative on my mother's side. A legendary captain of the famous Wasp, which disappeared in the mid-Atlantic in 1814 under mysterious circumstances."

"That's one way to put it," Will said.

"There's another way?" Splinter said.

"When you have time, read the article. The author speculates that the ship wasn't destroyed by cannon fire as many believed, but that it was sunk by an unnamed creature," Will said.

"He bases this on?" Lenah said.

"Sightings of what sailors called sea serpents," Will said.

Splinter chuckled.

"Don't laugh, there are many such sightings in the record and nobody laid claim to sinking the Wasp. If it had been the Royal Navy or one of their allies they would have crowed about it," Will said.

"My mom says her great grandfather thought the Wasp went under from a rogue wave," Splinter said. "A huge wave…"

"I thought it was interesting that you of all people had this connection," Will said.

"Yeah, me of all people."

The hum of the motor eased, and the boat slowed. Donny stuck his head into the cabin. "I think we lost it, or it gave up, or it didn't like going into the inlet," Donny said.

"Damn," Splinter said. "How far out from the inlet are we?"

"Mile or so. We're almost in," Donny said.

Splinter said, "Almost like it knows it shouldn't come close to shore."

"Where do you want me to drop you guys off? Will's car?" Donny said.

Splinter looked at Lenah, and they both turned to Will. "You mind?" Splinter said.

Will said, "What? Giving you a ride? Depends on where you're going. I think it's time."

"Yeah. It is," Splinter said.
"Mind telling me what you're talking about?" Donny said.
"It's time to go see the coasties," Splinter said.
Poseidon meowed.

26

Donny dropped Splinter, Will, Lenah and Poseidon off on Lenny's dock by the gas pump. Will said it would be a good idea to leave Poseidon at Lenny's until after they met with the coasties. Splinter was forced to agree, though the cat didn't. If Poseidon was with them and things went bad, and they somehow ended up in custody, Poseidon would go to a holding kennel. Not on Splinter's watch.

The three companions walked to Will's 2001 white Ford Taurus. It was the most unnoticeable car imaginable and exactly what you'd expect a retired cop on a pension to drive. Old, reliable, and it still looked pretty good, like Will. They piled into the car, Will driving and Lenah and Splinter in the back. The engine started, and Will drove through the boatyard, and out onto A1A.

Marsh land and Indian River ran by to the west, the Atlantic Ocean to the east. Splinter cracked a window and fresh air pushed into the vehicle. Will said, "Fort Pierce Coast Guard Station?"

"That's as good a place as any," Splinter said.

"Shouldn't we be going to the police?" Lenah said.

"The police do have some jurisdiction, but they're a land-based operation with limited resources when it comes to harbor patrol, and said resources are nonexistent out on the Atlantic," Will said.

"Plus, if things go the way I expect, the coasties will bring the local cheese in," Splinter said. His mind flashed back to the day of the tsunami, and the harassment he'd endured from the lady with the sombrero hat. She was gone, and most likely so was the cop. The idea brought Splinter no pleasure.

They hit the inlet and Will made a left onto Seaway Drive. The road curved and bent and Splinter saw a pizza joint, a diner and a supermarket. His stomach rumbled. The road turned around a cove and Will slowed and made a right into the Coast Guard station. He pulled around a circle and stopped at an airconditioned guardhouse where a coastie in a cleanly pressed light blue uniform shirt and dark blue slacks greeted them with a smile. Like a perfume huckster at a department store.

The coastie was an attractive young woman with golden eyes and light brown hair. A newbie, that was clear from the solitary basic training completion ribbon tacked above her breast pocket. She wore her lid straight, and everything about her said eager. "Seaman Apprentice Frazier at your service, sir, how may I assist you today?"

"We need to see the base commander," Will said.

"Oh, no, that's a problem. She's not here. Do you have an appointment?" Frazier said, a little rattled like a cashier being asked to handle a complicated return on her first day.

"Where is she?" Will asked.

"I'm sure I don't know. Surprisingly I don't have access to her calendar," she said. "Do you have an appointment?"

"No. Who's in charge in her absence?" Will said.

"Commander Peel, the duty officer is in charge today, but I doubt he'll have time to see you. He's very busy you know."

Will made a show of looking around. The base looked dead. A cutter sat docked in the small marina, and several SAFE boats with orange pontoons were moored next to it, but there were no groups of seamen walking about. No drills or calisthenics, nobody marching and singing those crazy songs. The base looked deserted. The Coast Guard had recently downsized, and Splinter figured most of the base personnel were either out patrolling and dealing with problems, or sleeping.

Will said, "Yes, I can see it's very busy today."

Frazier sighed and picked up a phone, but before she called ahead she asked, "And what is the matter in reference to?"

"Godzilla," Splinter muttered. He was losing his patience.

"I'm sorry? Come again?" the coastie said.

"Ignore my friend, he's an ass," Will said, and he looked over his shoulder at Splinter and mouthed, "Shut up."

Turning back to the coastie, he said, "We have important information concerning the recent shark attacks and we want to report what we've seen."

"I see, so you don't really need to see the base commander then, do you?" she said.

"I guess that's your call, but—"

"Great. One moment." It was clear she wanted them gone. Away from her booth and away from her. She dialed the old phone and said, "Yes, hi Marty. I've got three civvies here who claim to have information about the recent shark attacks."

Silence as she listened. Seagulls cried as they circled above, and a gentle breeze pushed through the mangrove trees that lined the base's property. "I think that would be fine. Send them through," Frazier said. "OK, good."

She hung up the phone and turned back to Will. "You'll be meeting with Petty Officer Child. He'll take a report. Head down the driveway until you get to the flat blue building. Go in and ask for him. He'll be waiting."

The gate blocking the road didn't lift.

"But first, I'll need you each to sign in and issue you temporary IDs," she said.

Twelve minutes later they were all stickered and named, and the gate went up and Will drove through with a mock salute.

Splinter said, "I notice you didn't mention Lenah and I are wanted for questioning by the police."

"Some information is best held until the appropriate moment," Will said.

"Which is?" Lenah said.

"Don't know yet. Let's see what this guy Child is like," Will said.

They made their way down the drive and parked where instructed, and they got out and walked through the early morning heat across the parking lot to the entrance. Inside, a man in the same uniform as Frazier greeted them in a similar fashion, and before Splinter could sit down, they were met by Child who guided them into a conference room.

The room was white, the long table was white, and the chairs around it were blue. Child fit his namesake. He looked twelve, with his freckled face and his buzz cut blonde hair. He held out his hand and everyone shook and greeted each other and sat down.

"So I see they've brought in the big guns," Splinter said.

Child chuckled and fiddled with his pen which hung over a form of some kind. "You'd like to make a statement?"

"We do."

And they did.

Will started, but soon Lenah and Splinter were adding details, and by the time they got to seeing the creature a second time, Child said, "Will you excuse me for a moment?"

Child left the conference room.

"Going to get the duty officer, Peel, I assume," Splinter said.

Will was nodding when Child returned with a tall lanky man that looked about fifty. He was all gray around the edges and his uniform was a bit wrinkled and worn. It was clear this guy normally lived on the sea and was stuck on land because the boss was off someplace being the boss. He said, "Pleased to meet you. I'm Commander Peel."

Greetings all around. Peel sat and took the stack of papers from in front of Child. He looked through what the Petty Officer had written, and his eyes flicked to Lenah and Splinter. "So before we start, I recognize your names. You ran from our cutter and several people said you drove the shark at the boat."

Splinter blurted, "That's not true."

"Two kids died and Ms. Brisbee's boat was seen fleeing the scene and ignored our hail." He pointed at Splinter and Lenah. "And the police want a word with you both. Shall I get them?"

"Sure," Splinter said. "We've got nothing to hide."

Peel nodded to Child, who got up and left the room. They sat there looking at each other, not speaking. Five minutes. Ten. After twenty minutes of silence, Child reentered the room with a blonde female police officer who looked put-out. She took a seat at the end of the table and pulled out her pen with a flourish, and sighed. The cop said, "Before we start, can I have a word with you in private, Ms. Brisbee?"

Lenah looked at Splinter and Will. "Whatever you have to say you can say in front of them," she said.

The cop sighed. A long, exasperated sigh that said people are so stupid it hurts my head. "Your call," she said. "Ms. Brisbee are you, or have you at any point, been held against your will?"

"No, ma'am," Lenah said.

The cop looked at Splinter, who stared right back at her.

"We were concerned you were an unwilling participant," the cop said.

"Nope. Just dumb, I guess."

The officer said nothing.

"Could you start again. From the beginning?" Peel asked.

It was Splinter's turn to sigh, but he told it all again, from first to last, pausing so the cop and Child could take notes on their forms. When Splinter finished, the cop said, "Why didn't you come in right away?"

"We kinda did," Lenah said.

"You kind of didn't," said the officer. Her nameplate read Bostic.

"Did you miss hearing and reading comprehension day at the academy?" Splinter said.

Bostic's cheeks turned red, but she said nothing.

"I explained that to you. We were trying to get proof, but things didn't go as planned," Splinter said.

"And they're here now. What's the problem?" Will said.

"The problem is your story is nuts. Crazy," said Peel. "You have any proof? A picture? Anything?"

Splinter, Will and Lenah exchanged glances.

"Didn't think so," Peel said. He gathered his papers, preparing to leave.

"Which is exactly why we didn't rush in," Lenah said.

"What changed?" asked Child.

"We've got this," Splinter said. He handed a piece of paper with the dart frequency on it to Peel.

"And this is?" he said.

"The tracking signal for a dart I put in the thing's ass," Splinter said.

"Really," Peel said. He leaned back and brushed lint off his pants. His patent leather shoes were dull, unlike Child's which might laser a hole in the wall if they reflected the sun just right.

"Really," Splinter said.

Peel handed Child the paper and without a word the young coastie left the room.

Peel said, "Did you know another piece of the missing child washed-up in Faber Cove? You've been seen over there recently."

Splinter said nothing.

Bostic shifted uneasily. "Where were you the night of—"

"Excuse me?" Splinter said. "Are you implying I had something to do with the boy's death?"

"Not implying. Just asking questions, and let's face it, you're not exactly a high character witness," the cop said.

Will coughed, and Lenah looked his way, but the fog was rising, the anger taking over. "What the fuck do you know about it, flatfoot?"

"I could arrest you right now and bring you downtown for fleeing the scene of a crime," the officer said.

"You and what army?" Splinter said.

Her hand dropped to her gun, and Peel said, "Officer Bostic, is that really necessary?"

She took her hand off her sidearm, but didn't take her eyes off Splinter.

Anger rose in him. All he'd done was try and help, and what did he get in return? Suspicion and disrespect. Just like the cop on the beach.

"What we've got here is a failure to communicate," Splinter said.

Lenah chuckled.

"Aren't you guys cute. Cool Hand Luke. Good flick, but can we get serious here?" said Peel.

An awkward silence ensued as they looked at each other, everyone unsure how to proceed.

The door opened, and Child entered, taking his seat next to Peel and whispering in his ear.

"It's not nice to tell secrets. Especially with people sitting in the room," Splinter said.

"No secret," Peel said. "They got a faint signal from your tracking dart. We were able to boost the signal and run it through the computer.

It's about seven miles off shore, in a hundred feet of water and it isn't moving."

"Been in the same spot for the last ten minutes, and if your description is accurate, I'd say the tracker isn't on your... fish," Child said.

Lenah's chin fell to her chest and Will sighed.

"Damn," Splinter said. "I know I hit it."

"Must have fallen out. You know how tough the thing's hide looked," Will said.

Officer Bostic chuckled.

"Something funny?" Will asked.

The cop said nothing.

"I'm retired PD, officer. Chief Hanley is my golf buddy, so before you do or say something that gets your ass busted down to crossing guard, perhaps we should split up this party," Will said. "Do you have any more questions for us?"

Bostic started to speak but her radio went off. She snapped it from her belt and put it to her ear, but it was so loud everyone in the room heard the call.

There had been a crocodile attack at Blue Hole Creek, and a young girl had been killed.

Bostic bounced up from her seat and tossed a card at Lenah. "Don't leave town. After my sergeant looks at these statements, we'll be in touch for a follow up." She shuffled out of the room.

Peel said, "That was pleasant. I need to get out of here. Want to take a ride over to the croc attack scene? See what's what over there? It could be your monster."

"We'd already know if it was. The report wouldn't have said crocodile," Splinter said. "In fact, there'd probably be no report at all."

Peel smiled like he was humoring a toddler.

27

The twenty-two-foot SAFE boat with twin 150HP Honda outboards skimmed across the bay, the bow lifting and falling as it cut through the light chop. Half the sun sat on the horizon and Splinter felt like he hadn't slept in days. He was dead on his feet and he didn't know how much longer he could go. Lenah didn't look much better. After their field trip they had to rest.

Mangroves lined the shoreline as Peel piloted the SAFE boat through narrow channels. Blue Hole Creek wasn't far, and they'd be there in a matter of minutes. Splinter couldn't shake the feeling that Peel had brought them for a reason because the Coast Guard typically didn't make a habit of toting around civilians.

Splinter said, "So why'd you really want us here?"

Peel chuckled. "You think I have an ulterior motive?"

"Don't know, but I follow the soldier's most basic rule: never volunteer. For anything."

Peel laughed again. "How do I know you never followed that rule?"

Splinter said nothing.

They hit a big wake from a fishing trawler and the SAFE boat skipped and bounced over the chop. Splinter gripped the command console to keep his balance.

"I know you didn't follow that rule because I know who you are," Peel said. He pushed down on the throttle and motors whined and the boat picked up speed.

"That's cosmic. Who am I? I'd really like to know," Splinter said.

"I made some calls when I saw you on the news. My gut told me we'd meet at some point. Not sure why, but here you are," Peel said.

Lenah's brow furrowed, and Will shifted his weight from foot to foot. Splinter said nothing.

"And why are we here?" Will asked.

"There's someone I want you to meet. He'll probably be at the scene."

"Who?" Lenah said.

"Not for me to say really, and actually, I don't know," Peel said.

"You want us to meet the guy, but you're not sure who he is?" Splinter said.

Now it was Peel's turn to say nothing.

Peel arced the SAFE boat right around an outcrop of mangroves and entered Blue Hole Creek. Avalon State Park stretched to the east, and beyond, the sound of crashing waves sounded over the dunes. Two police boats, a harbor patrol boat, and a coastie SAFE boat clogged the creek, and several men and women stood on the shoreline standing around a circle of red plastic flags. Peel piloted the boat past the clog of boats and further into the creek, where he spun the wheel and pulled back on the throttle as the SAFE boat crunched onto a rocky beach.

Peel jumped from the boat followed by Splinter and the others, and they crossed the beach to meet the group of uniformed men and women. When they got to the knot of people, Peel said, "How goes it?"

A coastie in a dark blue work uniform broke off from the group and briefed them. "How's it look?" the coastie said to his superior officer.

In the center of the red flags lay a blue tarp covering the body, and to the side the corpse of the biggest crocodile Splinter had ever seen lay baking in the sun. Easily fifteen feet long, the giant croc's mouth was open in death, huge teeth covered in blood filling the gaping maw.

"You got the thing?" Will said.

The coastie looked away, but said, "So says harbor patrol."

"And you believe them? How could they know this was the one without an autopsy? Did they see this exact croc attack whoever's under that tarp?" Peel said.

"No, and no," said the young coastie. He had dark hair and brown eyes, and his nameplate read Higgins.

"Doesn't matter," said Peel. "What worries me is these creatures don't normally attack without provocation."

"I'm telling you," Splinter said. "Whatever is out there is causing all marine species in the area to be aggressive."

"And you know that how?" Peel said.

"Open your eyes and look around," said a voice from over Splinter's shoulder. He turned to see a man standing on the beach. He wore a blue suit with a red tie and fancy shoes caked with mud.

"You are?" Will said.

"This is who I wanted you to meet," Peel said.

"Indeed," said the stranger. "Mind if they come with me back to the mainland?"

"Not at all," Peel said. He turned to Splinter and the others and said, "You know where I am." Then he walked away.

"Come with me, please," the man said.

"I'm not going anywhere until you tell us who you are and what you want," Will said.

"Easy Officer Dodge, I'm not the boogie man or the enemy."

"Then who are you?" Splinter said.

The man sighed. "Name's Harry Silva. I work for the government."

"In what capacity?" Splinter said.

"Let's just say I investigate abnormalities," Silva said.

"What agency are you with?" Lenah asked.

"All of them," Silva said.

They'd arrived at his boat, which was a gray Navy patrol boat with a large harpoon gun mounted in the bow.

"You going whaling?" Will said.

"Hardly," Silva said.

One by one they boarded Silva's boat and he directed them into the pilothouse where they took seats around a table.

"I suppose you've figured out why I wanted to talk to you?" Silva said.

"Our monster?" Lenah said.

"Yes," Silva said.

"What do you know of it?" Splinter said.

"More than you, I think, though I've only seen the creature once from a distance," Silva said.

Splinter jerked forward in his seat. "You've seen it? You believe us?"

"I have, and I do," he said.

"Then why isn't the ocean crawling with Navy and Coast Guard? Peel pretended he had no idea what we were talking about," Will said.

"He doesn't believe, I don't think. Would you believe if you hadn't seen the beast? I didn't. I believe in what I can see, taste, touch, or smell. Photos can be doctored, evidence faked," Silva said. "Plus, Florida's economy depends on tourism and fishing. If I created a panic with no plan on how to find the beast, what good would that do?"

"So you just ignore it?" Splinter said.

"You have to remember the ocean is a big place."

"You know what the thing is?" Lenah asked.

"Not exactly," Silva said. He reached behind him and took a brown envelope from a shelf. He undid the metal clasp and pulled out a short stack of photos. He laid them on the table before him and Lenah gasped. "Yes, impressive, isn't it?"

The pictures were of the creature.

"What you're looking at are pictures of what appears to be an extinct order of reptile known as *pliosaurs*. There were two major subspecies that we know of, each having a different size neck and tail. This particular creature doesn't fit any mold we know of, but it appears to be a mutant *kronosaurus*, the biggest known sub species of *pliosaurs*. Somewhere along the line crocodiles, or some other similar reptile species, mixed and evolved with a distant relative of the prehistoric beast. *Kronosaurus* were considered the lions of the sea at one point and were in direct competition with another ancient sea creature you may have heard of, *megalodon*. These apex predators date back to the early Cretaceous, over one hundred million years ago."

Will and Splinter exchanged glances.

Silva said, "I see you've heard some of this?"

"Not really," Will said. "But we did gather some information and make some wild guesses."

"Your beast is similar to the *kronosaurus* in that it has a large flat head with a tail that ends in a caudal fin, which the creature uses to swim. The jaw muscles are very strong, and its teeth are sharp, razor edged needle cones with a slight curve protruding from a long jaw like a modern-day crocodile. These beasts were larger and stronger than the kings of the land, including *tyrannosaurus-rex*, and until megalodon came along they ruled the seas. Here, look for yourself."

Silva shuffled the pictures, putting a shot of the creature taken from above. A satellite photo, Splinter thought.

Silva pointed at the head and said, "See these two holes? It's hard to see in these pictures, but those are the creature's eye sockets. A full grown *kronosaurus* head was flat-topped with powerful jaws, and each upper and lower jaw contained twenty-five to thirty teeth."

The pilothouse fell silent.

"Its body is sleek, but its hide is somewhat rough like a croc's on its back, but smooth along its sides and underbelly. Its body ends with a powerful tail," Silva said.

"Sounds like our boy, except for the tail. Our creature has a long tail like a croc," Will said.

"Like I said, I think we're dealing with a mutant of some type, not an actual *kronosaurus*, and there could be different types out there," Silva said. "*Kronosaurus* was believed to be a very fast swimmer, so catching a glimpse of it would be hard."

"How old do you think this thing is and where the hell has it been hiding?" Lenah said.

"Don't know, but however old it is the beast shows clear anatomical adaptations that make it different from any animal ever cataloged," Silva said.

Silva sifted through the photos until he got to a sideview that was taken from a submarine cruising on the surface. In the foreground the metal deck of the sub could be seen, and the creature ran alongside it.

"Again, it's hard to see, but look closely there and you'll see what appear to be gill slits," Silva said.

Splinter said, "No doubt. I saw gills as well. How can that be?"

"This creature has adapted to its environment. Not to be corny and quote Jeff Goldblum, but life found a way, and mutations most likely took place over thousands of years and many generations as these beasts lived in the depths out in the sea trenches and rift valleys," Silva said. "The dinosaurs went out with a bang, but prehistoric reptiles hung on much longer, and their extinction was more gradual due to a steady decline of sea temperatures."

"But if this thing is part croc, how can it live in the depths without sunlight? Don't reptiles need sunlight?" Lenah asked.

"They do, but the hydrothermal vents at the deepest parts of the seas are believed to provide chemicals, bacteria, and these creatures may rely on *chemosynthesis*, not *photosynthesis*," Silva said.

"You believe all this? That these creatures have been living at the bottom of the sea for thousands of years?" Will said.

"I believe in what I can see, smell, touch, and hear. What do you believe?" Silva said.

Splinter said nothing.

"Tell me your story. Leave out no details," Silva said.

So once again Splinter told the tale, Silva nodding his head, and Lenah and Will occasionally making an addition or correction.

"I agree about the tsunami. It's just too much of a coincidence that the creature showed up right after," Silva said.

"And all the fish?" Lenah said.

"Indeed. All connected," Silva said.

"This all sounds impossible," Will said.

"But it's not. The extinction event that killed the dinosaurs changed the planet dramatically, and suddenly *kronosaurus* would have been searching for warm water, and headed into the deeper, warmer parts of the world's oceans, where superheated water from hydrothermal vents warm the ocean to the point where the *kronosaurus* could survive and maintain its body heat."

"That's some pretty thin shit," Will said.

"Maybe. How do you explain what you saw?"

Nobody spoke. Waves lapped against the hull, seagulls squawked, and wind whistled through the open hatch.

"The question is, what do you plan to do about it?" Will said.

Silva put another picture on top of the pile. It was a cellphone camera shot of the tsunami as it came over the water toward the shoreline. In its center was a set of huge jaws, revealing rows of teeth.

"So far I haven't rung the panic bell. It's a shame you were unable to tag the beast. That would have been a big help."

"What now?" Lenah said.

"I keep watching, and when the time is right we'll take the thing down," Silva said.

"A shame. I'd bet a million scientists would kill each other to study this thing," Lenah said.

"They can study the corpse," Silva said.

Silva fired up the engines and took Splinter and crew back to the Coast Guard base to get Will's car.

As Splinter got off the Navy boat Silva handed him a card. "Call me if you think of anything or if you learn something new."

"Something new?" Splinter said.

"I can tell you're not going to let this go, am I right?" Silva said.

"Maybe," Splinter said.

"Keep me informed and take care, Captain Woods," Agent Harry Silva said.

"You too."

28

Back at the Coast Guard base they all piled into the Taurus and headed to Lenny's to collect Poseidon, who walked right past Splinter when he tried to pick the cat up. Clearly his feline friend was pissed. Will guided the old Taurus out onto A1A and made a right.

"You want me to drop you guys at Lenah's?" Will said. "I'm gonna drop Poseidon off at my neighbor's and catch some rest."

"Yes, please," Lenah said.

Splinter grunted. Lenah refused to go back to his "shithole" and she was justified. His half-sunken home was no place for a woman. Hell, it was no place for anybody, except maybe water rats.

They made the same left they had earlier onto Seaway Drive, and passed all the same places, but this time they didn't make the right into the Coast Guard station. Instead they drove on, past the aquarium, over the bridge to the mainland, and turned left on North 4th Street heading south.

Lenah's place was a well-kept two-story cape in Sunland Gardens that reminded Splinter of the house he grew up in. It was light green, with white trim, and there was a floral wreath on the front door and a sailboat on a trailer next to her garage. The lawn hadn't been cut in a while, and the thick blades of the St. Augustine grass swayed in the gentle breeze.

Will pulled into the driveway, and as Splinter got out, Poseidon jumped out behind him.

"Oh, no, you're with Will," he said to the cat.

Poseidon just stared up at him with glassy green eyes. She sat and curved her tail around herself. If that wasn't a no, Splinter didn't know what was.

"She can stay with us," Lenah said.

"No," said Splinter. "We don't know what's going to happen in the next few days and I can't be worrying about her."

"She can stay at my place when we're gone," Lenah said.

"Who's going to feed her? Let her out, etc…?"

Will said, "It's best if she comes with me. Toby will take good care of her, promise."

Poseidon hissed as Splinter picked her up, placed her in the front seat of the Taurus, and closed the door.

"Call you later," Will said.

"How?" Splinter said. "Lenah's phone is on the bottom of the Atlantic and I don't have one."

"We'll check in with you. I'm gonna get a new phone first thing tomorrow," Lenah said.

Will waved and drove off, Poseidon staring out the window at Splinter, her paws on the dashboard.

"Where's your car?" Splinter asked.

"Garage. I got a lift to the marina. Didn't want to leave my car there."

Lenah turned over a rock and picked up a key. "My keys are on the bottom of the Atlantic as well."

She opened the front door and went inside.

The foyer opened up into a living room, with the stairs to the second floor straight ahead. Splinter used the bathroom, and when he joined Lenah in the kitchen, she had various containers out on the table.

"I've got leftover spaghetti, and a couple of pieces of chicken, salad, take what you want," she said.

"Any beer or anything?" Splinter said.

Lenah went to a cabinet and pulled down a bottle of white wine. "Don't know if it's any good, but I figure you've earned it." She put it on the table.

It was a twist off, and Splinter opened the bottle and poured some into a coffee cup. "Want some?"

"Yeah, sure." She grabbed her own cup and he spilled some wine into it.

They ate in silence and when they were done Splinter took a shower and went to the guest room where he found sheets sitting atop an old futon. He opened it up, threw the sheet onto the worn cushion, and lay down.

In seconds he was asleep.

***

Splinter and Lenah slept in and had a late breakfast at a local diner. Then they went to the cellphone store in Lenah's 2015 Ford F150 and got her a new phone, which the clerk linked to her old account. Inside fifteen minutes, Lenah rejoined the twentieth century.

They grabbed coffee and parked at the end of Talbot's Pier.

"OK. We're rested. Fed. We have communication. What now?" Lenah said. "Oh, don't tell me, you want to swim out there and look for the thing."

"You're a riot, Alice. A real riot," he said. He sounded nothing like Jackie Gleason.

"My father loved that show," Lenah said.

"Mine too. I watched re-runs with him when I was a kid. I always thought Alice was way funnier than Ralph, though," Splinter said.

"Me too. I remember how the walls would shake when Ralph slammed the door. They were fabric stretched over wood frames," she said.

"Jackie Gleason was the first famous person to die that I actually cared about. I still watch the Honeymooners. Never gets old, no matter how many times you've seen them. That show could never be today."

"There are a million versions of it on TV right now," Lenah said.

"Copies, you mean. How do you think 'bang zoom to the moon' would go over today? It was always followed by Alice staring him in the face and saying 'just try' but still."

"I see what you mean. Never thought of that before," Lenah said.

"And that's good."

"Now that we know we share a love for classic comedy, what the hell are we going to do? We done here?"

"Not by a longshot. I'm just getting started," he said.

"Silva's on it. What can we do that he can't?" Lenah said.

"First off, we know the area. Second, he hasn't called in the cavalry yet, and until he does the thing needs to be hunted."

"Why us?"

Splinter laughed. "Who else?"

"So I ask again, what now?"

"You think Guppy would loan you one of his adventure boats? Those things are fast and have all kinds of neat equipment," he said.

She sighed. "I just dogged him. I don't know if he'll help, but I can certainly try."

"Agree to have dinner with him like you promised," Splinter said.

"And you'll come?"

"Sure."

Lenah called Guppy and he agreed to meet her at the Lobster Boat down in Palm City at five o'clock. That left them with three hours to kill. Lenah called Will and told him she bought a phone, and what they planned to do. He said the pets were fine, and he'd check in. Then she called Silva, but he didn't pick up, so she left him a message with her number, and said they'd learned nothing new.

"What about weapons?" Splinter said.

"Like what?"

"Like some big stuff. Grenades. Missiles. But we can start with guns," he said.

Lenah drove to Armed and Dangerous, a gun shop on the main drag of Fort Pierce. They agreed Splinter should stay in the car and let Lenah handle the transaction. There's a waiting period for handguns, but rifles and shotguns could be purchased, along with ammo, by answering a few basic questions and proving identity, which Lenah did with her passport. Her driver's license was on the bottom of the Atlantic.

She got back an hour later and put a long box with two smaller boxes in the bed of the pickup.

"I got two shotguns and a rifle, along with ammo," she said. "Cost me twenty-five hundred bucks. You got half?"

Splinter said nothing.

"Good thing Sal didn't cancel his credit card payment and I had a spare card," she said.

They drove on because it would take an hour or so to get to the Lobster Boat and she didn't want to keep Guppy waiting.

The Lobster Boat was a south Florida fixture. You entered through the hull of an old fishing boat, which had run aground on the very spot where the restaurant now sat. The back deck extended out over the water, and most of the joint's red paint was flaking off.

Guppy waited in the back of the dining room. It was early, and only a spattering of older folks were in the place at 5PM. Guppy's face registered disgust when he saw Splinter, and Lenah said, "You don't mind that Splinter is joining us, do you?"

"I do, but does it matter?" he said.

"No," Splinter said, and he sat down next to Guppy and made a show of putting his cloth napkin across his lap before he took a pull of water from a glass on the table, pinky held high.

Lenah sat across from Guppy and when the waitress came, they ordered drinks. A Jack Daniels Manhattan for Splinter, a glass of Pinot Grigio for Lenah, and a scotch neat for Guppy.

"So, why do I have a feeling this isn't a social visit?" Guppy said.

"'Cause it isn't," Splinter said. Lenah kicked him under the table.

"I'm sorry about the other day. Running out on you like that," she said.

"I'm used to it."

"I'm sorry anyway."

They drank, ordered their food, and ate, saying very little. Guppy was a human garbage pail, and he ate all the bread, two one-and-a-half pound lobsters, and a side of filet minion. Lenah had a salad with chicken, and Splinter had a T-bone steak. When they were done, Guppy said, "OK, out with it."

Lenah gave Guppy her "who me?" face, but Guppy wasn't that much of a guppy. "We need to borrow one of your boats," Lenah said.

Splinter smiled. He appreciated the directness.

Guppy laughed so hard his belly jiggled like a bowl full of jelly, like Santa Claus. "Why? Where's the Evenstar?"

Lenah looked down and started to speak, but Splinter jumped in. "It's got engine trouble. It's in dry dock for a few days over at Lenny's."

"So, lay low until it's fixed. Can't imagine you have many charters lined up. The fish have left the building."

"All the same, I'd like to get back out there. I do have a couple of charters lined up," she said.

"No way. All my stuff is in use. Plus, I don't..." He looked Splinter's way and Splinter stuck out his tongue. "Plus, I don't really trust your first mate."

"I'm the only mate, mate," Splinter said.

"You don't have anything in the yard you're not using?"

Guppy leaned back in his chair and looked hard at Lenah. "I've done a lot for you, Lenah, and all I seem to get from the relationship is rejection, disrespect, and lies." Guppy stood and threw his napkin on the table. "The answer is no, but thanks for dinner. You'll pick up the check, right?"

Lenah and Splinter said nothing.

"You know, for my help the other night. Do you have the rifle I lent you? That's an expensive piece."

Again Splinter jumped in before Lenah could tell him the truth. "It's back at Lenah's. I didn't want to drive around with it in the car."

"Of course, you get stopped by a cop and you'd get arrested. You are the butcher of Kabul, after all."

Splinter stood, the fog encroaching around the edges of his vision. Heat rose to his face and his stomach burned. Lenah stood beside him, her hand on his shoulder. "That wasn't called for. If you won't help, fine, but there's no need to insult anyone."

Splinter took a step toward Guppy, and Lenah tried to hold him back, but failed. "Listen you little shitbag. You talk to me like that again and you might just see the butcher of Kabul. Got me, Shrimp? Oh, sorry, I meant Guppy. Shrimp are too strong and smart for you to have that nickname."

Guppy turned red, but stepped back, and Lenah got between them. Guppy said, "Lose my number." He shook his head and left the restaurant.

"Nicely done," Lenah said. She rummaged through her purse. "Guess I'm paying. Again."

They got coffee at Bean Break on A1A and sat behind a high school to drink and talk.

"What's plan B?" Splinter said.

"Why do we need a plan B?" she said.

"Oh, I don't know, because plan A failed worse than that chain of cotton candy stores," Splinter said.

"I liked that stuff."

"You would," he said. "What do we do now?"

She smiled. "We take a boat anyway."

29

Lenah drove her pickup through the deepening night, route 70 twisting and turning toward Okeechobee. Saw palmetto and brown dried-out grass fields ran by on both sides of the road, and thick white clouds floated across a waxing gibbus moon. Oceanic Memories did adventure tours on both coasts, the keys, and Lake Okeechobee and its associated rivers and estuaries, and the town of Okeechobee was the company's central base of operations where it had its yard and maintenance facility. There wasn't much in central Florida, except small towns, swamp, and sugarcane.

"You sure we're not gonna get arrested for this?" Splinter said.

"When you see the yard you'll understand," she said.

Another hour slid away before she exited the highway and made a right on NE 14th Avenue, went a mile, and made a left on NE 3rd Street.

The yard where Oceanic Memories had its shop and dry dock was surrounded by six-foot chain-link fence with razor wire at the top. A pile of old boats sat at one end of the two-acre property and was overgrown with water reeds, everywhere else boats of various sizes were stored one next to the other like in a parking lot. At the yard's center sat the maintenance shed.

"Security?" Splinter said.

"You'll see."

Lenah slowed the pickup and came to a stop in front of a chain-link gate. A single floodlight on a pole illuminated the entrance, but it was the only light and the rest of the yard was dark.

Shep was an old German Shepard who sounded tough, but was in fact a teddy bear, if you knew him, which Lenah did. Guppy's mechanic Grady had worked on the Evenstar and she'd been to the yard many times. The old dog barked and growled at the stopped pickup, even though he'd seen it before.

Lenah got out and went to the gate, arms extended in welcome.

"Whatcha doin'?" Splinter said.

Shep growled and barked as she approached, but he stopped and started whimpering when Lenah entered the sphere of light. Lenah pet the animal through the fence, and then she fumbled with the lock and opened the gate. Shep jumped on her and licked Lenah's face, and she embraced the animal, kissing him on the nose.

When she got back to the truck, Splinter said, "OK, I'll bite. How'd you get the lock off the gate?"

"Guppy lost the key ages ago. He just lines it up to look like its locked," she said.

"No cameras or alarms?"

Lenah laughed.

She pulled into the yard, got out and re-secured the gate, and pulled the truck behind the maintenance building. Shep panted and waited for them to get out of the cab, but Lenah and Splinter sat in the darkness, waiting to see if anyone came out of the shop. Guppy's workers had been known to pass out after work.

Fifteen minutes passed and Splinter got out and surveyed the stored boats, but it was hard to see in the dark, so he reached back into the pickup and grabbed a flashlight. He clicked it on and trained its beam up and down the rows of boats. There were various sizes and shapes, ranging from small dinghies to big dive boats. Splinter said, "What do you recommend?"

"Size. Something we can mount a harpoon gun on," Lenah said.

"Where the hell are we going to… oh, right here," Splinter said.

An old rusted deck-mounted harpoon gun lay on its side next to the shop.

"It doesn't have any bolts, and it needs TLC, but it's better than nothing," she said. "Guppy was going to get it restored and mounted on his party boat and modify it to throw water balloons."

Splinter said, "It'll work. It's just a big speargun. I can make some incendiary harpoons. We'll mount it and I'll work on it while we search. We're lucky it's not a harpoon cannon. Those big boys need gunpowder and can't have rust or decay and only fire metal bolts."

Lenah nodded.

"You have a boat in mind?" he asked again.

"Just a type. He uses pontoon style boats for the basic tours, but he has bigger boats for scuba and deep-sea fishing. I'd like to get something with a sub," she said.

He laughed.

"I'm serious. The bigger vessels are equipped with Trident tourist subs. Might be useful."

They walked down the center row of inventory, and she said, "That one." It was three rows back and in a corner. "They won't notice it's gone for weeks unless its primary breaks-down and they need it."

The white rust bucket Guppy had named Sea Hunter IV didn't look like much, but it would do the trick. It was a thirty-two-foot ferry-like vessel with twin diesel inboard engines. It had no rear gunnel to make it easy to launch small craft, a pilothouse at its center, and a bow that rose above the deck four feet and surrounded a fifteen-foot Zodiac. Two underwater scooters were stored against the pilothouse, along with dive equipment, several harpoon guns, and fishing gear and poles. On the center of the aft deck an old Trident six-person Tourist-viewer submarine was held in place by large holding clamps, a gantry arm with steel cable lowered and tucked behind it. Two long benches sat in the bow behind the Zodiac where the tourists would sit while the boat was in motion. The ship rested on a trailer surrounded in weeds three-feet high.

"You sure it will run?" Splinter asked.

"Yup. He does his real He-Man expensive tours with these rigs. He keeps these back-ups ready to go in case a primary goes down. Guppy never cancels a tour. This one probably hasn't been used in a while because they constantly maintain the newer boats in the water. Especially the alpha ships."

They spent the next hour shifting boats around using Lenah's truck. When they had the Sea Hunter IV hitched and ready to roll Lenah crawled through Shep's doggy door and opened the shop. They scavenged gas, rebar, wood, a handheld grinder, a drill, some sheet metal, heavy-duty snippers, and some other tools, none of which would be missed right away. Splinter searched for shaft material for his harpoons and settled on two broom handles and a shovel handle.

Lenah and Splinter loaded everything into the pickup bed next to the guns and pulled the boat out of the gate onto the road. Then Splinter unhitched the trailer and they went back into the yard and put all the boats they'd moved back in their original spots. In the dark you couldn't tell the Sea Hunter IV was gone.

They said goodbye to Shep, closed the gate and lined-up the lock, and re-hitched the trailer. Lenah turned the rig around carefully on the narrow road. Last thing they needed was a jackknife. She headed back to route 70 and went east toward the Atlantic coast.

Splinter opened the windows, and the cool night air pushed out the rank stench of stale hamburger, fries and coffee. He said, "Last thing we need is some heavy artillery."

Lenah chuckled. "Any ideas?"

"There are people you can buy from in Miami, but it's dangerous and takes time because they check you out. Nobody wants to sell to some terrorist," Splinter said.

"How noble. Who do they expect them to be used on?" she said.

Splinter said nothing.

"You're looking for grenades? Missile launchers? That kind of stuff?"

"Ideally. I can make bombs, but as you know they'll be unstable, and hard to light and control."

"Don't see how we're gonna get any of the real stuff. This is Florida, but even down here you can't go buying missiles."

"Make them it is then. We should grab our supplies before we hit the water. We need a home improvement store and a supermarket."

"What are we doing here, Splinter? I thought the plan was to find the thing and call the fuzz?" she said.

"It is. It is," he said in his easy tone. She didn't believe it for a second and she frowned. The frown that said he was an idiot if he thought she believed that. "Just being prepared. We need food and supplies because I don't want to become food."

"I swam with it for ten hours," she said.

"And you never kissed it like I did. We're closer. Period," Splinter said.

She chuckled. "You're in a good mood."

"Ahh, I just like getting my way, and screwing Guppy is a bonus. What will he do when he finds out? Call the police?"

"Naw. I know too much about him, and he's given me that 'lose my number speech' before. He doesn't mean it. No, most likely he'll call me all pissed-off, but he'll get over it."

The Ford rumbled through the darkness, the horizon in the east getting gray with the coming day.

"Where you dropping us? Lenny's?"

Lenah said, "Yeah. I can leave my truck there and we can hide the trailer over by the scrap heap. He won't see it."

The sun was coming up and the gray of dawn covered the world when they stopped at the market and a lumberyard. Splinter picked up what he needed to make pipe bombs, and they bought all kinds of food, and even some beer. Traffic was light, and they made good time. Lenah made the left into Lenny's, spun the wheel and slipped the trailer down the launch ramp in one fluid motion. Splinter jumped out and worked the winch, but the boat didn't slide off the trailer.

"Give it a jolt," Splinter shouted.

Lenah came back slowly, then stomped on the brakes and the truck rocked the trailer and the boat broke free and floated into the canal. They loaded all the supplies onto the boat, including the old deck mounted harpoon gun, dumped the trailer, and hid Lenah's pickup in an overgrown section of the yard. They filled-up using Lenny's pump and her credit card.

They boarded the Sea Hunter IV and shoved off. The diesels fired right up, and they gurgled in the early morning dusk as the ship edged from the marina. Other fishing boats headed for the inlet via Indian River, but not as many as usual. The waterway wasn't closed, but a warning had been issued.

The sun came up, and sunlight shimmered off the ocean, the sky clear.

A Coast Guard cutter sat moored just inside the inlet, and several harbor patrol boats and coastie SAFE boats patrolled the inland sea.

"Looks like they're focusing close to shore," Lenah said.

"Makes sense. They're trying to avoid bad PR, we're trying to find the thing," Splinter said. "People are panicking and the community is demanding action. The authorities want to be seen providing and acting."

Lenah turned on the radio and cycled through the channels. "First sign we're calling Silva and the coasties. First whiff," she said.

Splinter said nothing.

"Where to? Our old spot off South Beach Park? With all the ships cleared out it might head back that way for seconds," she said.

"Good a place to start as any. What are we gonna do without your special sauce?" Splinter said.

"Don't worry. I picked up a few cans. We can whip something up. Won't be as good, but it'll be better than nothing."

"There's a bucket in the galley. You want me to get it going?"

"Yeah."

Splinter retrieved the bucket, along with the two jars of pickled pig's feet, fake meat dog treats, fish oil, chicken livers and moldy cheese. He mixed it all together in the bucket with a little seawater, and though it didn't smell as bad as Lenah's secret sauce, it was rank.

"All the oil will leave a good slick," she said.

Lenah turned the boat east, and they passed through the inlet, and into the sunrise, the Atlantic Ocean churning west in a steady rolling three-foot swell that cut across the bow. She pushed down on the throttle and didn't look back.

Splinter did look back, but all he saw was shoreline in the grayness, and the twinkling lights of Fort Pierce.

.

30

The Atlantic Ocean was flat and the air stifling, not so much a puff of wind to cool things down. Humidity was at eighty percent and sweat dripped down Splinter's back and his t-shirt was soaked through. Lenah hid her discomfort, but it was clear she was suffering. Wet stains under her armpits, a line of sweat running up the back of her shorts, her hair looking like she'd just stuck her finger in an electric socket, all told Splinter she was tired and uncomfortable.

"You want to take a nap while I keep an eye on things?" Splinter said.

The Sea Hunter IV drifted with the roll of the ocean off South Beach Park. Lenah had a good chum slick going, but there'd been no sign of the beast. Splinter cleaned and polished the old harpoon gun, but it would take a lot more work to make it usable.

"Yeah, I think I will. I'm washed out. Call me if you need me," she said.

Splinter nodded, and she disappeared into the cabin below deck where there was a couch in the galley.

The harpoon gun was steel, but it was so old most of the crucial parts were rusted or damaged. Splinter used WD-40, a rag, and elbow grease as he scrubbed and disassembled the old gun. Hours slipped away, and there was no sign of the creature, or any fish.

The sun passed noon, and it got hotter and stickier. Splinter took a break from cleaning the harpoon gun and started on the bombs. He'd purchased metal tiki candle lights, which were made to hold citronella oil. Splinter screwed the top off each candle and filled them with gasoline, being careful not to overfill them. The wicks were wide and full and took-up a lot of space in the can. Once all eight were filled, Splinter sealed each by threading the wick through the cap and twisting it back on the can. He'd have to be careful with them because they weren't sealed at the top, and the wicks would burn very fast.

Just as he was finishing, Lenah emerged from the cabin. "Yo. All good?"

"Yup. They're no more than Molotov cocktails, but they're better than nothing. You?"

"Hungry and thirsty, but better," she said. "I see you've been busy."

"We now have eight incendiary bombs and I made some progress on the harpoon gun."

"I can see that. Can I take a turn?"

"Yeah, and I think I'm going to lay down for a bit. Get some rest myself. I'm running on empty."

"Eat first?"

"Sure."

Lenah fixed them up ham sandwiches, and she had a water and brought Splinter a beer. "You deserve it," she said.

"Thanks." He popped the beer open and drank it down with one pull. Then he nibbled at his sandwich. When he was done he got up and stretched. "I'm going to take a nap."

"Any special instructions on this thing?"

"Don't cut yourself. Some of those old rusted edges are sharp."

Splinter went below and found the couch in the galley. He took off his shoes and lay down, hands behind his head. He was asleep in minutes.

Dreams of Kabul tormented him, but the creature was also there, interspersed in his nightmares like it had always been there, part of the history he fought to forget.

He woke to Lenah screaming.

"Splinter! Get up here. Splinter!"

He launched off the couch and ran up the steps onto deck.

"You OK? You scared me," he said.

"Sorry. Look," she said and handed him the binoculars.

About 500 yards off the port bow, a fin scythed through the water heading west, following the chum slick toward the shoreline. Whatever it was appeared not to notice them.

"What do you make of it?" Splinter said.

"Don't know, but I'm going to get on the radio," she said.

Lenah went to the command console and lifted the radio mic. She switched to the emergency channel and hailed the Coast Guard. No response. She pressed the button to hail them again, but she paused when she noticed the fin had disappeared.

"It's gone?" she yelled.

"Seems so. You already call it in?"

"Got no response."

"What does the fish finder say?"

"Got nothing big. Must have gone deep. You think it was our fish? It kinda looked like its caudal fin."

"Damn," Splinter said.

Lenah came back out on deck and the two companions studied the ocean, but saw nothing except the reflection of the fading day and the oily chum slick that left a nasty ring around the boat's waterline.

Lenah saw Splinter looking at the underwater scooters, and said, "No way."

"Come on. I need to see what's going on down there. An underwater view could tell us so much. A new perspective."

Lenah said nothing.

"I'll stay in radio contact and won't go far. Promise. I'll come right back at the first sign of trouble," Splinter said.

The underwater scooters looked like bicycles with thick square frames. The diver's tank sat beneath the handlebars, and a rear propeller pushed the scooter through the water, the rider's head covered in a dive helmet. Full throttle the bikes went about four knots. Not fast enough to outrun the crocosaurus.

"What if the thing goes after you? You can't outrun it," she said.

"I know, but these things are very maneuverable," Splinter said.

"Still, I'd rather you didn't."

Splinter sighed and went back to work cleaning and fixing the harpoon gun.

When the sun went down the beast hadn't returned, and Splinter was ready to mount the harpoon gun. Using the hoist arm used for the Zodiac, Splinter lifted the old gun and placed it in the bow as forward as he could. Then he started the arduous chore of drilling the holes for the mounting bolts. He was at it two hours and he only completed one when he called it for the night.

They ate another meal of sandwiches, and Lenah went below to sleep while Splinter took the first watch. The night deepened and moonglow shimmered off the Atlantic. Waves slapped the hull, lulling him toward sleep. Stars blinked, and seagulls circled overhead, drawn by the chum slick. Splinter poured more of the rank liquid into the sea.

Around 2AM Lenah emerged and took his place and Splinter slept, and this time his dreams were filled with the sound of water and howling wind. He'd had similar dreams for weeks after the tsunami, and they'd started up again in the last week, his subconscious warning him of danger.

The next morning dawned hotter than the day before, and Splinter gave up drilling the second mounting hole. Sweat dripped down his face and back, and he was already exhausted, so he switched to making harpoons.

He did this by cutting the rebar into two-foot lengths and using the grinder to fashion a barbed point on each. Then he cut and fit the rebar into a wooden shaft he made from the broom handles. In this way he was able to make four harpoons that fit within the old harpoon gun's sling.

Lenah took a turn drilling holes, then Splinter, and it took them the better part of three days before all the mounting holes were drilled, and the speargun mounted. Lenah moved the Sea Hunter IV several times, going out as far as ten miles and as close as two, drifting up and down the coast, but they saw no sign of the beast.

On their sixth day Splinter thought he saw the shadow of the beast off the starboard bow, and then again aft, but he couldn't be sure.

The sun was high, and rain clouds dotted the western horizon like puffs of smoke. Splinter felt the fog coming on, anger layered over fear and doubt. This thing was messing with him, playing games, and it had disappeared into the abyss.

"Not this time," Splinter said. He began removing the mounting brackets for one of the underwater scooters.

"No way, Splinter," Lenah said.

He didn't listen. He connected the hoist cable to a ring screwed into the base of the scooter. Working the winch remote, he lifted the bike and placed it gently on deck. He inserted a fresh scuba tank in its holder, checked the airflow to the dive helmet, and mounted the scooter. He placed the helmet over his head, checked his gauges, and gave the thumbs up signal.

Lenah stood her ground and shook her head. "I'm not helping you kill yourself."

He lifted the helmet and said, "I'm just taking a look. I'm not going to engage the thing."

Lenah went to Splinter and undid the clasps on the dive helmet and lifted it off his head. Splinter started to protest, but Lenah put a finger across his lips. "Breathe. Breathe," she said.

Splinter did breathe.

"You OK?"

Splinter would never be accused of being smart, but he had to agree taking the underwater scooter out wasn't the brightest idea.

"Put that gear away. You're not going underwater with that thing swimming around. I won't lose you that way. Not on my watch," she said.

"Let's head in, have a real meal, sleep in a real bed, and start fresh in the morning," Splinter said.

He'd been ready to jump in the drink with croczilla and had thought nothing of it. On an underwater tourist scooter that went four knots. Lenah pulled him from the abyss, saved him from himself. How much longer would she be there? What would he do when she wasn't? Splinter rolled his shoulders, trying to shake the unease. Maybe he would go to the doc at the VA and get some pills. How bad could they be? If it made Lenah happy, and allowed him to trust himself around her, and in civilization, it might be worth it.

Lenah eased the throttle down and the Sea Hunter IV shuddered and moaned as it pushed through the sea.

They didn't see the creature the next day, or the next, or the next. Splinter was starting to think the beast had departed. The coasties reduced patrols, and the harbor patrol was back on a regular schedule. So it was they saw no other boats as they inched through Fort Pierce inlet on a mid-summer Tuesday, the sun coming up in the east, the wind creating a blown-out chop.

Splinter used the ideal hours preparing their arsenal. The harpoon gun was mounted in the bow, and it was loaded with one of the handmade bolts. The guns were loaded and ready. Fire bombs prepared. The radio crackled with light local traffic. Most charters were only going out a few days a week, choosing not to waste money on gas. Only the larger fishing boats were still going out once a day. These boats toted families looking to save a buck and were happy to catch sea robins as long as the kids had fun. Some of the bigger boats were running 'search for the monster' trips.

"At what point do we give this up?" Lenah said.

"Will asked me that way at the beginning," he said.

"And what was your answer?"

"I don't know. Obsession is funny that way. Doesn't always discuss the rational options with you," Splinter said.

"Knowing you're obsessed should aid you in correcting said obsession."

"Yes, doctor, that's true, but way over simplified," he said. "Ask me why I'm hunting this thing right now? At this moment?"

Lenah said nothing.

"Because I've got nothing better to do," he said.

Splinter held a straight face for ten seconds, but couldn't stop himself from smiling.

They both laughed, and the Sea Hunter IV rumbled on into the rising sun.

31

Four more days passed with no sign of the creature.

They drifted from Vero Beach to Port St. Lucie, through a search grid of over 500 square miles, but they'd seen no sign of croczilla. Each day they left port a little later, and quit a little earlier, and Lenah complained about missing out on charters, though there weren't many to be had. The beast might be gone, but nobody had bothered to inform the fish, who were still mostly MIA. Rorey, a buddy of Lenah's, had told her he caught a few sailfish and a tarpon on his last trip, all keepers. This was the biggest success story they'd heard in over a week. If the fish were coming back, they were taking their time.

Lenah's new cell chirped at around 1PM, and it woke Splinter from his dozing. The Sea Hunter IV was six miles off shore, and communication signals were subject to the whims of the wind.

She read her screen and tuned the marine radio to 87.8MHZ. Static. Then a voice.

"Sea Hunter VI this is The Day After, do you copy?"

It was Will.

"You're on speaker," she said.

"Afternoon, Will," Splinter said.

"Yes, it is. How you guys holding up? I heard you were in the Bait & Switch the other night, talking all kinds of shit about the monster," Will said.

Bait & Switch was a pub off A1A where Splinter was known to imbibe. Splinter pretended not to see Lenah's scowl, and said, "Yeah. Thanks for pointing that out, pal."

"Don't mention it," Will said. "What did the boys at the bar have to say about your story?"

"Told me I should get off the sauce," Splinter said.

Lenah harrumphed and crossed her arms over her chest.

"Probably not bad advice, Captain."

"Did you call for a reason?" Splinter said. He knew Will was just trying to help, but he also knew he was warning Lenah. See what he does? He was saying. He's not over it, no matter what you may think. You can keep him dry while he's on your boat, but then... Splinter heard Will's voice in his head and it made him see red, and the fog crept in around the edges of his vision. Everyone always trying to control him. Tell him what to do. He was a grown man for shits sake. All he wanted was to be left alone.

An awkward silence ensued, and the wind howled, and the ocean cracked against the hull.

Will said, "You find anything out there?"

"Nothing. Nadda. Not a whiff," Lenah said.

"Donny and I were going out fishing today, so we figured we'd come your way. We can search as we fish, right?"

"Don't see why not, but you know you probably won't catch anything," Splinter said. "You have another reason for coming out here?"

Will said nothing.

Splinter thought he knew why Will was coming, and it made him angry. He was checking up on Lenah, making sure everything was OK. His friend no longer trusted him.

"Haven't seen you with you guys going all rogue," Will said. "Send me your coordinates. I'll bring lunch and we can chat and set up a search grid for Donny and I. We plan to be out there until after dark."

Lenah scanned the GPS.

Splinter put up a hand and shook his head. Will had always done right by him and Splinter couldn't say that about many people. Most people failed him, or didn't try. Will had literally picked Splinter from the gutter and took him into his home and nursed him to health. If it wasn't for Will, he'd be pushing daises.

Thing was, Will had known Lenah longer, since she was a young girl, and he had this fatherly thing going with her. He knew Splinter was unstable—Splinter knew it—but Lenah wanted to see the good in him. Splinter knew that. It reminded him of Luke Skywalker and how he refused to believe Vader wasn't all bad. In the end Luke was right. Could Lenah be?

"We're moving, Will," Splinter said.

Lenah's eyes grew wide as understanding dawned on her.

"Why?"

"New search area," Splinter said.

Will said nothing.

"Anything else?" Lenah asked.

Will grunted, as if he had to answer because Lenah had asked. "There is one more thing."

Splinter rocked back on his heels and threw up his hands in an 'I told you so' gesture.

"I got a call from Guppy," Will said.

"Do tell," Splinter said.

"He said you and Lenah stole one of his boats. Couldn't be any truth to that, right?" Will said.

"What do you think?" said Lenah.

"I think your Parker is on the bottom of the Atlantic. I think Splinter would do whatever needs to be done to get back on the water and hunt this thing. I think Guppy has always come through for you, so you figured why not ask."

"And?" Splinter said.

"He says he said no, but now one of his deep-sea vessels is missing. The high school kid who straightens-up the yard noticed."

Lenah sighed. "I'm sure I don't know what you mean."

"Of course not. Splinter is an altar boy and you're a choir girl. Got it. But if you had taken the boat, what would you want me to tell him? Hypothetically, of course."

"Hypothetically I'd ask, how mad is he? What does he plan to do?"

"Mad, and nothing," Will said. "That guy still thinks he's got a shot with you."

"Will, I—"

"I know. I know. You've set him straight many times, yet you still lead him on with your requests," Will said.

Splinter was getting angry. "What is it to you, Will?"

Will said nothing.

"What do you want us to do?" Lenah said.

Will sighed. "Nothing. He asked me to get in touch with you. Verify you had the boat before he called the cops. He doesn't want to get you in trouble, but the boat is worth $75,000 and he's justifiably concerned."

"Hypothetically, how much time would we have if we owned up?" Splinter said.

"Don't know, but I think you'll have a few more days. Assuming the Sea Hunter V doesn't crap out on him," Will said.

Lenah and Splinter looked at each other and made a mutual decision without speaking.

"OK, tell him we took it and we'll get it back to him by week's end," Splinter said. He didn't know if that was true, but he was having a hard time looking beyond the next hour.

"Thanks, Will. I know this could be sticky for you," Lenah said.

"Think nothing of it. My pleasure," Will said.

"When you get out here give us a call and we'll tell you where we're at, copy?" Splinter said.

"That's a 10-4. See you when I see you." Will cut communication and the channel went silent.

Lenah said, "What the hell was that?"

Splinter said nothing. He didn't know, but something gnawed at his insides, some worry that he couldn't identify. Was he bringing Guppy out with him? Was the fog creeping on?

"Will has done everything for us. Why would you be suspicious of him?" Lenah said.

"I'm not, it's just…"

"What?"

"We've been heading in regularly. Not hiding the fact. Spending time at your house. Why wouldn't he have stopped by? Asked to join us for dinner. Anything. But instead he waits until we're miles off shore? Doesn't make sense."

Lenah said, "Splinter, what the hell are you talking about? He wanted to go fishing and figured he'd check-in. What more could it be? Nobody's looking for us."

"That we know of," Splinter said. He knew that didn't make sense. They'd done nothing wrong and were free to go wherever they wanted. If Silva wanted to see them or talk, he and Lenah were a cell phone call away.

"Do you really want to move?"

Splinter gazed out over the turbulent sea. White stratus clouds drifted across the blue sky, the coast of Florida a brown and black line on the horizon. They'd laid a chum slick, but had no success. The rotted tuna they currently towed attracted a sand shark and seagulls, but nothing more. SONAR was clear, and radio chatter light.

An hour passed before the radio came to life again.

"Yello," Lenah said. A pause. "Hi, Will." Her eyes widening as she looked at Splinter, a question there.

Splinter nodded. If he couldn't trust Will, who the hell could he trust? Lenah was right. He was being over cautious.

Lenah read the GPS coordinates from the NAV screen and signed off. "ETA twenty minutes."

Splinter nodded, but said nothing. He stood at the transom, staring into the deep blue water.

Lenah chuckled. "Check this out."

Splinter turned and followed her gaze. A hulking mass of white steel pushed over the ocean like a brick, the upper and lower decks lined with people.

"Who is it? Boat looks full," Splinter said.

Lenah retrieved the binoculars and examined the horizon. "Looks like Ken Detmer's boat, Fate's Fortune."

"Isn't he the one that does whale watching?"

"Yeah, and lately he's been running ads about the monster. Come see a real-life sea monster from the comfortable confines of our large boat. Enjoy cocktails and fine food while you search for one of the world's mysteries."

"Are you shitting me? Nobody believes us, but they're selling tickets to see the thing?"

"Yup. Profit is as profit does. The existence of the creature doesn't really matter. It's the myth."

"And the stupidity of people," Splinter said.

"Say rather, people's need to explore the unknown."

"And see something their neighbor hasn't so they have a better story to tell at this year's block party."

The large ferry-like vessel left a thick whitewater wake, and the rumble of its engines echoed over the Atlantic.

"It's making a lot of noise," Lenah said. "You see The Day After?"

Splinter searched the horizon, but didn't see the black luxury fishing boat. "No." Splinter's stomach turned to ice. Lenah had a point. The vibrations that large boat sent into the depths would draw apex predators to the surface, but what could he do? He hadn't seen the creature in almost two weeks, so there was nothing to warn anyone about.

"Why do you think they came here?" Lenah said.

Splinter said nothing. He didn't know, but he had a guess. He had been talking a bit too loudly at the Bait & Switch, and maybe the guys at the bar were listening closer than he thought. There'd been plenty of scuttlebutt about what killed Aron Darnald, and words sometimes led to deeds.

"You think they know something?" she asked.

Splinter shook his head no.

The wind picked up and blew sea spray across the deck, coating everything with a layer of moisture. The sun had moved past noon and started its descent to the horizon, and beams of sunlight fought through the patchy cloud cover. Splinter saw something sticking from the water, moving toward the charter boat as it closed in on the Sea Hunter IV.

The creature's caudal fin broke the surface three hundred yards behind the charter. Splinter pressed the binoculars to his head, and his eye sockets hurt under the pressure. Worry rose in him like the tide. Fate's Fortune was a big boat. Made of metal, and there was no way the beast could bite a hole in it. But what if someone ended up in the water? Or the creature rammed and disabled the boat?

Splinter took the binoculars away from his eyes and saw nothing but the white glare of the sun on the water between the Sea Hunter IV and Fate's Fortune.

Splinter handed Lenah the binoculars and she gasped.
"What should we do?" she said.
"We go say hi."

32

Lenah eased down on the Sea Hunter IV's controls, and the diesel engines rumbled. Splinter was on the bow, watching the scene through binoculars. As the boat picked up speed, sea spray pounded him, but Splinter didn't move. He was a statue, a figurehead on the bow, unmovable and firm.

The creature slowed and was hanging back, and Splinter didn't think the captain of the charter saw it. He shouted over the moan of the engines, "Can you hail that ship? Get people away from the railings and into the interior?"

Lenah said, "Yes." She picked up the comm handset and hailed Fate's Fortune. Splinter opened the pilothouse door and stuck his head in.

"Yes, Fate's Fortune, we copy," said a scratchy male voice. "This is Captain Detmer. What is the nature of the problem? Do you need assistance?"

"No, but you're going to if you don't get all those people off the deck," Lenah said.

"What are you—"

Lenah stepped on his transmission. "Go look off your stern."

"10-4."

Silence and intermittent static as Captain Detmer did as instructed. Seconds passed. A minute.

"I see a caudal fin out there. Is it our sea monster?" said the captain of Fate's Fortune. The man sounded the wrong kind of excited.

Lenah said nothing. When she looked Splinter's way, he shrugged.

"We think so," she said. "I suggest moving all your passengers into the interior cabin and move from the area slowly and carefully. The more noise you—"

"Move away? We're out here to see this thing, over," Detmer said. He didn't close the channel and Lenah and Splinter could hear him giving orders to his crew.

"Ken, listen, this isn't a joke. This thing is dangerous," Lenah pleaded.

Splinter moved to Lenah's side, his temper rising.

"Appreciate the concern, Sea Hunter, but we've got a pretty stout vessel here. We could take a torpedo hit, so I'm not concerned. We will take all necessary precautions, I assure you. Fate's Fortune out." Detmer closed the channel.

"Stupid shit has no idea what they're dealing with," Splinter said.

"I think we need to show them. Look," Lenah said.

Fate's Fortune was tilted to port and looked like it was going to tip over as passengers crowded one side of the boat trying to get a peek at the creature as the ship turned. As the vessel passed the beast on the starboard side everyone shifted position and the boat yawed to starboard.

"The dumb bastards," Splinter said.

"What do you want me to do?" Lenah asked. Her face was dark with weariness, but her eyes were alight.

"Bring me in close and I'll stab this bitch, draw it away after us," Splinter said.

Lenah nodded.

"Oh, and call Silva," he said.

"Yeah," Lenah lifted her phone. "No signal."

"Text him and it'll go through as soon as we get a signal, then call the coasties on the radio. I'm sure Silva's monitoring communications."

Lenah nodded again, and Splinter went to the harpoon gun.

He had a general rule he always tried to follow. Never use a weapon you haven't personally tested. In the case of the harpoon gun, he'd been unable to test it without losing one of his prized homemade harpoons, so Splinter didn't know what was going to happen when he drew back the thick sling that would propel his bolt. He also had no idea how accurate it would be. It would probably take at least one shot for him to get his sights.

Remembering their arsenal of guns, Splinter ran back to the pilothouse and jumped down the galley steps two at a time. He retrieved a loaded rifle, a pocket of bullets, and scuttled back up onto deck. He leaned the rifle against the gunnel and gripped the harpoon gun's handles and brought it to bear on the creature. He pulled back the large black band and clicked it into the firing mechanism. So far so good. He loaded a harpoon and sighted the weapon fifteen feet in front of the beast's caudal fin.

It would take another minute for the Sea Hunter IV to get into range, which Splinter estimated at 50 yards.

The faint sound of laughter and excited screams floated over the water, and Splinter pictured parents taking photographs, and children gasping, asking if the creature was real. Could it hurt them and where had it come from?

Splinter couldn't wait any longer. His nerves jumped, the fog blowing over his subconscious. Worry climbed up his back and dropped a bucket of ice down his throat into his stomach. If he didn't act, the beast would attack the charter.

He picked-up the rifle, sighted forward of the creature's caudal fin, and fired. The faint chatter stopped, and the bullet plunked into the water and the monster rolled, its underside visible as the beast writhed.

Splinter drew back the bolt and slipped another bullet into the firing chamber and jacked the bolt closed. He fired again.

This time the beast bellowed and surged from the ocean. The Sea Hunter IV was one-hundred yards out and closing, and Splinter put down the rifle and gripped the harpoon gun again, closing his right eye and lining up the shot.

Seventy yards.

The fog came on, and rage rose in him. Anger at the captain of Fate's Fortune for being so cavalier after such a dire warning. Hostility toward the passengers who showed no respect for the sea and what it could do. Pissed at Lenah for helping him. Angry at himself for being where he was, doing what he was doing. Most of the people on the ship would look down their noses at him. The butcher of Kabul. Yet here he was trying to save their lives.

At sixty yards out Splinter pulled the trigger, but the harpoon didn't streak from its tube.

A loud twang resounded as the tension band snapped, and lashed Splinter on the arm, drawing blood.

"Shhhiiiitttttttttt," he screamed. He'd been afraid of this. The rubber was dry rotted, and he'd rubbed it with WD-40, but it hadn't been enough.

"What now?" Lenah said.

The beast was agitated, and it surged forward into the charter boat, rocking it and sending passengers sprawling across the deck.

A young boy fell over the railing into the drink. A woman, who Splinter assumed was the boy's mother, screamed and wailed, and climbed the railing to jump into the ocean, only to be pulled back. A life ring was thrown into the water, but Splinter could see it wasn't going to be enough.

The creature circled the ship, coming around the aft side, heading toward the bow where the boy flailed about, trying to stay above the rolling sea.

"Ram it. Now!" Splinter screamed.

Lenah hesitated only an instant, then dropped the throttle and the Sea Hunter pushed through the water, slamming through the waves.

Splinter grabbed the rifle and loaded a round. He sighted the weapon, but the beast was on the opposite side of Fate's Fortune and he couldn't see it. Frantic passengers ran around the ship's deck and children screamed.

Time slowed, and it felt like the Sea Hunter IV was moving at two knots. He balanced the rifle on the gunnel and aimed where he thought the beast would be when it emerged from behind the boat.

The creature didn't appear, and as the Sea Hunter IV came around the bow of Fate's Fortune, Splinter saw why.

The beast bore down on the child in the water, its flat crocodilian head rising from the ocean, long powerful jaws opening, sharp teeth shining in the sunlight. The boy screamed as he reached the life ring and made one last effort to swim away from the creature, but he was too slow.

The boy was jerked to the side as the crowd along the railing yanked the tether cord of his life ring. The beast chomped, missing the boy, and the creature wailed and dove as the boy was pulled from the ocean onto the deck.

A guttural shriek that sounded like a puppy getting dragged through a pool of cats rose above the commotion. No doubt the boy's mother.

The sight of the boy almost being eaten sent people running for the two cabin entrances on each side of the boat, pushing and shoving in an attempt to get inside.

"Mayday. Mayday. We are under attack. To anyone listening, we are under attack." It was Detmer on the emergency channel, too late to the party.

Lenah moved the Sea Hunter IV closer to Fate's Fortune, and Splinter took two more shots, but they didn't faze the animal. The beast turned and slammed into the large charter again, jolting and rocking the ship.

"Bring me alongside. Time to light it up," Splinter said. He retrieved the gas bombs he'd made, but as he prepared to launch one at the beast, he considered the consequences. The beast was close to Fate's Fortune. What if the charter caught on fire?

He strapped the two bombs to the gunnel using the bungies that held fishing poles.

"Brace for impact," Lenah yelled.

The Sea Hunter IV rammed the beast as it surfaced behind Fate's Fortune, and Splinter was thrown across the deck and crashed into the port gunnel. He dropped the rifle and it slid down the deck, past the submarine and off the transom into the water.

Splinter lifted one of his homemade harpoons and launched it at the creature's back. It struck home, and the beast thrashed, rolling toward Fate's Fortune and slamming into its port side.

When the beast righted itself, Splinter saw the harpoon sticking from the creature's torso just behind its right flipper. Blood leaked into the water, but the beast appeared undaunted. It shrieked, and its jaws snapped like a panicked croc. Flippers pounded the water, and the beast's caudal fin twisted as it dug into the sea.

Lenah backed the Sea Hunter IV away.

The monster breached in a dazzling knot of whitewater and launched at Fate's Fortune like a missile. Its thirty-foot body glistened, its flat head pointed upward, jaws flexing open.

The beast landed on the bow of Fate's Fortune, and the boat's transom lifted from the water, revealing the vessels two large brass propellers. Passengers got tossed like marbles about the deck, and several bounced over the railings into the sea.

The creature rolled off the boat back into the ocean, and the rear of Fate's Fortune dropped and smacked the water, causing a thunderous wave of whitewater. The surge pounded the Sea Hunter IV, and Splinter washed over the deck like a piece of chum. He slid aft, but managed to grab hold of the gunnel before he slipped into the Atlantic. The Sea Hunter IV bobbed and settled as Splinter got to his feet.

Fate's Fortune had taken on a lot of water, and the vessel tilted to port and aft, the bow lifting in the air as if looking to the sky for help. People in the water screamed, and lifeboats were lowered into the Atlantic as Fate's Fortune's emergency klaxon wailed.

Splinter looked to the horizon for help, hoping an armada of coastie ships powered toward them, or maybe Silva in a plane or helicopter. But he didn't see any of that. What he saw was the sleek black hull of Donny's Jarred Bay luxury fishing boat. It cruised toward them and Splinter smiled. Now it was three on one.

33

Lenah swung the Sea Hunter IV around, spinning the wheel and rotating the vessel with the maneuvering thrusters. Splinter grabbed a harpoon and ran aft, hoisting it to his shoulder as he went. Sweat dripped into his eyes, stinging them, and he rubbed at his face with his free hand, wiping away the perspiration as best he could, but it was like he'd sprung a leak and his insides were spilling from every pore. He felt overheated, and pinpricks of white light danced before his eyes as pain shot up his back.

Screaming and the panicked cries of parents and children rattled around in Splinter's head as the beast breached again, this time landing on Fate's Fortune's starboard deck, causing the boat to list severely. The creature rolled into the sea with a guttural yelp that sounded like a giant frog taking a shit. Waves surged toward the Sea Hunter IV and broke over the gunnel, swamping it again.

Splinter heaved his harpoon, but missed, the bolt striking the animal's tough hide and bouncing off and disappearing beneath the sea. Splinter grabbed the Benelli single barrel pump-action shotgun, which held six shells.

The beast surfaced on the Sea Hunter IV's port side, its giant jaws opening as it turned to make another attack run on the fishing charter. The passengers on Fate's Fortune scattered like quail, running and screaming like children on a playground.

Splinter braced against the gunnel and fired. He pumped the gun, loaded another shell, and fired again. He fired four more times, the explosion of each shot sending a jolt through his body.

He hit the beast. There was blood in the water. That made Splinter smile and reminded him of the subway train analogy he used when he was trying to impress someone. The passengers are riding along, minding their own business, like the people on Fate's Fortune, alone with their thoughts on the crowded train. Then the train goes dark as the power cuts out for a brief instant as subways are known to do, and in that instant everyone on the train is together, one concerned being that would deal with the problem together. Then the lights come back on and everyone is alone again, in the middle of a car full of people.

Were sea creatures like people? No, but blood in the water brought sharks, and that was both good and bad. Good because the great whites might help defeat the beast. Bad, because perhaps all the sharks would do is take sloppy seconds.

The crocosaurus circled the charter, disappearing around the bow to the port side.

Gunshots rang out and Splinter looked at the weapon in his hands, verifying it hadn't been him who'd fired. Donny's black luxury fishing vessel came into view. Will leaned over the gunnel and fired what Splinter figured was his old six-shooter service revolver. Will had missed the Glock era.

Fate's Fortune listed as people clung to railings, deck equipment, anything they could get their hands on. It reminded Splinter of that crazy scene in the movie Titanic, when the luxury liner's stern lifted from the water and people slid down the deck, with the star and his love interest bracing themselves on the aft railing. People aboard Fate's Fortune were doing that, trying not to fall into the water with the beast, but what good would it do? Fate's Fortune was going down, and there was no way to stop it.

Lifeboats were still being lowered into the water, but all it took was some fast math to see there'd be people left without a ride. There was no ship's crew controlling the evacuation and the lifeboats were leaving Fate's Fortune only half full, again similar to the Titanic.

The radio crackled to life, and Splinter barely heard it from his position out on deck. It was Will.

"Lenah, we've got to draw this thing away from Fate's Fortune before all these people end up in the drink," Will said.

"That's a 10-4, but how? We've tried everything we can think of."

Static. Then, "I'm going to put The Day After between the beast and Fate's Fortune. You position yourself on its opposite side, and we'll try and irritate it and nudge it along," Will said.

Splinter yelled from out on deck. "That's pretty thin."

Lenah yelled, "You got another idea?"

He didn't.

The Sea Hunter IV changed course and moved into position, as Donny piloted The Day After between the surging creature and Fate's Fortune.

The beast rose from the depths, building speed, its caudal fin digging at the sea, flippers pounding the water. Its great jaws opened and clamped down on a women and man holding each other in the ocean. There was a horrible crunching sound as bones broke and sinew and muscle ripped. Blood filled the white froth as the *kronosaurus* dove, jaws opening and closing as it chewed.

Lenah set the Sea Hunter IV on a due west course as The Day After moved east. The creature passed between them and Lenah rushed out on deck, a double barrel shotgun in her hands. She ran past Splinter to the bow, fury written on her face like a bad B movie scream queen. She opened up with the shotgun, and the blast tore into the creature's hind quarter.

The beast wailed and bucked, and a knot of whitewater rolled toward the Sea Hunter IV as the creature whipped its tail, caudal fin shooting from the water.

Splinter had a moment of panic, the fog rising before his eyes, red anger clouding his vision. The long tail rose like a sea serpent and came down with a shuttering crash on the bow of the Sea Hunter IV. It landed on Lenah, crushing her and knocking her into the sea.

Splinter ran to the gunnel, searching the ocean below, but she was gone.

Splinter screamed, all the anger coming out, the smell of gunpowder and roasting lamb filling his nostrils as Kabul came hurling back. He loaded the shotgun, and climbed up on the gunnel, preparing to launch himself at the beast when it surfaced.

But it didn't surface, and neither did Lenah.

It was a nightmare. Another death he'd caused, more blood on his hands. If it wasn't for him, she wouldn't have been out here. This was all on him. Everything.

For a heartbeat Splinter heard nothing. Fog engulfed him, and he wasn't one of the people fighting for his life any longer. He was the butcher of Kabul, and this animal was going to pay.

The Day After disappeared from view as it turned south and passed behind Fate's Fortune, picking people out of the water as it went. Splinter grabbed the two fire bombs he'd strapped to the port gunnel, all concern of burning the charter gone, all rational thought abandoned.

The giant crocodilian monster surfaced, its gray eyes studying the Sea Hunter IV. It opened its jaws, revealing blood stained teeth, and Splinter had a horrible thought. Was that Lenah's blood? Pieces of her beautiful body stuck in the teeth of the leviathan? Somewhere in the back of his mind he heard Lenah's voice trying to guide him from the fog. But he was too far gone. She was gone, and he had nothing left to live for except to exterminate the creature that had killed her.

Eighty percent of Fate's Fortune had passed beneath the waves. Passengers got sucked beneath the ship as it went down, people climbed onto the roof of the conning tower, but that would just delay the inevitable. Others jockeyed for position, and Splinter's anger rose. People were pushing and shoving, struggling to stay above the water at all costs, survival at its worst. All because they couldn't find anything better to do on a bright Florida day, and because a captain was desperate for charters to pay his bills.

Splinter went to the command console and spun the wheel, putting the bow perpendicular to Fate's Fortune. When the beast came up he'd ram the thing to hell.

The beast did come up, but on the opposite side of Fate's Fortune. Gunshots rang out, no doubt Will firing his peashooter. Splinter had one harpoon left, a loaded shotgun, and he'd use his hands if necessary.

That thought made him laugh, a full laugh from deep down, a bit fake and unhinged. That surprised him, and he remembered a book he'd read called Meg, in which the alpha hero cuts out the heart of a giant *megalodon* from the inside while it was still alive. Splinter remembered how stupid that ending was, then asked himself if he could do the same, even though he knew he couldn't.

"Splinter! Splinter!"

It was Will, The Day After had come around the aft side of the charter, and Will waved to him, gun in hand, yelling. Splinter couldn't move, every muscle frozen in place. He saw himself standing next to himself, and he was shaking his head admonishingly. His double said, "You killed Lenah dipshit. You didn't bite her in half, but you might as well have. Why don't you just give it up? Throw yourself in the sea. When Will finds out he's going to shoot you anyway."

Will continued to call to him, but Splinter had run out of time.

Croczilla launched from the sea, landing on the Sea Hunter IV's deck, flippers acting like stabilizing arms as it held itself up, staring across the deck at Splinter as Guppy's boat sank beneath the waves, bow lifting to the sky. The beast's jaws snapped open and closed, head thrashing.

Then Splinter saw it was chewing on something. The remains of a person.

Oh, Lenah, I'm so sorry.

The beast pushed forward, driving the Sea Hunter IV down, and Splinter was forced to jump into the ocean to avoid being caught in the beast's flexing jaws or sucked under with the boat.

He hit the water hard and lost the shotgun as he went under. Sounds from above were muffled and nondescript, and as he sank into the depths he felt at peace, the fog fading, his life finally to coming to a close. A life that would have been better had it never been. The world was better off without him, and Lenah was gone so what did he have to live for?

He didn't fight as the ocean pulled him down. He let go of his burdens, everything that had weighed him down since Kabul, and perhaps long before that. He was finally going into the abyss and he smiled.

Something snagged under his arm, and he fought to free himself as he was pulled upward. He broke the surface sputtering and coughing. Will hung over the side of The Day After, a long telescoping boat hook fully extended, its hooked end tugging at Splinter's armpit.

Splinter floated in the Atlantic, staring up at Will who was yelling and waving his arms, but Splinter ignored him. He didn't want to hear him. All he wanted was the sweet embrace of the abyss, and an end to his constant anger and worry.

Will swatted him on the head with the tip of the boat pole and Splinter's head went under and he took in a mouthful of water. This cleared the fog, and as his head bobbed above the waterline, he heard Will screaming.

"Shark! Shark!"

Splinter searched about him and didn't see any sharks. What he did see was a three-foot dorsal fin slicing through the water, coming toward him, throwing spray like it had a propeller.

Splinter smiled and waited for the peace and finality of the abyss.

34

Pop! Pop! Pop!

Splinter struggled to stay above the surging sea. Will braced against The Day After's gunnel, firing his six-shooter. The shark veered away, wagging its caudal fin. It was a big one, and the twelve-foot great white smiled at Splinter as it darted past.

Splinter floated dumbfounded. Had that just happened? Splinter's death wish fled like the coward it was, and like a switch had been flipped, he wanted to live.

Fountains of blood and whitewater sprouted from where the .35 caliber bullets hit the shark, and the beast thrashed. Croczilla threw itself sideways into The Day After, and the thirty-four-foot sport fisherman rocked, tuna-tower swaying, but the vessel bounced back level. Donny gunned the engines in an attempt to get the *kronosaurus* with the propeller, but missed.

Croczilla dove, its white shape gliding beneath the boat and disappearing off the port bow. The shark turned west, making a slow arc back toward Splinter. Will tossed out a life ring, and Will and Donny pulled Splinter to the dive platform where he climbed from the water and scrambled up the stainless-steel ladder to the main deck as the shark snapped at his heels.

"Good to see you, buddy. Saved my ass again," Splinter said.

"Not yet," Donny said. He rushed back to the controls. The Day After was drifting into the sunken Sea Hunter IV, which was upside down, floating listlessly in the rolling waves. Passengers from Fate's Fortune had climbed onto the sunken ship, struggling to stay out of the water.

"Where's Lenah?" Will asked.

Splinter said nothing. He looked at Will, a tear leaking from his right eye. His left eye would never betray him like that. It was his aiming eye.

"Splinter? Oh, no, Splinter. What happened?" Will said.

"She's gone, Will. I've lost her," Splinter said. Then like a dam breaking, Splinter's emotions spilled out in a series of crying jags, screams of pain, and constant streams of self-deprecating excuses, none of which he was able to sell himself.

Will said nothing, anger, fear, then sorrow passing across his face like flashcards of emotion.

Donny yelled from the command console, "What do you want me to do?"

"Find it!" yelled Will before Splinter could answer.

Splinter nodded and clapped his friend on the shoulder.

Will turned to him with a face that made Splinter understand this old man, his friend, had once been a cop. "We're not done. This just isn't the time," he said, and turned away and went down into the galley.

Splinter stood there alone, mind spinning out of control. Lenah left a crater hole in his life, and its dark maw beckoned to him, another abyss of his making. He struggled to keep from falling, fought the urge to embrace the fog and end it all.

Croczilla wailed and the *womp womp* of helicopter blades cut through the moist air. A copter came in from the west, a black spec sliding across the clear blue sky.

Silva. Below the whirly-bird, several coastie and harbor patrol boats formed an armada as they headed for the emergency scene, their wakes leaving a thick white line of foam. Lifeboats trailed away in jagged lines as survivors tried to put ocean between themselves and the monster.

The beast's caudal fin surfaced behind the sunken Sea Hunter IV, its flat head lifting from the sea, jaws opening.

Splinter grabbed the gunnel, but there was nothing he could do but watch the beast take a bit out of the Sea Hunter IV, along with three people, who yelled and screamed as they were eaten alive, the creature's jaws smacking down, cracking bones and ripping muscle. Blood filled the water and the shark knifed through what the creature had left behind like a cub following a lion.

Donny spun The Day After around, putting the boat's bow on the Sea Hunter IV wreck.

The sound of the helicopter grew louder. Soon they'd have help, the copter was now a large black smudge, but it was still a couple of minutes off.

The beast turned in a wide arc, its flippers digging into the sea, caudal fin thrashing back and forth as it lined up for another attack run.

Will came back out on deck, his gun by his side, and for an instant Splinter thought he might raise it and point it at him, but he didn't. His eyes shot daggers, and most of them pierced Splinter's heart. Will was right to hold him responsible for Lenah's death. He'd brought her out here. She'd done it all for him, and like everyone else who cared for him, now she was dead.

Donny brought The Day After in closer as the beast plucked another person from the sea like a pelican snagging shiners. Screaming and wails of pain, snapping bones and tearing flesh filled Splinter's mind as the creature chewed, the shark circled, and the fog came on.

Will screamed and opened up with his six-shooter as the creature arced past the sunken Sea Hunter IV and lined up on The Day After. He fired until the gun clicked empty. Will dug through his pockets, pulling out bullets and stuffing them into their cylinders, rotating the housing and slipping in bullets.

Donny stopped The Day After so Will could line up a steady shot and put six more down the thing's gullet.

A white HH65 Dolphin helicopter with an orange strip came in fast, buzzing over the scene. Wind tore at Splinter's hair, and Will grabbed the gunnel to brace himself.

Splinter watched the helicopter, and saw Silva waving his hands, pointing.

The creature rose from the water and Will held his gun out before him, sighting the beast's head.

The top of the creature's head surfaced, and its caudal fin whipped as the beast surged toward The Day After. It was fifty yards out, but still Will didn't fire.

Forty yards.

Splinter's gaze flicked from the creature to Will and back to the beast as it dove beneath the waves.

At thirty yards Will opened up, pulling the trigger in a steady rhythm, firing a shot a second, trying to line them up on the beast's forehead like he was at the firing range.

The monster slammed into The Day After and Will pitched over the gunnel into the sea.

It was happening again. All of it. Roasting lamb. Gunpowder smoke. The blood and brains of one of his men splattered on his fatigues.

Splinter ran to the gunnel and grabbed a life ring. Will was treading water next to The Day After, but the creature knifed at him.

Donny gunned the engines and The Day After moved back, closer to Will who was slipping away from them with the rolling waves. The coastie copter came in low, wind tearing at the Atlantic, a rescue harness descending from the whirly-bird's open bay door. Silva was there, next to a coastie in a dark blue work uniform who wore a white flight helmet with a blast shield covering half his face. Silva wore his suit like a g-man, his dark shades making Splinter smile.

Just like Saigon, hey slick.

"Yes!" Splinter yelled. He couldn't get to Will in time, but Silva would.

The creature came on. It was fifty yards from Will, and the life ring was only ten feet from the surface and his friend would soon be in it.

Three coastie SAFE boats arrived like a fleet coming out of hyperspace, and they started rescuing passengers and firing on the beast. "No," he yelled. "No!" If any of them missed, they could easily hit Will, who was putting his arms through the rescue harness. Will gave a thumb's up, and the copter's engines cycled up, and Splinter breathed a sigh of relief.

But even as Will was pulled from the sea the creature rocketed from the water, launching itself at Will, jaws flexing open. The beast hung there for an instant, suspended in the air, a mound of whitewater holding it up. Will was silhouetted between the creature's jaws, then they closed on his friend and Splinter yelled so loud he thought he blew out his vocal cords.

The monster fell back into the sea, its jaws slamming up and down, blood and flesh flying from its long flat mouth.

Splinter couldn't move, fury built in him like a volcano preparing to erupt. The fog descended like an old friend as he climbed onto the gunnel and pulled his dive knife from its sheath strapped to his leg. He was going to crawl inside this motherfucker and cut its heart out, just like Jonas Taylor.

The beast disappeared off the port bow as it circled The Day After.

"Splinter you crazy shit, get down from there," Donny said. He grabbed Splinter around the waist and tugged him off the gunnel and the two men toppled across the deck.

Splinter sprang at Donny and grabbed him by the throat, pinning him. "What the hell are you—"

Donny held up a grenade. "I th…o…"

Splinter let go of the man's throat, and Donny rubbed it, pure contempt written on his face.

They got to their feet and Donny tossed the grenade to Splinter, who caught it. "I thought this might help," Donny said.

Splinter stared at the bomb in amazement, then looked up at Donny.

"Friend of mine smuggled it home from Iraq. It's live and has a ten second delay."

Splinter said nothing, but a smile crept across his face that felt more like a sneer.

"Just pull the pin and make sure you're nowhere near the thing when it goes," Donny said.

"No shit. I was a SEAL, remember?"

"You are a SEAL. Now go get it, Splinter. You go get it, god damn it! For Will and Lenah."

Splinter checked the pin to ensure it was securely fastened, then headed to the bow, where he pulled the gantry arm free and attached the hoist cable to the Zodiac. The black fifteen-foot Mercury inflatable had a small side console with a stainless-steel wheel and throttle arm. The 20HP outboard was up and in the locked position.

He activated the winch, and the Zodiac lifted from its holding cradles. He stopped the winch and nudged the dinghy over the gunnel railing, the arm swinging to a ninety-degree angle.

Splinter lowered the tender into the ocean, grabbed the lead line, and worked the dinghy around to the dive platform.

He looked back at Donny, who saluted him.

Grenade in hand, Splinter leapt into the Zodiac. He pulled back on the engine cover and undid the bolt that held the motor in the up position. He eased the outboard into the water, and it locked in place with a click.

He moved the throttle switch to neutral and yanked on the starter cable. Nothing. He primed the motor and pulled again, and the motor sputtered, but died. Third time was the charm, and the Merc roared to life.

Splinter flipped the throttle switch to full speed, and jerked the control arm right, and the Zodiac cut left, heading straight for the monster.

35

The Zodiac bounced over the waves, the Merc whining. The scene had become a knot of boats. Three SAFE boats rescued passengers, and the whirly-bird circled overhead. Fate's Fortune had disappeared beneath the waves, and what was left of the Sea Hunter IV floated upside-down, covered with survivors. Donny fell in behind Splinter with The Day After as they pressed toward the monster.

Fog obscured his vision. Splinter rammed the creature's side, turning hard to starboard at the last moment. The Merc's propeller dug into the side of the monster, and the beast bucked and heaved, tossing the Zodiac from the water.

The inflatable landed with a jarring crash and Splinter pitched into the sea. Waves broke over him as the Zodiac floated away. He heard Lenah's voice in the back of his mind, but it wasn't saying he should let go and join her. It was telling him to fight.

The creature flipped, and its massive flat head crashed into the sea five feet from the Zodiac. Its jaws chomped and snapped, but that only pushed the inflatable closer to Splinter, who used the momentum of the surging whitewater to haul himself back into the dinghy. He pulled on the starter cable and the outboard roared to life. He slid the throttle switch to maximum and pointed the Zodiac west.

The monster fell in behind him, gliding along the surface, steel gray eyes focused. Its caudal fin swayed back and forth, its flippers pushing through the sea.

Splinter smiled as the scene of chaos receded into the distance. He'd lead the beast into the confined sea walls of the inlet and ram the Zodiac and grenade down the sea monster's gullet.

The *womp womp* of rotor blades cutting through the air made Splinter search the sky. The Coast Guard whirly-bird tracked the chase as Splinter drew the creature away from the chaos.

Splinter pressed on toward the setting sun, the Zodiac bouncing and heaving through the chop. The fog engulfed him, and his nerves shivered, and Splinter shook himself, trying to ease the feeling, but he couldn't. He piloted the boat through a tunnel of light that had but one end; the mouth of croczilla. It seemed fitting, and that realization warmed his cold stomach and soothed his jumping nerves. Perhaps this was his destiny? Why everything had happened. So he could be in this time and place.

He jumped a large set of waves and the Merc chirped and moaned, but didn't stall. The coastline was a dark smudge in the grayness of the fading day, the red navigation light on the tip of the jetty at Ft. Pierce inlet still a mile off. Splinter looked back, and it was hard to see the creature as it knifed through the dark water.

The helicopter thundered overhead, hanging back, waiting for Splinter to make his move, but Splinter wasn't ready. He wanted to tire the beast out, disorient it, bring it to a spot where it had limited options, turn it from hunter to prey.

As if reading Splinter's mind, the beast torpedoed from the sea, its jaws snapping closed, feet from the Zodiac. The monster crashed back into the Atlantic and the ensuing surge of whitewater lifted the inflatable and pushed it down the face of a six-foot wave.

Splinter jerked the control arm, and the outboard's propeller grabbed the face of the wave. Water spilled overhead as the Zodiac was engulfed in the wave's barrel.

The rubber boat shot from the cave of seawater like a kid from the end of a water slide. The dinghy skittered over the surface, the outboard fighting to grab water. Splinter steadied the control arm and brought the boat straight, pointing the bow at the inlet, and the outboard dug into the sea.

A sharp pain pierced Splinter's neck and he slapped a hand over the area, killing a wasp. He held the dead bee between his thumb and forefinger, examining it in its death throes. The sound of the wind, the crashing waves, the pounding of helicopter rotors, all fell away like Splinter had passed into a bubble of silence. The wasp gave one last attempt to wiggle free of Splinter's grasp, then fell still.

What was this lone soldier doing out at sea all by himself? Wasps could fly up to ten miles a day, but clearly this guy had been lost. It made Splinter think of his long last relative, the captain of the Wasp. Was that long dead seaman trying to tell him something? Don't join me in the locker?

Fort Pierce inlet opened before him and Splinter guided the Zodiac into its mouth. Mangroves and beach ran by to the north, houses and seashore to the south. Ahead the bright lights of Fort Pierce glowed over Indian River as the sun sank below the horizon.

When Splinter reached the inner bay, he spun the Zodiac around, the Merc sputtering and wheezing because of the sharp turn. The creature sliced through the water, one-hundred yards out and coming right at him.

He had it boxed into the inlet and there it would end. Splinter smiled. He'd always loved a good game of chicken.

When he was a boy, he'd played chicken on the railroad tracks with his friends. They'd wait in the woods until the train was a half mile off then run onto the tracks. The train's conductor would throw on the brake, and sparks would fly as the metal wheels slid over the steel tracks.

Splinter always won. He'd stay on that track until the shadow of the train fell over him, diving off at the very last instant. Once he cut his foot on the side of the train as it tore by because he'd been so close.

The creature was ninety yards out, and it rose in a knot of whitewater.

Splinter flashed back, and he was on the Parker, floating over the Atlantic. The entire sea turned red as the shark's head burst from the ocean and splattered him with blood. The shark's cold wet eyes searched his, and it smiled as if it knew something Splinter didn't. The sea bubbled with red foam, and Splinter saw the faces of all those he'd killed staring up at him from the depths. This was his atonement. He'd make everything right.

Eighty yards.

Splinter heard the wail of the boy swimming by the yacht in the moment he realized he was going to die. The sound of breaking bones and tearing flesh forever etched on his brain. The wail of the child's mother. And more blood red sea.

Seventy yards. The Zodiac jumped a wave and the Merc sputtered.

Splinter saw a boy's severed hand in his mind's eye. A tiny body covered in a tarp. Flashbulbs in his mind. Snapping. Reminding him.

Sixty.

The leviathan rising from the depths. Sucking people into its maw.

Fifty yards. The creature's white teeth glowed as it opened its giant jaws.

The fishing charter listed in the rolling ocean, people falling into the sea, screaming. Sharks circled, the animals fed, and Splinter stood by helpless. Frozen. A coward. Unable to do anything. Just like his entire useless life. All he was good for was killing and getting people killed.

Forty yards. A caudal fin tore through the water as the beast picked up speed for its attack.

The scent of roasting lamb and gun smoke. A woman and an infant with one bullet. There was no way to atone for that. No explanation or justification that could put his mind at ease.

Thirty yards. Splinter slipped his finger through the loop at the end of the grenade's firing pin.

Lenah. No. Lenah.

She held his head in her hands. She was smiling, her eyes shining with life and energy. Her lips curled into her perpetual smile. She flattened his hair and said, "You need a haircut and a shave."

"I'm sorry, Lenah," he said, but there was no one there to hear.

Twenty yards. Splinter killed the outboard.

"Hi, my name's Will. You OK?"

Splinter's mind spun. He couldn't trust this guy. Who the hell was he? What did he want?

"Come on. I'll get you some food," Will had said.

"Don't waste your time on me, mister. I'll only disappoint you."

"I know people. You're worth the risk."

Ten yards.

Splinter pulled the pin on the grenade and dropped it to the deck of the dinghy. The sound of the helicopter faded, and peace settled over him. This was right. Everything was right.

The Zodiac skittered across the ocean, right into the creature's opening jaws.

Pain jolted Splinter's back as his survival instinct kicked him in the ass, and he heard Will and Lenah yelling at him. There was nothing right about this. Being chow for croczilla wasn't what he deserved, was it? He'd done his best and failed. He was guilty of that, but he'd earned the right to live, and now as death held the door open Splinter decided he'd like to stay outside for a while.

The creature's massive jaws engulfed the Zodiac and Splinter dove into the sea.

The grenade detonated, and Splinter was thrown like a ragdoll in the maelstrom, the Atlantic, pieces of the creature and the dinghy swirling around him like a tornado. He saw Lenah's face in his mind's eye, and he smiled as the abyss took him.

36

A mosquito sucking blood from his cheek brought Splinter awake. He slapped at the little vampire, smacking himself in the face but missing the bug. He scratched the bite and rubbed his eyes. Seagulls cried, and a gentle breeze rattled leaves.

He lay on a tangle of branches in the shade, stray beams of sunlight leaking though the mangroves. Splinter's back ached, and he shifted position and almost fell into the water that sloshed beneath him. Splinter smiled. The sea had placed him on a natural platform as the tide washed out.

Splinter laughed. And laughed. And laughed.

***

Splinter was dead, and he liked it that way. Nobody noticed him or looked at him with reproach. He was a ghost like everyone else, lost in the mass of humanity.

He sat at a round table outside Bagel Boss, sipping his coffee and watching strangers. Nobody would recognize him even if they knew who he was because he'd shaved his beard, dyed his hair, gotten new clothes, and wore a Miami Dolphins cap and large mirrored sunglasses.

He took a bite of his everything bagel and glanced through the plate glass window of the bagel joint. The clock above the checkout counter read 8:47AM. His funeral wasn't until 9:30, so he had time.

A three-day-old copy of the Miami Herold lay on the table before him with a flyer on top of it. The leaflet was clearly Lenah's work, and it announced Splinter's memorial service at South Florida National Cemetery in Lake Worth, which was an hour south of Fort Pierce. The announcement said retired police officer William Dodge would also be honored at the ceremony, though his grave marker was to be placed next to his wife's in Coral Gables at a later date, and no service information had been announced. The flyer noted that next of kin were out of state.

Splinter didn't know how Lenah had managed to get him into the national cemetery, but since the police were calling him a hero, Splinter figured Silva cut all the red tape. The news coverage depicted Splinter as the man of the hour, and Silva was front and center, saying he'd seen

Splinter drive the Zodiac into the mutant's mouth and detonate the grenade, thus sacrificing himself to save others and atoning for his sins. Many mourners were expected at the service, especially since it was for Will as well. Though Will had no local family left, he'd been a cop in the area for many years, and half the people in St. Lucie county owed him a favor.

Splinter picked up the paper and sipped his coffee. "Heel to Hero" was the headline, and below surrounded in text was a picture taken from Silva's copter showing Splinter driving the Zodiac toward the beast's open maw. The article described the creature as a large crocodile. Splinter figured that was also Silva's doing. No need to worry the populace about things they can't control, he'd say. Lenah had only a small mention in the article as one of the survivors rescued by the Coast Guard, but it had made Splinter cry like a baby. Even Guppy got an honorable mention for his posthumous donation of the Sea Hunter IV, which Splinter was sure would be replaced with a new boat thanks to insurance.

He folded the paper, put it under his arm, and took a long pull of coffee, finishing it. He wiped his mouth, put the paper napkin in the empty cup, and got up and stretched. The paper fell from beneath his arm and landed open on the concrete. Heel to Hero. Funny, he'd never felt like a heel, and he certainly didn't feel like a hero.

He picked up the Herald, tossed everything in the garbage, and headed for the bus stop. The 9:11 would bring him to the cemetery by 9:26 if it was on time.

Splinter didn't feel like a hero because his decision to keep his survival a secret, even from Lenah, weighed on him, but he couldn't shake the feeling she was better-off without him. With him out of the way she'd be forced to move on with her life and find a man who could give her what she needed and make her happy. Do all the things he couldn't. It was better this way, the man he was going six-feet-under.

Air breaks chirping broke Splinter from his daydream and he got on the bus and dropped change into the ticket stand. The bus pulled away and made a right on Lake Worth Road, bumping along. A boy sat next to his mother staring at him, and Splinter crossed his eyes. The boy laughed and when the child's mother saw Splinter entertaining the boy she smiled. What a difference a haircut and shower made.

He swayed in his seat as the bus made a right on US-441 south. They passed Target and a housing development to the east as the bus rolled through the morning humidity. Rows of white tombstones stretched out beyond a metal fence to the west, and the bus's air brakes squeaked as it stopped before the cemetery gates.

A computerized voice burst from a speaker, "South Florida National Cemetery."

The boy waved goodbye to Splinter as he got up and went to see his final resting place.

Splinter pulled the bill of his cap down and blended in with the crowd that worked its way down a gravel road toward a gathering of mourners. Splinter chuckled. He didn't think he'd met this many people in his entire life. News vans lined the narrow lane closest to the main road, satellite dishes raised, generators humming. He kept his head down, met nobody's gaze, and stayed behind a man and woman who walked side by side, the man's arm around the woman's waist.

Dirty-white tombstones stretched out in all directions, like dominoes waiting to fall. Grass filled in the gaps, and lines of people stretched away from a center mass where Lenah stood. Splinter's grave marker and a headshot of a young Will in his uniform and wearing a watch cap sat on an easel next to a podium.

Splinter hung back and leaned on a palm tree, a thick crowd of people before him.

The PA system crackled to life, and Lenah tapped the microphone with her index finger. The system squealed, and she stepped back, hand on heart.

She leaned back in and said, "Sorry." Lenah looked down at her notes. Someone coughed. A child whined. "This is hard for me, so bear with me." She folded her prepared speech and put it in her pocket. "It's hard because I loved Splinter Woods and Will Dodge. In different ways, but with equal strength, and to put them both to rest today is an open wound I know will never heal."

Mice ran up Splinter's neck, the little claws of worry and concern digging into his nerves like needles. Someone had seen him. Was watching him. Splinter scanned the crowd, but it was no human searching for him, it was a cat.

Poseidon sat at the edge of the small dais, peering into the crowd. When the shifting and swaying of the mourners was just right, Splinter saw his friend, who stared in his direction and appeared to have spotted him. Galatia and Nereus sat behind Lenah and appeared half asleep. He missed his friends, but they too were better off with him dead.

Lenah was going on about Will. His service in the Navy, his marriage and two children, all but one having died and left him. Sadness washed over Splinter at the thought of never seeing Will again. To never hear his laugh, see that bright gleam in his eye Splinter wished he had. The gleam that said, "Yeah, whatever, move along, you aren't the droids we're looking for."

The crowd murmured, and Splinter looked up. Lenah was dabbing her eyes with a white handkerchief.

"Who was Captain Matthew Woods, who everyone called Splinter?" Lenah paused and laughed. "That's right. He got under your skin. He was a pain in the ass. But you know what else? He loved this country. What it stood for. Let me give you a brief accounting of his honors." Lenah paused and shuffled some papers.

"Hey, mister," a young boy said. A red-haired freckled youngster stood before Splinter, looking up into his sunglasses. "That guy asked me to give you this." The boy handed Splinter an envelope.

"What man?" Splinter stepped behind the palm tree.

"That man right…" The boy pointed to an empty spot along the road. "He was there." The boy walked off and kept looking over his shoulder back at the road.

Splinter opened the envelope and found Will's police badge with a note folded around it. It read, "Splinter, I'm glad you made it. Maybe I'll see you down the road. Go find some peace. Enclosed is Will's badge. I thought you should have it." It was signed Silva.

Splinter pulled down the bill of his cap and slipped the badge in his pocket along with the note. He looked to the north and saw a bus chugging down US-441 south. If he walked fast, he could catch it.

"Captain Woods earned a Silver Star and Meritorious Service honors for service to his country. He earned two Purple Hearts…"

Lenah's voice faded. Kabul faded. Splinter left it all behind.

He arrived at US-441 just in time to catch the bus. He waved, air brakes chirped, and then he was heading south, bouncing and swaying with the roll of the road, destination unknown.

THE END

Edward J. McFadden III juggles a full-time career as a university administrator, with his writing aspirations. His novels THROWBACK and The Breach were recently published by Severed Press, and his short story Doorways in Time appeared in Shadows & Reflections, an estate authorized Roger Zelazny tribute anthology with an introduction by George R.R. Martin. His other novels include AWAKE, The Black Death of Babylon, Our Dying Land and HOAXERS (Crossroad Press.) Ed is also the author/editor of: Anywhere But Here, Lucky 13, Jigsaw Nation, Deconstructing Tolkien: A Fundamental Analysis of The Lord of the Rings (re-released in eBook format Fall 2012 – Amazon Bestseller), Time Capsule, Epitaphs (W/ Tom Piccirilli), The Second Coming, Thoughts of Christmas, and The Best of Pirate Writings. He lives on Long Island with his wife Dawn, their daughter Samantha, and their mutt Oli.

CHECK OUT OTHER GREAT
DEEP SEA THRILLERS

SHARK: INFESTED WATERS
by P.K. Hawkins

For Simon, the trip was supposed to be a once in a lifetime gift: a journey to the Amazon River Basin, the land that he had dreamed about visiting since he was a child. His enthusiasm for the trip may be tempered by the poor conditions of the boat and their captain leading the tour, but most of the tourists think they can look the other way on it. Except things go wrong quickly. After a horrific accident, Simon and the other tourists find themselves trapped on a tiny island in the middle of the river. It's the rainy season, and the river is rising. The island is surrounded by hungry bull sharks that won't let them swim away. And worst of all, the sharks might not be the only blood-thirsty killers among them. It was supposed to be the trip of a lifetime. Instead, they'll be lucky if they make it out with their lives at all.

DARK WATERS
by Lucas Pederson

Jörmungandr is an ancient Norse sea monster. Thought to be purely a myth until a battleship is torn a part by one.

With his brother on that ship, former Navy Seal and deep-sea diver, Miles Raine, sets out on a personal vendetta against the creature and hopefully save his brother. Bringing with him his old Seal team, the Dagger Points, they embark on a mission that might very well be their last.

But what happens when the hunters become the hunted and the dark waters reveal more than a monster?

CHECK OUT OTHER GREAT DEEP SEA THRILLERS

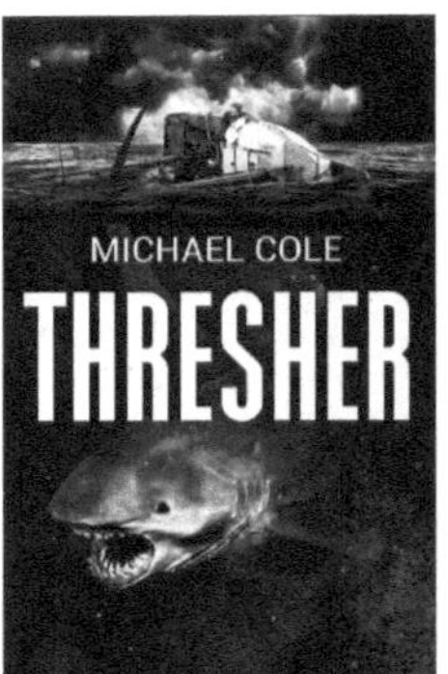

THRESHER
by **Michael Cole**

In the aftermath of a hurricane, a series of strange events plague the coastal waters off Florida. People go into the water and never return. Corpses of killer whales drift ashore, ravaged from enormous bite marks. A fishing trawler is found adrift, with a mysterious gash in its hull.

Transferred to the coastal town of Merit, police officer Leonard Riker uncovers the horrible reality of an enormous Thresher shark lurking off the coast. Forty feet in length, it has taken a territorial claim to the waters near the town harbor. Armed with three-inch teeth, a scythe-like caudal fin, and unmatched aggression, the beast seeks to kill anything sharing the waters.

THE GUILLOTINE
by **Lucas Pederson**

1,000 feet under the surface, Prehistoric Anthropologist, Ash Barrington, and his team are in the midst of a great archeological dig at the bottom of Lake Superior where they find a treasure trove of bones. Bones of dinosaurs that aren't supposed to be in this particular region. In their underwater facility, Infinity Moon, Ash and his team soon discover a series of underground tunnels. Upon exploring, they accidentally open an ice pocket, thawing the prehistoric creature trapped inside. Soon they are being attacked, the facility falling apart around them, by what Ash knows is a dunkleosteus and all those bones were from its prey. Now...Ash and his team are the prey and the creature will stop at nothing to get to them.

CHECK OUT OTHER GREAT DEEP SEA THRILLERS

THE BREACH
by Edward J. McFadden III

A Category 4 hurricane punched a quarter mile hole in Fire Island, exposing the Great South Bay to the ferocity of the Atlantic Ocean, and the current pulled something terrible through the new breach. A monstrosity of the past mixed with the present has been disturbed and it's found its way into the sheltered waters of Long Island's southern sea.

Nate Tanner lives in Stones Throw, Long Island. A disgraced SCPD detective lieutenant put out to pasture in the marine division because of his Navy background and experience with aquatic crime scenes, Tanner is assigned to hunt the creeper in the bay. But he and his team soon discover they're the ones being hunted.

INFESTATION
by William Meikle

It was supposed to be a simple mission. A suspected Russian spy boat is in trouble in Canadian waters. Investigate and report are the orders.

But when Captain John Banks and his squad arrive, it is to find an empty vessel, and a scene of bloody mayhem.

Soon they are in a fight for their lives, for there are things in the icy seas off Baffin Island, scuttling, hungry things with a taste for human flesh.

They are swarming. And they are growing.

"Scotland's best Horror writer" - Ginger Nuts of Horror

"The premier storyteller of our time." - Famous Monsters of Filmland